At the Edge of the Sea

KAREN M COX

Meryton Press
Oysterville, WA

AT THE EDGE OF THE SEA

Copyright © 2013 by Karen M. Cox

ISBN: 978-1-936009-27-5

Graphic design by Ellen Pickels

Dedication

For my parents…

My father, who taught me that the world is more colorful
and interesting when seen from outside the box

And for my mom. My life has been generously sprinkled with fortunate
circumstances. The very first one was that she became my mother.

Acknowledgments

Publishing a book is a contradictory experience comprised of solitude and teamwork. *At the Edge of the Sea* would not exist without the generosity and hard work of several wonderful people. I want to express my eternal gratitude to the staff at Meryton Press: Michele Reed, for her willingness to step a little off the beaten path with this book; Ellen Pickels for crossing I's and dotting T's with elegance and efficiency; Gail McEwen, my intrepid editor, who pushed me to take chances but always tempered it with her trademark gentle honesty; and the ever-patient Zuki, who put such care and artistry into the cover design.

Additional thanks go to the readers at *A Happy Assembly* for their interest and comments on an earlier version of this story. I am extra grateful for my beta readers: Jane Vivash, Terry Jakober and Karen Adams who gave their time, their opinions, and their friendship. Terry also found the book's title. Those three ladies are very dear to me.

Finally, I thank my family: My daughter, who keeps me grounded in the present; my son, who coaxes me to see the possible; and my husband, who walks the thousand journeys with me.

The Bookend on the Left

A PROLOGUE

August, 1982

The late afternoon sun slanted across the trees farther inland, saying its 'good night' to the ocean until the next morning. A little farther ahead, I spied Kevin, my youngest, leap up from his intricate sand castle and run toward the boardwalk where his mother lounged on a blanket, her umbrella leaning toward the afternoon sun. She was the perfect portrait of a woman at leisure. I walked toward her, hands in my pockets, the softer, drier sand folding up around my wet feet. Kevin flopped down beside her on the blanket, digging in our beach bag.

"What are you looking for?" I asked him.

"Here it is!" He pulled out a folded-up kite and a wad of tangled string and then thrust the whole mess out between us. "Can you help me unwind it?"

I gave it a dubious look. "I dunno, son. It's awful tangled up. Besides, there's hardly any wind today. I don't think it will be a good afternoon for kite flying.'"

He looked crestfallen, and I realized I was probably frowning at him in that stern fashion my wife accused me of.

Gathering my patience, I replied, "Well, let's just take a look, shall we? It can't hurt to try."

His face brightened, and we spent the next ten minutes untangling kite string. When we finished, he ran toward the ocean, calling, "Thanks, Dad!"

over his shoulder.

I shook my head and turned back around, smiling at the woman now propped on her elbows, watching.

"Hi ya, handsome. Whatcha up to?"

"Guess he'll never give up on getting that kite to fly, will he? I believe it's a lost cause though."

We watched Kevin running back and forth a few minutes, trying to get the wind to lift the kite into the air.

"Maybe I should try to help him," I murmured.

"You always were a soft touch for lost causes."

"You think so, huh?"

She nodded. "I know so."

I settled beside her and leaned over to kiss her cheek. "No good cause is ever truly lost, honey. Just like no person is beyond redemption. Remember how, of all Jericho, the Lord's people spared Rahab and her family. She made a choice to hide their spies, and it changed her future."

"And then, Rahab the harlot became the great-grandmother of King David."

"She did."

I stared out over the sea, contemplating the exciting, massive, yet frightening body of water in front of me. Because of my upbringing and my own sentimental nature, I saw symbols everywhere, in everything. Now, I saw the sea as a symbol of life—not an original comparison, perhaps, but a valid one. These days, as I approached middle age, my life was sometimes intense, like brutal, bright sunlight reflecting off the surface of the water. With all the challenges this stage of life entailed, I frequently found myself on the hot seat: raising teenagers, working harder at my job than I ever had, and all the while wondering whether the sunset years on my life's ocean would bring storms or calm.

Without thinking, I reached over and clasped my wife's hand for reassurance. I had navigated this earthly life pretty well I thought, but, like Rahab, I never could have predicted the twists and turns God had in store. Some events that shaped my life were obvious: my mother's death, going away to school, the births of my children. But sometimes, little events that had far-reaching effects crept up on me unexpectedly, like the tide easing higher on the sand...

Chapter One

Summer, 1959

The 1949 Oldsmobile rumbled up the gravel road, red dust flying out behind us. I looked over at my father, who was humming "Nearer My God to Thee" in an absentminded way as he fanned himself with his fedora. It was ninety degrees and humid as the steam from a teakettle, but Dad still wore a suit and tie. Dad always wore a suit and tie. It was the first Friday in June, and we were heading into Orchard Hill, the next stop on Dad's traveling ministry. More than a few small-town Methodist churches couldn't afford a full time preacher, so after Mama died some years back, my father deposited me with my Aunt Catherine and took on the mission of serving the rural areas of the state. He made it around to each church every few weeks, performing christenings, a wedding or two, and evangelizing to the salt of the earth.

In the summers, instead of staying with my aunt, I accompanied him. Dad said it was good for me to take time away from the carefully orchestrated elegance of his sister's home and see how the other half lived. That summer I'd really see the other half up close because I was spending almost twelve weeks with his friend Alvin Miller, M.D. before starting medical school in the fall. After his Sunday sermon, Dad planned to move to the next town on his circuit, leaving me in Orchard Hill to shadow Dr. Miller and learn about the life of a country doctor.

Dad had been driving for four hours. That particular leg of his circuit was a remote one and we had almost forty more miles to go. On backcountry roads, that might take another hour and a half, putting us in Orchard Hill at almost six forty-five. I was in awe of my father's stamina. But then, his endurance had always been inspiring. For a middle-aged man with gray at his temples, he was spry and energetic, and his sermons lit up the congregation with bursts of fire and brimstone to make the most resolute sinner tremble in his boots.

What a lot of people didn't understand about Dad was that, even though his sermons gave the impression he was a hard, judgmental man, underneath, I knew he wasn't. He had a strong calling to minister to the flock in ways they could understand. So, in addition to leading hymns, he also helped arbitrate disputes, raise barns, and fix leaky roofs—anything that needed doing. He often said we are called to bring the sinners to the Lord—and the Lord to the sinners—in any way possible. The two of us had no idea how that conviction was about to be tested.

I'D ALWAYS LIKED DR. MILLER. He was kind, and he talked to me like I was a man instead of a boy. A couple of years before, when I decided I wanted to be a doctor like him, he told me all about what I would need to learn and the schooling I'd have to take. Mrs. Miller was a quiet woman who kept a well-run household, and the food from her table was some of the best on the circuit. They had three grown children: Louise was the oldest, Marlene the youngest, and Charles was in the middle. He was just a year younger than me, and we hung around together whenever Dad and I came to town.

We pulled up to the Miller house on Cavanaugh Street right around suppertime. It was a stately, two-story Victorian with a rose arbor over the front sidewalk and gingerbread trim on the eaves. Dr. Miller's practice was in the little shotgun house next door, and that's where I would be staying —in one of the patient rooms in the back.

The doctor and his younger daughter, Marlene, were sitting on the front porch waiting for us, and they both descended on the car as soon as we pulled in and turned off the engine.

"Alvin!" my father boomed, "How are you, my brother?"

Dr. Miller stuck out his hand and gave my dad a broad grin. "I'm well, Reverend, doing very well. And yourself?"

"It's a hot one today, but the Lord saw fit to give us good weather for our travels, so I can't complain."

"Well, come in and kick the dust off your boots. Martha's got supper almost ready."

I walked around to the trunk to get our travel bags and almost jumped out of my skin when Marlene Miller appeared right at my elbow.

"Hi, Billy Ray Davenport—long time, no see."

"Hi yourself," I replied. Her hair was pulled back in a sleek blond pony-tail, and she smelled of some kind of cloying, flowery perfume. She wore a navy, polka-dot dress that tied around her neck, leaving her shoulders bare. The skirt stood out all around her like a moat around a castle. A pink belt cinched her tiny waist and emphasized her chest. I knew a lot of the guys at my college would think Marlene Miller was the cat's meow. She was pretty, no doubt, but although she looked like a nice girl on the outside, I hadn't seen any evidence she was nice on the inside.

She batted her eyelashes at me. "Here, let me get one of those bags for you."

I lifted the suitcases, setting each one on the ground beside me, and slammed the trunk shut. "Now, whaddya think my dad would say if I let a girl carry my suitcase?" I shook my head and grinned at her as I leaned over and picked up one bag then the other.

She stood stock-still, blinking and staring at me for a second. Then she seemed to come around, shrugging her bare shoulders. As I started toward the house, she slipped her arm in mine, making me lean over awkwardly to keep from bumping her with the suitcase.

"It's really cool that you're staying all summer. I've told all my friends you're here, so we'll get invites to all the big bashes in the county."

"I'm here to work, Marlene, not play around." She pouted and pulled away from me, hands on her hips. "College hasn't changed you a bit, has it? You're as square as you ever were."

"That I am." I left her standing there and hurried up the front porch steps. As I set our bags just inside the hallway, Charlie came hurtling down the stairs, grinning from ear to ear. He reminded me of the Cheshire cat in *Alice in Wonderland,* a story my mother used to read me. I couldn't help smiling back at him.

"Billy Ray!" He shook my hand and clapped my shoulder. "How you doin'?"

"Right as rain, and you?"

"Never better. Come on in. Supper's almost ready, and I'm half-starved."

I followed him into the dining room, and we sat at the sleek mahogany table set with china plates. That was the other thing I liked about the Millers' house: formal, sit-down dinners with lots of conversation. Dad and I conversed over meals at times, but Aunt Catherine hardly ever said a word at the table.

About ten minutes later, the rest of the family gathered for the evening meal. The rumbling sound of Dad's voice saying grace washed over me in a familiar, comforting wave—that is, until his words mashed together in an abrupt pile-up because somewhere in the middle of the blessing, Marlene's hand found its way to my thigh and gave it a firm squeeze. She was lucky I didn't leap right out of my chair with a yelp. Last summer, the flirtatious smiles and batting eyelashes were bad enough, but now it was apparent that the girl was on a serious mission to get my attention. After Dad declared 'Amen,' I glared at her, but she just responded with a smug little smile. Trying my best to ignore her, I tucked into country-fried steak, mashed potatoes and green beans, listening closely to Dr. Miller as he told my father the plight of one of the families in the Orchard Hill community.

"Quinlan had some wind damage to his barn during that awful storm last month."

"He hasn't fixed it yet?" Dad asked, passing me the butter for my cornbread.

"He bought the lumber but has no one to help him do the repairs. He's got all those girls, you know—no sons to help him out, and no other family around these parts."

Dad frowned, and I remembered that he didn't care much for Tom Quinlan. Tom himself never attended church, and Dad thought he was too lax with his parenting responsibilities and impractical with his money. But in spite of all that, I knew what the next words out of Dad's mouth would be.

"Well, what better way to lead a man to the river of salvation than to help him pull his ox from the ditch? I'll drive over there tomorrow and offer to help. Will you come with me?"

Dr. Miller smiled. "I thought I might be able to talk you into it. I'm already scheduled to make a little trip out that way. I have to check on Mrs. Quinlan because she's just had another baby."

"How many does this make?"

"It's her seventh delivery, although only the four girls have lived to see their first birthday." Dr. Miller sipped his coffee.

I tried to conjure up an image of the Quinlan family, but only a vague recollection of hand-me-down clothes and solemn faces swam before my mind's eye. They rarely attended worship services, and because we typically blew in and out of town over a weekend, I'd had little opportunity to socialize much around Orchard Hill outside of church.

Dr. Miller went on. "I imagine we can get some of the other men in town to pitch in as well, being as tomorrow's Saturday. I'll make some calls after supper."

"I'll go, Pop," Charles said through a mouth full of green beans.

"Thank you, son." Dr. Miller nodded in approval.

"Charlie, please chew with your mouth closed," Mrs. Miller admonished.

"Sorry, Ma." He grinned at me with a 'there-she-goes-again' expression that indicated an affectionate forbearance. His mother was a stickler for propriety and manners.

"He just wants to go out and get a look at that Lizzy Quinlan." Marlene sneered. I turned to her, struck by the vehemence in her tone.

"That's not true," Charles said, indignant as he threw his napkin across the table at his sister.

"He'd rather get an eyeful of Jeannie." Louise nodded her head as if she knew everything about it.

Charles blushed.

"Now, Jeannie Quinlan is a nice girl," Mrs. Miller began.

"But Lizzy..." Louise stopped cold at a stern look from her father.

Mrs. Miller sighed and said no more.

"She's a slut," Marlene blurted out.

"That's enough!" Dr. Miller said in a sharp tone.

"Marlene, your language! And in front of Reverend Davenport and his son." Mrs. Miller gasped in dismay and turned crimson with embarrassment.

"Well, it's true," Marlene muttered under her breath.

I watched the whole interchange in fascination. Family squabbles were always interesting to me because I'd never had one.

Dad spoke up, ready to smooth the waters in that decisive way of his, like King Solomon might have all those years ago. "I believe this is when the preacher is supposed to say, 'He who is without sin should cast the first stone,' but you all know that story already, and this kind of sordid talk is hardly an appropriate topic for the dinner table. So I'll just leave it there, shall I?"

"I think you owe the Reverend an apology." Mrs. Miller put down her fork. Apparently, her daughter's lack of decorum had stolen her appetite.

"I'm sorry, sir," Marlene mumbled.

"You don't owe me an apology, Marlene." Dad wiped his mouth with his napkin and laid it beside his plate. "But you might look into your heart and see if you can genuinely repent and request forgiveness from your Lord." He looked up at our hostess and smiled. "Excellent dinner, Mrs. Miller. You bless us with your hospitality, and we humbly extend our gratitude."

Mrs. Miller looked a bit uncomfortable still, but she told Dad he was very welcome, and she offered us some warm cherry cobbler. Then, thankfully, the conversation turned to more pleasant topics.

Chapter Two

We were working on the Quinlans' barn by nine o'clock the next morning. About a dozen people showed up to help, and I noticed a fair number of stray looks toward to the house—from the young guys mostly but even from some of the men. About eleven o'clock, those looks were rewarded with a slam of the screen door and a holler.

"Daddy, if y'all are hungry, we got your dinner up here."

"Thank you, Lizzy," Tom replied. "We'll be up in a minute or two."

I turned my head toward the sound of the girl's voice and promptly hit my thumb with the hammer. Somehow, I managed to squelch my yell, and as I stuck my thumb in my mouth to soothe it, I carefully took in the captivating sight of Lizzy Quinlan.

She was not very tall. I was probably head and shoulders above her, but her figure was—there was no other word for it—voluptuous. It was made even more so by the denim cutoffs that hugged her hips and the sleeveless red-gingham blouse that stretched and strained against the buttons across her chest. She'd left the ends of the blouse unbuttoned and tied them in a knot around her middle, showing the hourglass curve of her waist. She was barefoot, and long, lush dark curls were drawn back in a ponytail that bounced when she walked. Her lips and her toenails were painted what I'd overheard Aunt Catherine call 'harlot red' when she thought I wasn't listening. Marlene Miller had called Lizzy Quinlan a slut, and I didn't want to judge a book by its cover, but I had to admit she kind of looked the part. She took springy running steps to the barn, leaping like a gazelle over rocks and two-by-fours until she reached her father. They spoke briefly, and then he turned to the rest of us and said, "We're mighty grateful to y'all for your help, so my girls have fixed some victuals. It ain't much, but we'll share what we got. If you want to go into the kitchen and grab a plate, the food's in there, and we can sit at the picnic table out back."

Several men mumbled their thanks as they passed by Mr. Quinlan and Lizzy. She looked each one straight in the eye, a smug, calculating smile on her lips. Real smiles, however, were saved for Charles and his father. That's when I noticed her eyes, dark and sparkling like fireworks in the night sky. She turned those fine eyes my way, and I felt my face get hot. She whispered to Charlie and pointed, and I simply stared back at her. And I continued to stare as she approached me.

"Aren't you a little old to be sucking your thumb?" she asked, a teasing lilt in her voice.

"What? Oh…" I hadn't realized it was still in there and dropped my hand to my side quickly. "I hit my thumb with the hammer."

"Let me see." She took my hand in hers and inspected it. "Can you bend it?" she asked.

I nodded then realized her head was bent forward so she couldn't see me. "Yes, ma'am, I'm sure it's fine." My breath stirred the strands of curls that escaped her ponytail.

In slow motion, her face rose to meet mine, and I caught the faintest glimpse of something puzzling in her expression before she covered it with her teasing smile. "Oh, poor baby." She rubbed the base of my thumb, kneading it with her fingers. Her lips formed a little pout, and in a throaty whisper she said, "Does that feel better?"

I jerked my hand back. "Yes, thank you." I started toward the house, and ran right into a stern, troubled look from my father. I kept my back to Lizzy Quinlan and walked straight into the kitchen.

When we finished the repairs to the barn about three o'clock that afternoon, my father stayed with Dr. Miller and a couple of the other men to visit with Tom Quinlan. Everyone seemed to have an agenda: Dr. Miller wanted to assure himself the new baby was doing well, Dad wanted to sound out Tom Quinlan about christening the little one on his next visit to Orchard Hill, and Charles had his eye on the oldest Quinlan girl, Jeannie.

She was a blonde, blue-eyed beauty, pink-cheeked and soft-spoken. Charlie asked if she'd like to take a walk with us over to the quarry. There was a lake there, deep and cool, and maybe they could take a swim since it was such a hot day.

Jeannie stammered, blushed and said she'd ask her father. He waved her off, but then he called her back, and I overheard him say, "Take Lizzy with you. I don't want you off by yourself."

That meant I was stuck with Lizzy Quinlan while Charles chatted up her sister, and I was annoyed and bothered at having a girl foisted on me like that, especially a girl like her.

"Charles," I hissed under my breath. "I don't want to walk out with her. My dad's the minister here."

"So?"

"I don't want people to get the wrong idea," I said, remembering my father's stern look.

"Because you're walking to the quarry with Lizzy and Jeannie and me?" Charles shook his head. "Don't pay no mind to Marlene's rumor mill. She's just being spiteful. Besides, Jeannie and I will be there too. Nobody will say anything."

"I saw how the other boys looked at her—some of the men, too. What Marlene says about her is right, isn't it? She's fast and loose."

Charles sighed. "What they say doesn't matter. You—" He froze, and I realized that the subject of our conversation was most likely right behind me. I whirled around and found myself face-to-face with wounded eyes that hardened the instant I looked into them.

"Don't worry; fast and loose isn't catching. So you can keep your pristine reputation, you son of a…preacher man. A square like you is safe from the likes of me." She spun around and marched toward the house in a fascinating display of incensed feminine indignation.

Words of apology stuck in my throat. Charles looked dismayed and went after her. I heard her say, "I'll still go, Charlie, so Jeannie can go out walking with you. But keep that arrogant, holier-than-thou jerk away from me, okay?"

When we started out a few minutes later, Charles immediately forgot his promise, and he and Jeannie quickly fell back, walking hand-in-hand and talking quietly. Lizzy forged ahead, stalking toward the quarry as fast as her shapely legs would carry her.

It was hot. Sweat plastered my hair against my forehead and temples and beaded on my upper lip. Walking behind Lizzy didn't do anything to help me cool down either. Her hips swayed enticingly from side to side as she stalked up the path, and the curls in that ponytail kept bouncing up and down, up and down. It was downright distracting. Even though I was twenty-one years old, I really didn't know all that much about girls, just whatever I'd managed to overhear in the boys' locker room. I led a pretty sheltered life, and no one shared his girl knowledge with the preacher's kid. But I knew enough to realize Lizzy Quinlan upset my equilibrium, and I didn't like that one bit.

We arrived at the lake in about twenty minutes. Lizzy plopped down on a tree stump a few feet from the water. When I stepped up to the shoreline, I could hear her muttering to herself. She gingerly peeled off her shoe and her harsh intake of air caught my attention.

Concerned, I approached her. "Are you all right?"

"Fine," she snapped, turning to the other shoe.

I kneeled in front of her, frowned and picked up her foot to inspect her heel.

"Get your hands off me!"

"You're bleeding," I stated without emotion. I picked up the shoe and studied it. There was a flat heel, but the leather was stiff and unyielding and the toes were pointed so much they must have hurt her feet. "No wonder. Why would you wear these impractical shoes to hike out here?"

"Maybe they're the only ones I've got."

"Are they?"

"No," she replied hastily, but I wasn't convinced. I'd seen the condition of her family's house.

"Come on." I held my hand out to her. Words of apology for what I'd said would sound empty at that point, but I could show her some kindness. That would restore my faith that I was, in fact, a Christian and a gentleman.

"Where are we going?" She was wary.

"I'll help you down to the water. It will feel good on your blisters, don't you think?"

"Perhaps."

She took my hand, and we sat on a large rock near the water's edge. I let her go as soon as she was settled with her feet dangling in the water. Touching her made my hands tingle, and that was probably not a good thing. If that was the way she affected all the males of the human species, no wonder they watched her from barn windows and from behind farm implements. I stood and looked behind us at Jeannie and Charles; they were sitting on a boulder more than twenty yards away, heads together, shoulders touching.

Lizzy Quinlan followed my gaze. "No matter what you think about me or my family, my sister is a nice girl." She stuck her chin out, her tone defensive.

"Charles seems to like her."

"He does—and don't you ruin it either by lying about her. She deserves to be happy."

"I don't lie," I returned, starting to feel defensive myself. I had no opinion on the matter—no knowledge of whether Jeannie was a nice girl or not. I picked up a stone from the water's edge and skipped it across the lake.

"I know what you think about us. I can see it in your disdainful little scowl, hear it in your haughty voice," she muttered.

She leaned back on her elbows, her feet splashing and churning the water under them. The sun lit her hair in a coppery halo around her head, making her look like a fiery, avenging angel. Her eyes blazed flames at me too, and I stood, mesmerized for a long minute, drinking her in.

Suddenly, her expression changed. The fire in her eyes was gone. I was sorry to see it go because it drew me like a moth to a flame, but what replaced it was even more alluring—and disturbing. It was as if the clear bright flame had been doused by water, turning it to a heavy, smoldering steam. I swallowed—hard. Never before had I understood what people meant by a 'come hither smile,' but now I saw one right in front of me, and knew it for what it was. Before I was even aware of what I was doing, I 'went thither'; my feet propelled me over, and I sat on the rock beside her.

She cast a quick look along the shore line, and behind her to Jeannie and Charles' now empty rock. They must have taken off into the thicket of woods. I wanted to throttle Charlie for leaving me in the clutches of Lizzy Quinlan—and clutched was definitely how I felt at the moment.

She started unbuttoning her blouse.

I leapt to my feet and backed up a couple of steps. "What are you doing?!" My voice sounded harsh and cold, but my heart was pounding.

She smirked. "Going swimming. We are at the lake after all. Don't worry, preacher boy, I'll keep my undies on."

She slipped off her blouse, primly folded it and laid it on the rock. Then she shimmied out of her shorts. Standing up, she stretched her arms high over her head, and looked at me, cocking one eyebrow up in challenge. Then, clothed only in bra and panties, she jumped into the lake.

I watched her disappear beneath the surface and then dark, wet curls appeared a few feet from where she had gone under. She squealed, "Oooh, it's cold!" and wiped the water out of her eyes. "It feels good though. You should get in 'cause it's a long hot walk back. Or can't you swim?"

"Oh, I can swim," I assured her.

"Then why don't you get in?"

The water looked inviting, and so did the mischievous look she was giving me. I stripped off my shirt, socks and shoes, and tossed them in a pile next to hers. "I'm not taking my jeans off."

Her white belly rose to the surface as she glided away from the water's edge. "Suit yourself, but they'll get awfully heavy in the water and mighty clammy feeling on the way back."

She kept treading water about ten feet from the rock. "And if you come back with wet clothes, everyone who saw us leave the house together will know you've been swimming with me."

I thought of my father's stern countenance. She had a point there. I put my hand on my belt and then stopped. "Turn around."

"You don't got nothing I ain't seen before." She was deliberately provoking me now. If it had been anyone else but me, I might have even laughed at the absurdity of the situation.

"If you want me to go swimming with you, you'll turn around," I insisted.

"Sissy-pants," she huffed, and turned her back.

I quietly slipped into the lake. My feet touched the bottom, and the water was up to my waist, but I knew there was probably a steep drop off a few more feet out. She had exaggerated how cold it was, although it was refreshing. Moving silently through the water, I swam up behind her, dove under the surface and tugged on her foot. Even underwater, I heard her shriek. I popped up, right beside her, grinning.

"Why you little...!" She sputtered, wiping water out of her eyes. "You scared me!"

"Well, how about that? It is possible to scare the rough and tough Lizzy Quinlan."

She swam back to where she could touch the bottom and the water came up to her shoulder. "Who said I was rough and tough?"

I shrugged and did a lap out and back a few yards. When I returned, she looked at me with eyes dark as a midnight sky.

"Don't believe everything Marlene Miller tells you about me. She hates my guts because, once upon a time, her boyfriend broke up with her and asked me out. He said she was a pricktease."

I'd never heard that word before, but I had a pretty good idea what it meant. "Did you go out with him?"

"Yep."

I didn't respond.

"Don't you want to know what we did?"

"Nope." I paused. "So I shouldn't believe anything Marlene says about you?"

She grinned. "Believe what you want."

"I want the truth."

"The truth? Who cares about the truth? According to the Orchard Hill gossip ring, every boy in town's had a piece of me."

The blood drained from my face at the vehement disdain in her tone, and then it rushed back into my cheeks after I realized what she meant. To hide my embarrassment, I leaned back to lie on top of the water, my face to the sky, and closed my eyes. "And ye shall know the truth and the truth shall make ye free. John 8:32." I opened one eye and looked at her. "That's what my father would say."

"What would your father say about you skinny-dipping with me out at the quarry?"

"We aren't skinny-dipping—that means swimming without any clothes on."

"Like he would believe that we kept any clothes on."

"He would believe it if I told him it was the truth."

She said nothing, and I sneaked a peek at her out of the corner of my eye. Her eyes were open and she was floating on her back a few feet from me. The white fabric covering her breasts stuck up above the water, and the outline of her nipple was visible. I felt my insides leap in response and closed my eyes again.

We floated that way for several minutes. She was apparently lost in her thoughts, and I was trying to control mine.

Suddenly, I felt her wet head bump my rib cage. We both spluttered and flailed in surprise, and I inadvertently pushed her under me. She wriggled in panic, and I grabbed her around the waist and lifted her back up above the water. She was coughing and trying to catch her breath.

"Are you okay?" I was breathless and trying not to think about her bottom so close to my hip. "Can you stand?"

She shook her head and held onto me. "The water's too deep." Suddenly, she was very still. I was confused until I realized what she must have just felt with her leg. Embarrassed, I almost hurled her toward the water's edge. She regained her footing, and the smoldering, come-hither look was back. I stared at her, breathing hard from being so startled—or that's what I told myself anyway. I turned and stared across the lake, trying to get myself under good regulation. And that's when I felt her warmth up close behind me. Small, wet hands slipped around me and pressed my back to her front. She laid her cheek against my back, and I felt her hands glide down the sides of my body.

I seized them and held them away from me. "Why are you doing this?"

"Why not? Aren't you the least bit curious, Billy Ray? I'll bet my bottom dollar you've never been this close to a girl before."

"Curiosity has nothing to do with it. Men and women shouldn't touch each other like this until they're married."

"Is that what your father says?"

I looked over my shoulder at her, trying to recruit my best scowl. "Yes."

"Does this mean you're going to marry me now?" Her eyes radiated amusement, and I rolled mine and faced out toward the lake again.

"No."

"No," she went on softly. "I didn't think so."

I let her hands go, and she moved back a little, but was still close behind me. The eddies created by the motion of her hands and legs were like liquid fingers swirling around my body. It was almost as if she continued to touch me, except I felt it everywhere.

"So does your father preach about the virtues of chastity?"

"Sometimes."

Her laugh had a bitter quality to it. "He'll have a helluva time convincing the guys around here to give it a go."

"That doesn't mean he isn't right." I finally got up the nerve to turn back around and face her.

"You're such an innocent, Billy Ray." Her face was serious for a minute and perhaps a little sad. Then, a wicked glint lit up her eyes. It was such a rapid transformation that I was smiling before I could stop myself. She moved farther out into the lake.

"What?" I asked, following her.

"You better hold me up, son-of-a-preacher-man, or I'll drown."

"No, you won't; you can swim just fine."

"Maybe I can, and maybe I can't."

I ignored her.

"Maybe I will, and maybe I won't."

I frowned at her and started toward the shore. "I don't like playing silly little games."

"Hold me close," she warned. "I'm going under now." She slipped beneath the surface.

I snorted, knowing she'd be up in a second.

I waited, telling myself that the water wasn't that deep. She was so still though, I couldn't even tell if she was there.

I knew she was pulling my leg, but she didn't resurface, and now I was starting to get angry. I pushed through the water and reached under until I found her arms and hauled her up, crushing her against my chest while I planted my feet on the lake bottom. She was laughing, sputtering and gasping for air, and I shook her a little and growled, "That isn't funny!"

"I beg your pardon, but it is too funny."

I bent my face over hers, glaring at her. "Being reckless like that is a sure-fire way to get hurt." My scowl bore into her, and her lips parted as the silly smile dimmed. We stayed like that, our eyes locked together for half a minute, and then I pulled and pushed her toward the shallow water. As soon as I knew she could stand, I thrust her away from me. "Stupid little fool!"

After slipping and losing her footing, she grappled for balance and stood up, returning my glare. "Why do you care if the town slut drowns?"

I strode past her and turned to sit on the edge of the rock, arms folded across my chest. "I didn't call you that—and I certainly wouldn't want you to drown."

She seemed angry, and for the life of me, I couldn't figure out why. If anyone had a right to be angry, it was me. After all, it was me who was the butt of her joke.

"Oh no," she said sarcastically. "Then everyone would know we were together, and it would look so bad on your reputation and weigh on your conscience. You have such a big...conscience."

I picked up my clothes and headed off for the thicket, where I could wring out my boxers and get dressed in private.

"No sense of humor," she shouted at my back.

I whirled around and strode back to the water's edge. She was out of the lake now, sunning herself on the rock in her bra and panties.

"Okay, fine. I don't have a sense of humor about tricks like that. It's petty and cruel to make people afraid for you, just so you can laugh in their faces. And furthermore, drowning isn't funny. That's how my mother died."

I turned my back on her and approached the cover of the trees once more. I yanked on my pants and left my shirt unbuttoned and flapping in the breeze. I carried my shoes and socks in my hand, and beat a path back to the Quinlan house without looking back. I didn't care if she, Jeannie or Charlie stayed out there all night. Lizzy Quinlan might say she was the town slut, and maybe she was and maybe she wasn't. I had no idea and didn't care. But she had a mean streak about her, and I didn't have to bear the brunt of it.

Chapter Three

After supper, Dad walked me over to Dr. Miller's office where I would sleep for the summer. Mrs. Miller had set up a nice cot for me in one of the patient rooms. There was a bathroom just down the hall, and before we arrived, she had Charles and his dad carry over a chest of drawers to store my clothes. It was plain living, nothing like my upscale room at Aunt Catherine's, but it was a lot cozier than many of the places Dad and I had stayed during our traveling summers. Sometimes, we'd even camped out under the stars.

Dad sat on the cot, watching me hang up my shirt and finish unpacking my things.

"You sure you don't want to stay in the Millers' guest room? I know you're grown, but you might get lonely over here by yourself."

"I'll be fine. It will be good for me to get used to staying alone, and I'm kind of in the mood to be by myself anyway."

"I saw you come back to the Quinlans' before the other young people. Something you want to tell me about?"

I shook my head.

"Ask me about?"

I hid a smile, knowing he was referring to the birds and the bees. We'd never had 'the Talk.' I'd found out about adult relationships between men and women through books and the gossip that ran through small towns like this one. I wouldn't put Dad through the agony of explaining something so embarrassing. That's why I had always tried to spare him those conversations if I could find things out some other way.

"No, Dad."

"Well then…" his voice drifted off.

"Actually, now that I think on it, there is something I want to ask you."

His guard went back up immediately. "What is it, son?"

"What makes some people mean?"

"Mean?"

"Yeah, not evil or horrible, but just a little bit…I don't know…mean?"

"I think people can become mean for a lot of reasons—pride, jealousy, selfishness, greed… Wait, are you talking about the Quinlan girl? The dark-headed one? I saw her leave with Jeannie and you boys."

I nodded.

"Ah. Well, I don't know for sure about Miss Quinlan, of course, since we barely know her. I do wish Tom Quinlan had been more faithful about bringing his family to worship service these last few years. Those girls ought to have been brought up in church; perhaps life would be different for the lot of them." Dad rubbed his chin, deep in thought for a second. "But back to your question—think about this a moment. What does a wounded animal do if you approach it?"

"It snarls at you. It growls."

"And if you try to help it?"

"It might bite," I answered, anticipating the obvious place he was taking this analogy.

"That's right. Now a beloved pet, like a dog or a cat, might let its master help it—maybe—because it's known the kindness of its master's hand. The master pets it, feeds it. But the wild animal has never known that kindness, so it is very likely to bite anyone that gets too close."

"I understand."

"Not that well-loved house pets don't bite their masters, because you and I both know that sometimes they do, even if the master has been kind."

I waited.

"From what I've seen and heard, Lizzy Quinlan is acting a lot like one of God's wounded wild creatures—one who may not know the kindness of the Master's hand, which, as a minister, distresses me. So you should show her Christian compassion, witness to her."

"I thought that's where you were going with this."

He smiled very briefly; then he sobered. "Just remember, the wounded don't always recognize kindness for what it is. They might try to bite you regardless of your intent. Be careful, Billy Ray."

I straightened up and closed the armoire. "I'll keep that in mind."

He stood and patted me on the shoulder. "I'll see you at breakfast. Good night, son."

"Good night."

After Dad left, I turned the little fan on my dresser to a low hum, undressed, and lay on top of the covers, hands folded behind my head. A cool, damp breeze fluttered the curtains and drifted over me. As my body cooled off, so did my angry thoughts. In their place, shame flared up as I remembered the rude comment Lizzy Quinlan overheard me say to Charlie. I wish I'd never uttered those words. They were beneath me. It bothered me to know that I was guilty of repeating gossip and disparaging another person. Lizzy might be wounded, but something told me she really didn't want to hurt anyone. Perhaps I should practice a little more compassion in these situations, like I'd been taught. I wondered, though, what had happened to make her as prickly as a porcupine. Then I wondered if perhaps she was too injured to ever recover, even under the best kindness others could offer.

THANKFULLY, THE NEXT DAY WAS cooler. A breeze blew all morning, chasing white clouds with gray centers across the sky as we walked into church, sitting atop a little knoll on the outskirts of town. It looked like almost every other church on Dad's circuit—white clapboard exterior with chipped paint revealing gray, weather-beaten wood underneath. One simple, stained glass window adorned the front, and a few plain windows were scattered along the sides. Inside, an aisle divided the dark wooden pews down the middle. The floor was the same dark wood with a burgundy aisle-runner, frayed at the edges, leading the way to the altar. The pulpit was a rich golden brown, pock-marked and marred but heavy and eternally solid. A deep, reverberating thud issued forth whenever my dad struck it with the palm of his hand to punctuate a point in his sermon.

The Quinlan girls were lined up in the second to last pew. Jeannie was obviously the leader of the crew in the absence of their parents. Next to her were two younger girls—Carla looked to be about eleven or twelve and Lily was about six or so. Lizzy sat at the other end of the younger two Quinlans, bookending them in conjunction with Jeannie. I stole a couple of looks at her. Her curls hung down around her shoulders, the sides pinned back with some kind of hair doohickey that girls use. The dress she wore was simple, modest, but stretched tight across the bosom like her gingham shirt was yesterday. Her lips were still painted that red color. It looked almost garish in the morning light and against that prim little dress. Our eyes met once before church began, but after giving me a long, serious look, she turned her head and I couldn't attract her gaze again. Not that I was trying to, of course.

I was sitting near the front with Dr. Miller on one side of me and Charles on the other. It had been touch and go there for a minute whether I'd have to sit next to Marlene, but under the guise of being gentlemanly, I gestured for the Miller ladies to go first and then waited, out of respect, for Doc to enter the pew before me. That seating arrangement saved my sanity because Marlene couldn't carry a tune in a bucket. And I wouldn't put it past her to try and give my thigh another squeeze when she thought no one was looking—even if we were in a church pew.

I leaned slightly toward Charlie and whispered, "Why aren't you sitting with Jeannie?"

"I didn't know she was coming with her sisters in tow. It's been ages since they were all here together. Mr. Quinlan stopped coming to church years ago, but Mrs. Quinlan would still bring the girls till about the last three or four years. Now they come sporadically at best when Mr. Collier conducts the service, but the girls are all here today, and Jeannie wanted to sit with her sisters. Their mother is still recovering from the baby, so she stayed home."

I almost laughed at how much of an expert on the Quinlan family Charlie had become, but he wasn't finished yet.

"Actually," he opened the bulletin and folded it back, creasing it so it was inside out. "Jeannie said Lizzy insisted on coming to worship this morning." He shrugged. "I guess it's good that both Jeannie and Lizzy are here. Carla will sit quietly no matter what, but Lily needs the two older girls to corral her."

I didn't comment further because Dad had begun his sojourn from the back of the sanctuary, which meant service was about to start. There was a buzz of excitement throughout the congregation. Having the minister in town was a special occasion of sorts. I had the feeling the services led by the lay minister, Mr. Collier, left something to be desired.

Church went long that morning, because Dad had baptisms to do in addition to the sermon. People wanted to talk to him after the services too, and after waiting alone in the stuffy church for at least twenty minutes, I decided to go outside for some fresh air.

There was a cemetery out back, a variety of headstones—some new, some ancient and sticking up, snaggletoothed, above the grass. A lot of people are afraid of graveyards, but I always found them peaceful, except for the one where Mama was laid to rest. That one just made me miss her.

A cluster of trees bordered one side, so I walked around the fence toward the welcoming shade. One of the trees was split in two, all the way to the ground, so I braced my back against one trunk and put one foot against the other. My eyes caught a flicker of movement, and I saw Lizzy Quinlan walking toward me, her skirt whipping around her legs. The warm breeze tossed her hair in a frolicking, chaotic dance around her head and shoulders. Her eyes met mine, but she didn't look angry, nor did she give off the sparkling fireworks I'd seen when she spoke with Charles and his dad. It wasn't the sultry, disturbing look from the day before either. Instead, her gaze held the barest hint of a warm glow, like a candle flame flickering in the breeze. I had planned on waiting for her to speak, but found myself greeting her first anyway.

"Morning, Lizzy Quinlan."

A shy smile crossed her lips, and she looked down at her shoes. I noticed they were the same shoes she wore to the lake yesterday. "It's afternoon now, Billy Ray."

I stayed very still, afraid to make a noise, afraid to move. If I did, I had the distinct impression she'd bolt, and something told me that would be the end of ever seeing behind that hard shell of hers. What I wanted to see there, or why I wanted to see it, I had no idea.

She inhaled and exhaled deeply, straining the buttonholes on her dress to their breaking point. Out in the sunlight, I noticed that her lips didn't look quite as lurid as they did inside the church.

"I was afraid you wouldn't speak to me after yesterday. You ran off before I could say anything. By the time I got back home, you and your Daddy were gone back to Dr. Miller's."

I folded my arms across my chest. "I was mad at you."

"I know, and I had all night to think about it." She closed her eyes briefly and then looked me directly in the chest. "I'm sorry for teasing you and for pretending I was gonna drown myself. I didn't know about your mama, honest."

Now, that took me by surprise. An apology was the last thing I expected from the girl who acted so prickly the day before. I paused a minute, but given who I was, what I'd been taught, there was really only one thing I could say—even though I didn't feel it.

"I forgive you." The words tasted like sawdust in my mouth, false and dry —a rote response to repentant words I'd heard uttered many times before, between many other people.

Then, her eyes darted up to look in mine, and the whole world stopped turning on its axis. I was trapped, suspended by her stare and frozen in time. It took me a minute to realize she'd kept on speaking.

"I almost lost my mama a few years back. She about near died when one of my brothers was born. I was really scared, 'cause I can't imagine life without her."

"I didn't know you had any brothers."

She nodded. "Two. That one was stillborn. The other one died when he was three months old."

"I'm sorry." That sounded a little warmer, a little more like the real me, rather than the dutiful minister's son.

Pulling my hand out from under my crossed arms, she tugged me along behind her. "Come here, I'll show you." She led me to two little gravestones side by side. One said *Thomas Quinlan, Jr.* and the other said *Jeremiah Quinlan.*

"Having Jeremiah almost killed Mama. He was the one after Lily. That's why Doc was so concerned about her when Baby Susie was born last month. Thomas was born after Carla. He died of crib death when I was eight."

"How old are you now?"

"Old enough," she replied, a wicked grin spreading across her features. But I kept staring her down, and she shrugged. "I'll be nineteen in November."

A little girl's voice called across the yard. "Hurry up, Lizzy! We gotta go home now!"

"Coming!" She turned to me. "See ya round."

"Would you like me to walk you home?" I wondered what on earth had put that idea in my head.

Her expression turned wary. "Aren't you riding back with your dad?"

"He'll be tied up at the church for a while. He's used to me getting back to wherever we're staying on my own."

"I live on Linden Road, so it's out of your way."

"I'll walk you to the turn-off then."

"Okay." She seemed almost nervous.

"If you'd rather not be seen with me..." I began, half-smiling.

"Oh no! No. It's fine if you want to walk me home." She shrugged. "I was just surprised that you'd want to when Jeannie and Carla and Lily will be there too. I won't be alone. Usually, fellas aren't too interested in being with me unless they can get me somewhere by myself."

"I'm not most fellas," I declared.

"Sure you aren't." She shot me an amused look as we started walking toward the road. "I overheard Dr. Miller tell someone that you were going to stay and work with him this summer."

"Mm-hmm. I'm going to be a doctor, and Charlie's dad was kind of my inspiration so..."

"Doc is one of the best people I know. I can see why you would admire him. Are you going to medical school this fall?"

I nodded.

"So, you'll be here all summer?" She turned and walked backwards as she talked.

I smiled, and she stopped in her tracks for a second, staring at me, lips parted. Then she shook her head and kept walking. Jeannie and Carla were up ahead of us by several yards, and Lily was skipping along behind them.

"Charles is nice, like Doc," she continued, "but those sisters of his are horrid. Hanging around with them won't be any fun."

"I'm not actually staying in their house. I'm living in one of the patient rooms at the doctor's office."

"Oh, that's better then. If you were at Millers', you might wake up one morning with Marlene curled up in your bed with you. She's been talking all over town about how she's got you all to herself this summer, and saying that by September you'll be hers." Her words were glib, but I caught a hint of warning under the sarcasm.

I stopped, shocked that even Marlene would make such a forward suggestion. "She's mistaken. I'm here to work with Dr. Miller, not run around with her all summer long."

"Oh, I knew she was lying. She's a liar." A bitter note crept into her voice.

I put my hands in my pockets and looked off in the distance.

"Just like a preacher's son. You won't talk bad about her, will you? Even if she talks about you first?"

"I was recently reminded how much gossip hurts people. I'm trying to do better." I wondered if I should say the apology that was on my lips, but she reached over and squeezed my forearm. Her eyes shone and told me she'd just received my sentiment loud and clear, but I said it anyway.

"I was wrong to repeat the rumors I heard about you. I won't do that again."

Her voice was very soft, and it warmed a place deep in the pit of my stomach. "Thank you. I'll try to do better, too, and not tease you anymore."

We walked a while in silence until we came to the turn off for Linden Road. Her sisters were standing there waiting for her, Jeannie eyeing me with a cool, appraising stare.

"Bye, Billy Ray. I'll see you around." Lizzy's face broke into a bright, happy smile, summoning an involuntary grin from my own lips.

"See ya," I said, before continuing up the road that would lead me back to Millers' and a pot roast Sunday dinner.

Chapter Four

Dad left the next day, leaving me in Orchard Hill under Dr. Miller's tutelage. Our parting this time was like so many previous goodbyes—a heartfelt hug and a "God bless you and keep you." We had said farewell a hundred times before, during the school years and when I went to college, and we were well practiced at it.

From the very start, I loved working at Dr. Miller's office. It was one interesting place to be; that was for sure. We saw food poisoning, cuts that needed stitches, a broken nose from an errant baseball, and a case of heat stroke. We took care of them all, except for one man who fell off a roof and broke his arm—him we had to send to the hospital in the next town.

One surprising thing I discovered was that not everyone was treated with the medicines that lined the shelves of Mr. Lucas's pharmacy around the corner. This came to light one morning when I was fetching a chart for Doc.

The front doorbell rang, the door opened slowly, and I realized that the person behind it was having trouble getting in. The bottom end of a cane poked through then stopped. I strode over to the door and gradually opened it so as not to startle the person or make him lose his balance.

But it wasn't a *he;* it was a *she*—a tiny, wizened thing with white hair and a hunched posture. She smelled faintly of liniment and, if I wasn't mistaken, cats.

"Thank you, young man." Her voice was thin, and it crackled like yellowed paper when you wadded it up. "That door gets heavier every time I come in. Sooner or later, I'll just have to wait outside until someone comes in or goes out." She cackled at her own joke.

"Are you ill, ma'am? Do you need to see Dr. Miller?"

"Ill? Oh no—no more than usual. Just old: ninety-one years old to be exact. I've lived out my time, and now I'm borrowing someone else's." She squinted up at me. "Who are you, sonny? You look familiar."

"Billy Ray Davenport, ma'am."

"Hmm. Do I know your mama?"

I suppressed a smile. Boy, if I had a dime for every time I heard *that* question! "No, ma'am, I'm not from here."

"Oh. Could've sworn I'd seen you before." She began to hobble over to a chair, so I took her arm.

"You here to see Doc too?"

"No, ma'am. I work here."

"You work here?" She sat down with a big sigh and eyed me again. "You're too young to be a doctor, ain't ya?"

"I'm not a doctor. I'm just helping out this summer. What can I do for you?"

"Oh, well then. I'm Mrs. Long, and I'm here for my tea. So just scamper along and get it for me, and I'll be on my way."

"Tea?"

"Yes. I've brought my money too, so you needn't worry about that."

Now I was considerably more confused.

"Your tea?"

"Yes, for my rheumatism. Be quick about it now. I don't want to take time away from all the sick people."

I looked around to be sure, but there was no one else in the office. Having no idea what she was talking about, I went to fetch Doc. He smiled and said he'd be in to talk to her in just a minute.

While I waited with her, she asked me again who I was, why I was there, who my mama was, and what was wrong with me. Finally, much to my relief, Doc came into the waiting room.

"Good morning, Mrs. Long. What can I do for you today?"

"I need my tea for my rheumatism." She leaned forward and whispered, "This handsome young man you've got working here is very well-mannered, but I'm afraid he's not too bright." She touched a gnarled finger to her temple. "He doesn't seem to know what I'm talking about."

Dr. Miller winked at me. "Well, Mrs. Long, I'm afraid I don't have your tea here."

She sat up straight—well, as straight as she could. "You don't?"

"Mrs. Gardener makes your tea for you, remember?"

She sat for a second. Then she laughed. "That's right. You'll forgive an old, forgetful woman, won't you, Doc?"

"To be sure." He patted her shoulder gently. "In fact, I'll go one better than forgiveness. How about if you wait here in the office where it's nice and cool, and I'll send Billy Ray down to fetch it for you?"

She cracked a big smile. "Oh, that would be lovely. It's so hot today." She fished in her purse. "Here, young man. Here's the money for it."

Doc pulled me aside, and scribbled something on a scrap piece of paper. "Mrs. Gardener's house is at 212 Adalia Street."

"What on earth"—I pointed to Mrs. Long—"is she talking about?"

"Mrs. Gardener is the local midwife, and she brews up some of the old Indian and folk remedies and sells them."

"You've got to be joking! Sir," I added hastily.

He chuckled. "I don't use her concoctions for everything, and I know that some of the effects must be placebo, but many of them do seem to help my patients with chronic symptoms, like Mrs. Long. I check up on the ingredients and the mixtures to make sure they're not harmful, and then I look the other way."

I thought the world had just turned upside down. Dr. Miller, a man of science and medicine, advocating the use of potions and other pharmaceutical chicanery?

"Don't be so shocked, my boy. Do you really think I'm arrogant enough to insist I know everything under the sun about healing the sick?" He patted my shoulder. "Now, get going. It's quiet here right now, but you never know what the next hour will bring."

I walked out into the hot sunshine, four blocks down to the intersection of Cavanaugh and Adalia, and began counting house numbers. I remembered that I'd run across Lizzy Quinlan walking down this street a couple of days ago. We had nodded and greeted each other, and when I turned back around, curious to see who she might be visiting, I saw her disappear into the house I was standing in front of now.

Mrs. Gardener's house was a pristine white dwelling with blue shutters and a picket fence. No sinister wisps of smoke or noxious odors greeted me when I stepped up to the porch, so I knocked on the door.

Through the open window, I heard a melodious alto call out, "Can you get that door for me, honey? I'm elbow-deep in brew right now."

The door flew open.

"Billy Ray!"

"Lizzy?"

"Um, hi."

"Hi."

"What are *you* doing here?"

"I came to pick up something for," I looked down at my note. "Mrs. Long." I handed her the paper. "Doc wrote it down for me."

She took it and stepped back from the door. "Okay, I'll let Mrs. G know. Come on in." I followed her, taking in the pretty, blue sundress she wore and the ever-present bouncing ponytail. It looked like she had new shoes too, some kind of strappy white leather with a buckle.

"You look nice."

She smiled, and I was rewarded with sparkly firework eyes. "Thanks."

A woman, maybe forty years old with a few wisps of gray scattered through her otherwise black hair, stepped through the doorway, drying her hands on a clean white towel. She had a calming, pleasant smile, which she directed at the two of us. "Can I help you, young man?"

Lizzy gave her the note. "Doc sent him to get this for Mrs. Long."

Mrs. Gardener read it and shook her head, chuckling. "She always forgets that she's supposed to come here instead of the doctor's office."

"Here's her money."

She counted and pocketed the coins I gave her. "Interesting that she can't remember where to get it, but she always remembers exactly what it costs. I guess it's no coincidence that Doc's office is a shorter distance from her house, either." She paused, but I was looking at Lizzy and didn't notice right away.

"You two know each other?" she asked, a trace of amusement in her voice.

Lizzy looked from me to the lady of the house. "Oh, sorry. Mrs. Gardener, this is Billy Ray Davenport. He's Reverend Davenport's son, and he's working at Doc's office this summer."

"Nice to meet you." She held out a hand and shook mine. It was clean and soft and smelled of lavender.

"Billy Ray's gonna be a doctor too, just like Doc." Lizzy smiled up at me in a rare display of honest admiration.

"Doc Miller's a good one to learn from. They don't make many like him anymore." She turned and went back into the kitchen.

Lizzy and I stood there, looking at each other and then at the ground. It was an awkward silence but sort of pleasant too.

Mrs. Gardener came back in, a mason jar in each hand. She looked down and checked the labels. "Here's yours, Lizzy." She handed her one jar. "And here's Mrs. Long's." She handed me the other. "Well, I got to get back in the kitchen and then out to the garden before dinner."

"Thank you for this, Mrs. G. It seems to help Mama."

"You're welcome, child. Good to meet you, Mr. Davenport."

I nodded. "Mrs. Gardener."

I opened the door for Lizzy, and we went back out into the heat.

She picked up a bag sitting beside the door and drifted down the steps. She had this light, graceful way of moving that made me expect her to start floating a couple inches above the ground any second.

"I'll walk you to your turn-off today. Cavanaugh Street is on my way back to Linden."

She held open the gate for me, and I nodded and smiled to her as I passed. She didn't move for several seconds, staring at me, until I turned around to face her.

"What?" I asked, walking backwards and grinning.

She looked away and shook her head, trying to hide her expression. "You really have no idea, do you?"

"About what?"

The gate banged shut behind her as she fell in step beside me. "What that smile of yours does to us girls," she teased.

"What do you mean?"

"It melts us till we're just puddles on the floor."

I flushed a bright red and turned back around, walking forwards again. How was I supposed to react to that?

"It's a good thing you don't wield that smile too often, Billy Ray. You'd be spoiled rotten with all kinds of womanly favors."

I blushed hotter and kept walking.

"I didn't mean to embarrass you."

"You didn't embarrass me," I lied.

We walked almost a block in silence.

"Why are you all dressed up today?"

"Oh, this old thing?" She laughed. "It really is an 'old thing.' Mrs. G found it for me at a second-hand shop. I don't think it looks second-hand though, do you?"

I cast my eyes quickly to the side. "It's pretty."

"Mrs. G says it suits my figure better than Jeannie's old dresses. Jeannie's the oldest girl, you know, so I get a lot of her hand-me-downs."

"Mm-hmm."

"But Jeannie's smaller around the chest, so her dresses don't always fit so well. See, this one has a v-neck, and it crosses over in the front, so there's more room."

I picked up my pace a bit. I didn't have much to contribute to a conversation about how girls' clothes fit across their...

I glanced quickly at Lizzy. She wasn't looking at me as if she was teasing though. She just as easily could have been talking about the weather or her breakfast. Suddenly, she seemed to notice I wasn't talking anymore.

"At least, that's what Mrs. G says."

I kept looking at the ground in front of me as I walked.

"The shoes came with it. Are these shoes more practical than my other ones, Billy Ray?"

"Do they hurt your feet?"

"Not yet."

"Then I guess they're more practical."

"It's real nice of you to get Mrs. Long her tea."

"Doc didn't want her walking in the heat."

"Makes sense. She's about ninety years old, and she forgets things like drinking enough water. That's another reason the tea helps her. It keeps her fluids up. I think that's one of the things about the tea that helps Mama too. This stuff," she held up the jar, "is supposed to help her milk production, but Doc and Mrs. G say the extra water helps as much as anything."

"I was surprised that Doc sends his patients to a wise woman."

Lizzy nodded. "It's unusual, I guess, for a doctor to do that. But there are a lot of people around here needing help, and Doc is just one man. I think he learned that folks were better off if he worked with Mrs. G rather than against her."

"I see."

"That really started after Mama had Jeremiah. Doc almost lost her, and Mrs. G helped him save her with that squaw vine mixture that helped the baby come out. That shook him up some, you know. They started talking with each other more after that happened. Mrs. G told me though, that she would've lost Mama too if it hadn't been for them antibiotics he give her when she got the childbed fever."

Lizzy Quinlan said the darnedest things sometimes.

"It takes a mighty big fella to ask for help when he's at a loss and everyone's looking to him to make it all right." She looked at me pointedly. "*That's* what makes Doc a great man."

"I will lift up mine eyes unto the hills, from whence cometh my help. My help cometh from the Lord, which made heaven and earth."

"Huh?"

"It's from Psalm 121. My father says although all help comes from the Lord, sometimes it takes an unexpected form, and we need the Lord's guidance to see it for what it is. I guess that happened to Doc and Mrs. Gardener —and to your mama."

"Do you have an answer for everything in that Bible of yours?"

"It's your Bible too."

"Hmmph."

"I have yet to find a problem or question I can't use the Bible to help me solve. Big meaningful questions I mean, not things like two plus two."

She giggled at my joke. "You think about things real deep, don't you?"

My shoulders lifted in a half-hearted shrug. "I just try to make sense of what I see, that's all. And traveling around with my father, I've seen a lot."

"I imagine you have."

We reached the turn off to Cavanaugh Street. "Well, here's my street," I replied. "I'll see you later, Lizzy. I hope your mama gets to feeling better."

"Thanks."

I waited till after she left, given what she'd said earlier, but I couldn't keep from grinning as I watched her walk down the road. Her fine eyes and her unique outlook just made me smile.

Chapter Five

From the time I was a little boy, I always liked Westerns—movies, comic books, TV shows like *Gunsmoke* and *Northwest Passage*, and, of course, Western novels. Some of my friends thought they were boring and predictable, but to me, forging new territory in the untamed West seemed like an exciting adventure. Then again, I liked the familiar feel of the stories, comforting as an old blanket—mountains and prairies, cowboys and noble Indians, determined settler families and gunslingers. Everyone knew good from evil, and was clear on which side he stood. When my father saw me with another book in my hand or heard I was going to see a western movie, he'd just smile and shake his head.

"Those stories make the right thing seem crystal clear, but it isn't always so easy to discern in real life, Billy Ray."

And I'd just smile and say, "You're right, Dad." I knew that the real Old West wasn't quite as exciting as the stories. After all, I'd been to college. I knew my American history. But my Westerns—those stories had rules: rules for how men behaved toward women and how women behaved toward men, rules that made it easier on all the townsfolk to get along and unite against the outlaws, and the bad guy always lost in the end. I found no better escape than a well-told cowboy story.

There was no TV in Doc's office, of course, and no bookstore in Orchard Hill, and I was really missing my Westerns that summer. I could have spent my evenings in the Millers' living room watching television, but I didn't. I had grown tired of Marlene's snide gossiping by the close of the first evening after Dad left town, and by Thursday of that week, I'd had it with her.

By that time, I had already learned to claim the wingback chair to the side. The sofa had the best vantage point for watching TV, but when I sat there, Marlene couldn't resist all that open chenille-covered space beside me.

Thursday was *Zane Grey Theater* night, and it was an anthology series, not one continuous story like *Gunsmoke,* so you had to pay attention to know what was happening. As the opening credits faded from the screen, and I got ready to lose myself in the story, Marlene started in over and above the sounds of gunfire on the show.

"Who's that girl on TV?"

"Diane something-or-other," Louise replied. "I think she's pretty."

"I don't like the look of her. She reminds me of that Sheila Robinson down at the dress shop. You know who I'm talking about, Louise. The girl who acts like she's better than everyone else because her mother was a Thompson, of the Bedford Thompsons."

Marlene looked at me expectantly. I suppose she was waiting for me to ask about the Thompsons from Bedford, but I couldn't care less, so I ignored her and leaned toward the TV set.

"She might be related to the Thompsons, and her uncle might be a state senator, but that sure doesn't make her the envy of every girl in Orchard Hill. Her teeth are crooked, and she has a face like a donkey's."

Mrs. Miller glanced at me. "That isn't kind, Marlene."

"But it's true."

Her mother pursed her lips and let out a little sigh of frustration as she jabbed her needle into the fabric she had stretched tight across some kind of round frame. Her face looked as tight as that fabric, but she made no reply.

Marlene scooted over until she was sitting at the corner closest to my chair. She leaned over the sofa arm and twirled her ponytail around one finger. "Besides, if the Robinsons are so important, what are they doing here in Orchard Hill anyway?" She sat back. "I certainly wouldn't live in this tired old place if I could live over in Richmond or London, would you, Billy Ray?"

For me, not wanting to live in Orchard Hill had more to do with Marlene being there than anything else, but of course, I couldn't say that in her mother's living room after I'd just eaten from her table.

"Once I'm through school, I'll have to move anyway. I probably won't have much choice in the matter." I turned back to the TV set.

After a couple of minutes of blissful silence, she tried to engage me in conversation again. "And look at that actress's hair! My goodness, what a mess! Reminds me of the way that Lizzy Quinlan looked on Sunday—all wild and sticking out all over."

I felt an involuntary jolt at the name. Casting a quick look at Marlene, I saw her watching me closely. "But then again, there probably isn't a comb in the whole Quinlan household."

I still said nothing.

"Or maybe she was still disheveled from a tumble with some fella in the churchyard."

Louise snickered, and Mrs. Miller implored, "Marlene, please!" She laid her needlework to the side and stood up, desperate to provide a distraction. "Billy Ray, would you like a scoop of ice cream?"

"No, thank you, ma'am. I'm still full from dinner."

"I'll have some," Louise piped up.

"None for me," Marlene replied without looking toward her mother.

Mrs. Miller looked between the three of us and went into the kitchen.

Marlene leaned toward me and lowered her voice so her sister couldn't hear her. "You sure disappeared fast after church on Sunday. Did Lizzy Quinlan haul you off behind a bush too?"

I stood up.

"Oh, sit down, Billy Ray. Don't get all in a huff; I was only teasing." Her smile was bright, but it had a cruel undertone to it.

"I'm going to bed. I've gotta work early in the morning, and I've missed the first part of the TV show anyway."

"Suit yourself then. Good night. Sleep tight." Marlene leaned back against the sofa. She looked confused, and if I read her right, a little miserable too. Then a smug smile crossed her face. "Think about me."

Mrs. Miller was standing at the doorway with Louise's ice cream in her hand. Her eyes widened at Marlene's remark, but she didn't respond to it.

"Turning in so early, Billy Ray?" she managed to say over her embarrassment.

"Yes, ma'am. Big day tomorrow. Thank you for dinner."

"You're welcome, of course."

As I left the house, I could hear the strained voices filled with family strife as Mrs. Miller scolded her daughter. I couldn't make out the words, but then again, I didn't try very hard.

I was still trying to clear my head of the image of Lizzy Quinlan hauling me behind a bush.

I TRIED A COUPLE MORE times to join the Millers after dinner, but then I gave up. Without a preacher's presence to rein her in, Marlene was merciless regarding parishioners from church, the store clerks in town, and the young women who worked at the bank. Even the seventy-year-old postmistress didn't escape her sharp tongue. I was confident that Doc wouldn't have let her get away with talking like that, but he was usually in his office reading, so he didn't hear her, and Charlie was hardly ever home, spending more and more evenings at the Quinlans' house visiting Jeannie—not that he corrected his older sister even when he was home. Louise agreed with everything Marlene said, and Mrs. Miller tried her best to ignore the venom spewing from her daughter's lips as she sat in a stuffed rocking chair, working on her mending or knitting or some kind of needlework she called 'crewel.' Poor Mrs. Miller—I almost felt sorry for her in spite of my opinion that she didn't exert her parental authority nearly enough. Periodically, she would sigh at some egregious remark, and then she would cast me a nervous glance, probably wondering what I was telling my father in my letters. Marlene made her mother so uneasy that I began to wonder if the gossip was an unusual occurrence, something done for my attention. I decided to take Doc's example and find myself a nice, quiet place to read.

And that was how I ended up at the public library that sunny afternoon about a week after Dad left Orchard Hill.

The building was one of those old, white-brick Carnegie libraries built all over the country in the last century, complete with uneven wood floors crowded with endless stacks of books—and enough historical and western fiction to keep me occupied all summer. When I walked in, Mrs. Martinson, the librarian, was speaking in low tones with a volunteer. She looked the librarian part for sure—hair rolled up in a twist on her head, wire-rimmed glasses, sturdy shoes, dark navy dress with a white lace collar. Dr. Miller told me she was nice, so I went right up to the front desk and stood there, patiently waiting for her to finish.

She looked over at me, and I smiled to let her know I wanted help. She stood there a second and blinked at me. I saw an opening to interrupt her, so I took it.

"Excuse me, ma'am? I'd like to get a library card. I don't live here all the time, but I'm staying here for the summer, helping out in Dr. Miller's office. My name is Billy Ray Davenport and—"

"I know who you are, Mr. Davenport. Your father officiated at my wedding and christened my baby," she replied, dismissing the volunteer and coming over to help me herself. She plucked a pencil and a yellow sheet of paper out of a drawer. "You can fill out this form here, and I'll see you get a card."

I stood at the desk and filled in the boxes, and Mrs. Martinson said I could pick up my card when I came back to check out my books. I high-tailed it over to the fiction shelf to look for Louis L'Amour, one of my favorite authors. Before I knew it, I had an armful of books, too many to check out at once, and found myself wondering which ones to choose. Well on my way toward quenching my thirst for a good Western, I paused when felt a charge in the air, almost like the crackle of electricity. I glanced at the back door, and sure enough, there was Lizzy Quinlan, breezing through the center aisle with three or four books under her arm.

She strode in like she owned the place—a woman on a mission. Without a thought, I took a step toward her but stopped when I saw the ice form in Mrs. Martinson's eyes. Oh, she was polite enough, saying, "Hello, Lizzy, how are you today?" But her expression conveyed it all: suspicion, envy, distrust. A trio of young women at one of the tables whispered and snickered behind their hands.

Lizzy ignored them, gave Mrs. Martinson a bright, brittle smile, and pulled a note out of her jeans pocket. After reading it, the librarian pointed her down the aisle next to mine, and something in that cold interchange made me duck back behind the shelf instead of speaking to her as I'd originally planned.

I could hear her whisper Dewey Decimal numbers and could almost see her trailing a finger across the book spines. "47, 61, 86…"

"Hey, Lizzy." The male voice startled me out of the trance she put me under with her low, sonorous muttering.

"Oh, hey Johnny Lee."

"What are you doing here?"

"Checking out a book, ya' dope. What's it look like?"

I stifled a grin.

"Well, excuse me. Didn't know you liked to read or nothin'."

"Well, I do." I could see her when I peeked through the shelves, hands on her hips, chin up. "I know you don't like to read, so what are *you* doing here?" she asked him right back.

"Me and my brother come over and read the *Sports Cars Illustrated* mags and stuff."

"Oh."

I heard Lizzy's voice move farther down the row and saw a larger shadow pass by me as this Johnny Lee person followed her. My spine stiffened as I moved with them, close enough to listen, but careful to keep myself hidden.

"We got some beer and sodas in the truck, and we're going fishing later. You wanna come?"

"Who all's gonna be there?"

"Me, and Hank, and maybe Jerry Wayne, some of the other guys."

"Where?"

"Down by Lock Six."

I was appalled. Did this goon actually just ask a young woman to go alone with a bunch of guys who were drinking, out in the middle of nowhere?

"I gotta get home early tonight. Got chores."

I relaxed a little, glad that Lizzy Quinlan had some sense after all.

"Aww, come on Lizzy. You can have a little fun with us. You're a fun girl."

How would he know that? Had she been down there with him before? She *was* kind of quick to take off her clothes and go swimming that day we went to the lake.

"I am a fun girl," she replied, "but sitting down with a bunch of you yahoos getting drunk and slinging fishing line doesn't sound all that fun to me."

"Maybe you'd rather us be alone?" I heard him move closer, and saw him put a hand up on the bookshelf above her head, so he could lean over her.

"I told you, I got chores." She stood her ground. "Now, back up. I gotta find this other book...for Jeannie."

"Your loss, baby doll."

"Mm-hmm."

"Me and Hank, we can wait for you. Give you a ride home if you want."

"I'm not going home yet."

"I thought you had chores..."

"Oh, good Lord Almighty, Johnny Lee! I told you I wasn't going with you. Go on and git. Your buddies are waiting for you. And I got stuff to do."

"You're missing out." He sing-songed, "Lizzy, Lizzy, you make-a me dizzy!"

She laughed. "Yeah, right. I'll make you dizzy when I clunk-a you on the head with *Atlas Shrugged*."

"Who?"

"Never mind."

"But Lizzy—" He clutched his chest. "You're breakin' my heart."

"I bet. So that wasn't you at the drive-in with Nancy Jo Moffett last Saturday?"

"Guy's gotta keep his options open."

"Hmmph. You're a mess. I'll see you later."

He left then, softly singing "Dizzy Lizzy, Dizzy Lizzy." I thought Lizzy would leave too, but she stayed right there in the stack.

Now, if that Johnny Lee hadn't backed off, I'd have said something; I know I would have. Wouldn't I? That's what I wanted to tell myself. But if that were the case, why didn't I speak to Lizzy and let her know I was there if she needed me? I was going to say hello—honest I was—but something in that librarian's expression made me hesitate. And while I was hesitating, I began to notice just how many people would see me talking with Lizzy, and I wondered what they would think of me. Or what they might tell my father.

My father. His image behind the pulpit flashed in my mind. I could almost hear his booming voice declaring, 'Let he who is without sin cast the first stone.' It was a principle he preached often enough, and he tried to live it—both he and my mother did. Kindness virtually radiated from her. *She* would have spoken to Lizzy, if she'd been there, and that made me feel ashamed of myself. Because, if I thought about it, Mama *was* there. She lived on in me.

Just when I was about to step around the end of the aisle and say she was right to tell that local redneck "no thank you," I heard her exhale in something that sounded suspiciously like relief.

"Oh, good, it's you."

I stopped. Had she seen me hiding behind the shelf and eavesdropping?

I could just barely hear Jeannie Quinlan's soft, gentle voice. "Why? What happened?"

"Oh nothing. Just that stupid Johnny Lee wanting me to go down to the lock with him and a bunch of those hoods he hangs around. I told him I had to get home, and then he wanted to drive me home in his truck with his two-headed brother in tow. Are they gone yet?"

"I think they just left. You about ready?"

"Yes, I believe I am. You want any books while we're here?"

Jeannie laughed. "You know better than to ask me that. I don't have time for reading anymore."

"Oh, that's right. You got a boyfriend now," Lizzy teased.

"Stop it, you. Come on. I want to look in Mrs. Holloway's Dress Shop on the way home."

I went to the end of the aisle and watched the Quinlan sisters walk toward the front desk to check out. On the way over there, a couple of little girls, giggling and not watching where they were going, ran straight into her, dropping their books on the floor. She squatted down to pick them up, talking with the girls while they showed her the books they picked out. She laid a hand on one of the curly heads and told how she liked that book when she was their age too. The mother came over and took their hands, frowning as she led them away without so much as a by-your-leave. One of the girls turned back and gave Lizzy a little wave, but the mother didn't stop until they were out the door.

Lizzy watched after them a second then squared her shoulders and resumed her walk to the desk, head held high.

I, on the other hand, felt like slinking out the door in shame. I'd been taught better; my mother had shown me better. So, I made myself a promise that day I hid like a coward in the book stacks. If I had another chance to come between Lizzy and other people's unkindness, I vowed to do it, because, well, it was just plain right.

Chapter Six

One evening, about ten days after Dad left, I walked down to Lucas's Pharmacy to grab a root beer float. I had a hankering for one, and it gave me something to do after dinner besides hide out in my room or suffer through Marlene's Review of Orchard Hill Gossip. Mr. Lucas had a soda fountain in the drugstore, and on Wednesday and Saturday evenings, he stayed open until eight o'clock. I was walking back along Elm Street when I heard the squeal of brakes and turned to see a pick-up truck halt in the middle of the street. There were some excited female voices, and then the door opened and Lizzy Quinlan popped out of the passenger side. She was laughing as she ran behind the truck and hoisted a large canvas bag off the asphalt and over the tailgate. She looked up, saw me on the other side of the street and gave me a big wave and friendly smile.

"Hey, Billy Ray!"

I jogged across the street. "Hey, Lizzy. You girls got some problem with your truck?"

"Nah. Nothing we do could hurt old Harriet here."

"Harriet?"

"That's what Lily named Daddy's truck." She grinned. "She names everything."

"Oh."

"We just lost one of the laundry bags."

Jeannie called out from behind the wheel. "Come on! We gotta get to the laundromat so we can get all the clothes done before it closes."

"Hold your ponies; I'm coming." She turned back to me. "I'll see you around, Billy Ray Davenport!" She hopped in, and the truck rumbled down the street, leaving a dull quiet in its wake. Lizzy Quinlan always seemed to electrify the air wherever she went. I watched until the truck turned the corner, and then I kept walking up to where Elm intersected with Cavanaugh Street.

When I got back to my room, I tried to read for a bit, but I couldn't concentrate. I thought about writing Dad a letter, but found I had nothing to say. My mind kept turning back to Lizzy and laundry, which led me to realize I had a bit of a dilemma myself. I was out of clean clothes, and Dad told me not to ask Mrs. Miller to do my wash—not that I would have anyway. He left me some money for the laundromat, but I wasn't sure exactly where the place was or how much money I'd need, so I walked over to the house to ask Charlie.

"It's on Hanover," he replied, "next to the railroad tracks."

"What is?" a voice piped up from behind me.

I cringed. Nosy Marlene was always in my business. I was anxious to get over to the laundromat right away, and I wanted to get over there alone.

"The laundromat," Charlie answered her.

"Why do you need the laundromat, Billy Ray? Mama will wash your clothes for you."

"I'm not going to ask her that. She has enough to do already."

"Then I'll do your laundry." She sidled up to me. "I do the wash very well."

The thought of Marlene handling my underwear made my skin crawl. "No thanks, I always do my own."

Charlie laughed. "You hate doing wash, Marlie."

"I'd do Billy Ray's though."

"I'll bet you would." Charlie chuckled and shook his head.

I picked up my laundry bag and walked toward the door. "I'll see you all at breakfast."

"Aren't you gonna come sit on the porch swing with us?" Marlene asked with a flirtatious flip of her long, blond hair. "It's a nice, clear night."

"I won't be back in time. Good night." I hurried off, before she could offer to go with me.

THE DOOR TO THE LAUNDROMAT was propped open with a cement block. The

49

dank, soap-perfumed heat of clothes' dryers poured out into the evening air.

A heavyset woman sat at the counter reading a magazine.

"Need some change, honey?"

"Yes, ma'am. Enough for two loads." I handed her some bills. "And I need some soap too." I took a quick look around, but there was no sign of Lizzy. I hoped I hadn't missed her after all. I wanted to make up for not speaking to her at the library the other day—even though she had no idea I was there. I had something to prove to myself.

"Here you go." The laundry attendant pushed the coins toward me, followed by a little box. I put my clothes in two side-by-side washers, read the directions on the lid, added soap and coins, pushed the button—and just about jumped out of my skin when I heard a blood-curdling shriek behind me. A blur of brown curls and a faded cotton dress raced from the back room toward the front door.

The attendant looked up from her magazine and frowned, grumpy but not irate. "Get that hellion out of here! She's a menace."

"Sorry, Miz Turner."

I knew that voice. It set my stomach to flipping about like a trout on a fishing line. Lizzy Quinlan seemed unsurprised to see me, though.

"Oh hey, Billy Ray. I thought I heard you talking; fancy meeting you here. Hold on a second…"

She blew by me and rounded the row of washers near the door. "All right, Lily, you little imp! I counted to fifty, and I found you fair and square."

"Only if you catch me before I get back to base!" a little voice emerged from behind the washers on the next row. Lizzy pointed to the other end near the doorway to the next room and mouthed at me, "Head her off down there."

I walked to the end of the row and stood in the door frame, arms folded, my best scowl in place. Lily came barreling down the aisle, squealing and laughing, looking behind her so she couldn't see where she was going—and ran right into me.

"Hey you!" I tried to frown, but the shock on her face was so funny, I couldn't keep it up. She looked up at me with big brown eyes, her face drained of all color.

Lizzy swept in from behind, put her arms around her sister and twirled her about, laughing. "I got you! I got you! Now *you're* It, Lily Lou!"

"No fair!" But now Lily was laughing too.

"Go back and check on our clothes, squirt," Lizzy said.

Lily ran into the back room, and Lizzy turned to me. "So, Mr. Davenport does his own laundry. Couldn't get Marlene to wash your undies for ya?" She grinned.

"She offered. I refused—obviously."

Lizzy looked at me with a thoughtful expression. "Hey, c'mere a sec." She started walking back to the room where her sister and their clothes were. "You been to college; I wanna ask you something."

I followed her, my eyes dropping to her blue jean-clad bottom, bouncing up to her ponytail and then down again. She had an oversized man's shirt tied around her waist, and I wondered how a girl wearing men's clothes could be so appealing. She stopped beside a couple of brassieres hanging over the side of a basket, feeling of them to see if they were dry.

"I, ah…" Swallowing nervously, I gazed up, down, anywhere but at her underthings.

"Your prissiness tickles me." Her lighthearted laugh rang out. "No, I didn't want to ask you about my underwear, College Man."

I breathed a sigh of relief.

She picked up an old, thick textbook, and flipped back a couple of pages. "There." She pointed. "How do you say that one?"

"Tanacetum parthenium," I repeated. "It's feverfew—see here?" I pointed to the next line. "There's the common name."

"Then why don't they just call it feverfew?" she asked with a touch of exasperation.

I tried to hide my smile. "It's Latin. All the plants are organized into categories. The first name is called the genus, the group name. The second is the species—the group within the group. Like with animals—all cats belong to one genus, bobcats are a specific type."

She was watching me with wide-eyed interest, and it was strangely gratifying to have her hang on my every word.

"I didn't know you were interested in botany."

"Oh yes," she nodded. "I like to learn about plants. Mrs. Gardener got me started, but now I read on my own too."

"Don't they teach botany at the high school here?"

She shook her head. "Just chemistry and earth science—not enough teachers."

"Did you get the book from Mrs. Gardener?" I picked up the thick volume and turned it over in my hands, looking at the spine.

"Nope—the library. It's an old book, but you gotta start somewhere, right?"

I grinned and handed it back to her. "Right. Botany doesn't change that much anyway."

"Plants fascinate me." She thumbed through the book and shrugged her shoulders. "They seem so common, just your run-of-the-mill greenery growing in the field or beside the road. But hidden inside them is this amazing power. Some of them nourish or heal, but some of them can kill. The deadliest plants can appear so ordinary."

"See? I'm not the only one that thinks about things real deeply—or looks for answers in an old, familiar book." I tapped the cover to illustrate my point.

She looked away as Lily came back in the door and tugged on her sleeve.

"I want some ice cream. Can I walk over to the Dairy Queen? You said I could, if there was money left over."

"Can you wait a bit? I don't want you crossing the street by yourself, and the clothes are almost done anyway."

Lily sighed in frustration while Lizzy counted out coins. It looked like she had just enough for one small cone.

"I have an idea." I reached into my pocket and pulled out a bill. "An ice cream sounds good to me, so if you two ladies would get me one when you get yours, I'll treat. And I'll watch your clothes till you get back."

"Deal!" Lily grabbed the bill from my hand and pulled Lizzy along behind her.

"You don't have to—"

"I insist."

Lizzy looked from me to her sister and finally acquiesced. "Lily, what do you say to Billy Ray?"

Lily curtsied. "Thank you, kind sir."

I bowed, just a bit. "You're welcome, gentle lady."

She giggled and pranced out into the twilight where the Dairy Queen sign glowed like a beacon across the street.

"Make sure you keep an eye on my brassiere," Lizzy called out as she left. My face got hot, but I smiled anyway.

I watched over the girls as they crossed the street, and that's when I heard the loud rumble of a pick-up truck pulling into the ice cream shop's parking lot. Loud, bawdy male laughter filled the humid air, and Lizzy turned her head to say something to the goons in the truck. I couldn't make out her words, but they laughed again, and she proceeded up to the window to order.

I kept my vigil as she came back across the street, an ice cream in each hand, and tensed when the pick-up squealed out of the parking lot and did a u-turn in the street, pulling up between the girls and my post at the laundromat's front door.

"Hey, Lizzy, you want a lick of my cone?" The passenger snickered loudly, and the other redneck guffawed.

"Got my own cone tonight. Maybe some other time, boys." I heard the brittleness in her laugh and felt a low rage start to burn in my blood. She had such a joyful heart, and these boys were trampling it with their vulgar innuendo. Lily had come back in and stood in front of me, holding her hand out.

"Here's your change, Billy Ray."

I took it without thinking and without taking my eyes off the jerks in the truck. Their heads swung around toward Lily and me, then back to Lizzy.

"Oh, I get it; the preacher's kid gets his cone licked tonight." She ignored them and started to cross in front of the truck. The driver stepped on the gas and the break simultaneously, revving the engine and lurching the truck forward. It startled her if her little jump was any indication, so I decided to intervene. Without saying a word, I walked out and took one ice cream from her. I slipped my other hand to her back as I stood between her and the ugly orange truck and guided her gently the rest of the way across the street.

"Have a good evening, preacher boy!" one of them joked. "You're in for the ride of your life!"

"He'll be confessin' plenty on Sunday," the other said in a mocking tone. I gave him my best scowl, and he let out a whoop of laughter as they peeled away.

"Bye, Lizzy!" The driver's hand lifted in farewell as they disappeared into the night.

"Bye, Stan! Bye, Nate!" she called.

I tried to read her expression, but it was completely closed.

"Friends of yours?" I asked, taking a bite of my ice cream.

"I know 'em. Why?"

"Why do you let them talk to you that way?"

"What way?"

"That…disrespectful way."

She let out a bitter bark of laughter. "You say that like I've got a choice about how they talk to me."

Hopping up on the concrete table outside the laundromat, she put her feet on the bench. "Besides, if I let them get to me, haven't they already won?"

I followed her, finishing my ice cream in three bites and tossing the cone in the garbage can. "Tolerating it only gives them your tacit approval."

"Why should I disapprove? Boys like me; why is that a bad thing?" Her ice cream sat forgotten on the table beside her.

"Do they like you, yourself—or just some superficial part of you?"

"Maybe I don't care. Maybe I like the attention like everybody says." Her eyes were blazing, the way they did that day at the lake when she defended Jeannie against my perceived judgment, except this time she sounded hotter, angrier. That heat made me feel singed and raw.

"When I'm with a boy and we're doing…whatever, I call the shots. I have the power over him. He'll do anything—promise anything. For just a moment in time, I can pull his strings and make him dance any way I want." She moved her hands up and down as if she was manipulating a marionette. Her face was stony, immovable. "I can even make him say he loves me."

I should have been offended by her words or at least angry, but I wasn't. I had a sneaking suspicion she could make me promise those things too if she tried. I couldn't blame those boys for wanting to touch the light and life inside Lizzy Quinlan. It must make them feel invincible. And knowing that I wasn't any better, any stronger than all the rest of them? Well, it was a disconcerting thought.

But I hated that hard, unyielding expression of hers and wished I could rub it off to show the eager, innocent face of the girl I talked with earlier —the girl learning the Latin plant names. Without considering my actions too closely, I laid my hand gently against her cheek. "Love is long-suffering, is kind," I whispered. "Love envieth not; love is no vain boaster, is not in-flated with pride, doth not act unseemly, seeketh not her own advantage." I brought my hand down slowly. "Is that what you feel when those boys say they love you?" I called them boys because no real man worth his salt would lie to this precious soul. I watched her eyes gradually fill with tears, and she shook her head slightly. Her hands came up as if to reach for mine and then fell back to her sides. She got up from the table and started to walk away, but I planted my feet in front of her and refused to move. I put one arm around her and drew her head to my shoulder with the other. Her arms slipped around my waist, and I could sense a hesitant tension in her, so I pulled her a tiny bit closer to soothe that unease away. To my surprise and delight, a shaky sigh exited her mouth, and I felt her relax just a bit. I turned my head to lay my cheek on top of her hair and met the incredulous faces of Charles and Marlene Miller not ten yards away.

The sneer on Marlene's face made my blood run cold. Charles just looked shocked beyond belief. My whole stance grew taut, and Lizzy turned to see what had taken my attention. She looked up—to gauge my reaction, I'm sure—but I couldn't look back at her right then. Marlene turned around without a word and stalked off.

"Uh…" Charlie stammered. "We came by to…well, Marlene wanted… um…" He shook his head, and a nervous chuckle escaped him. "Do you need any help carrying your stuff back to the office?"

"No, thank you, Charlie," I said in a grave tone, praying he would just go home. He looked at me for a long time, and as if he had read my thoughts, he said, "Well, okay then. See you tomorrow."

My gaze returned to Lizzy's upturned face, watching the emotions play across it like the changing patterns on a kaleidoscope. Embarrassment, sorrow, triumph, guilt and some other emotion I couldn't name but thought might be desire—they were all there. Her arms were still around my waist, but she snaked them tentatively up to my shoulders, rising on her tiptoes to reach around my neck. I'd never felt as alive as I did at that moment, and a smile came unbidden to my lips. She gave me a tremulous smile in return and cast her eyes down in an almost modest gesture.

"Oops," she brushed her fingers against the collar of my shirt and began to sing in a sultry, low voice about lipstick on my collar. Her fingers rested against the side of my neck, my pulse hammering into them at a fevered pace. I was afraid to move, afraid I'd chase her away if I said a word. When she came to the part about you and I being through, she stopped as if she'd had a sudden jolt of reality and abruptly pulled her hand away.

"Billy Ray Davenport, what on earth do I do with you now?"

"Lizzy," I began, "I promise, I—"

She stepped back. "Please don't say anything. Don't promise anything."

"Why not?" My voice did not sound like my own. It had a rough, gravelly quality I'd never heard in it before.

She closed her eyes. "Because I won't be able to bear it when it turns into a lie." She turned and walked back into the laundromat just as Jeannie pulled up in the pick-up. "Lily! Jeannie's here," she called. "Did you get our clothes folded?"

I stood there—immobile, just absorbing the emotions, the night, the whirling dervish inside me—until she came out carrying a basket under one arm and, over her shoulder, a large laundry bag with US Navy stamped on the side. Lily paraded along behind her with a basket of her own.

"Thanks for the ice cream, Billy Ray!" Lily called out cheerfully.

"You're welcome."

Lizzy smiled up at me, but there was sadness in that smile. "Good night."

My voice dropped into bass register. "'Night, Lizzy."

I watched her pile the laundry in the back of Jeannie's pickup and climb in the passenger side after Lily. She looked ahead, didn't wave. I remained there, watching the taillights disappear into the darkness, and stayed put for I don't know how long after they left.

Mrs. Turner stuck her head out the door. "Your clothes are dry, son. Come back in and get 'em so I can close up shop."

"Of course." I folded my laundry and put it back into my bag, hoisted it over my shoulder and walked slowly back to Dr. Miller's.

I walked through the back door of the office and into my dark room, closing the door behind me with a soft click. Moonlight shone through the window and illuminated a figure sitting on the bed. I almost jumped out of my skin.

"Hello, Billy Ray."

"Good grief, Marlene! You scared the living daylights out of me!" Willing my heart rate to slow, I put my bag down with shaking hands and started putting my clothes away. "How did you get in here anyway?"

"Daddy's spare key."

I made a mental note to go to the hardware store in the morning. Surely, they had a privacy lock I could buy to latch the door from the inside.

"Yes well, speaking of your daddy, if he finds you in here, he'll fire me on the spot and lock you in your room till you're thirty."

"I don't care about that."

"You're being foolish, Marlene. Go back to the house before they miss you."

She stood up and walked over to me, putting a hand on my shoulder. "What do you see in her?"

I ignored her and kept on putting clothes away. She slipped her arms around my waist.

"If you show me how, I'll do for you what she does; I promise." Her voice was soft at first, and I almost felt sorry for her, but then it took on a hard edge. "Except I'll do it only for you, not for every Tom, Dick and Harry in Orchard Hill."

I shucked her hands from my body and made my voice as firm as I could. "Stop it, Marlene."

She stepped back, and I turned to face her—to frighten her off with my scowl. I found it extremely disturbing that this harridan and her wounded pride could somehow manage to heighten my senses to a level just below arousal. We were alone, at night, in my bedroom, for heaven's sake! And though we were both completely clothed and not near any swimming hole, Marlene made me feel shame in a way that Lizzy never had.

"People always say the preacher's kids are the wildest."

I went over and held the door open. "I would tell you it isn't what you think, but I doubt you'd believe me."

She sauntered past, her sweet, sickening, flower perfume wafting over me. "Just think about it. I would never embarrass you in public the way she did tonight. It would be a secret—just between us."

I didn't respond—kept on standing there, waiting. Then, thank goodness, she left. I shut the door and shoved a chair in front of it. I sat heavily on the bed, dropping my head in my hands. Sleep would be a long time coming.

Chapter Seven

The next morning I rolled out of bed at quarter till seven. I had no desire to walk into the Miller's house and face Marlene, but that's where the food was, so I took the risk. I worried for naught though; Marlene was not yet up when I sat down to biscuits and gravy, and I managed to inhale the entire meal and leave the premises before she appeared downstairs.

I always started work by seven thirty in the morning, bright and early, and unless he was swamped, Doc would let me go about three in the afternoon. Mrs. Miller didn't serve dinner until somewhere between six and seven, so that gave me time to myself most afternoons. I usually spent the time reading or walking around town, or writing letters to Dad, Aunt Catherine or a couple of friends from school.

But that day, I found myself walking out away from town, following a creek that ran near Linden Road. Up on the bank, I could see the side of the now-repaired Quinlan family barn. I thought about stopping to talk to Lizzy, but after last night, it seemed, well…awkward. Marlene's assumptions about Lizzy and me—and the subsequent vulgar offer she made—rankled more than I cared to admit. It angered me that those assumptions tainted the innocent fun Lizzy and I had talking about plants and playing tag with little Lily. I wondered if Marlene was vicious enough to tell lies about us all over town, or if her pride was so decimated that she wouldn't say a word. I hoped for the latter, but honestly, I expected the former.

Still, if she and Charles had seen that embrace Lizzy and I shared, other people in town probably saw it too. That, in combination with the crass insinuations made by the Pick-up Truck Goons, would probably make for some fine gossip. I figured it was too late to worry about my 'reputation.' Strangely enough, that didn't bother me half as much as I thought it would. It seemed to rouse some part of me that longed to shock people—to show them I was in charge of my own life, and that I wasn't just the preacher's son.

I kept on walking, trying to rid my mind of this ambivalence and following the stream so I wouldn't get lost. My thoughts and feelings were a jumble. First and foremost was rage at the town's unjust treatment of Lizzy. Hadn't these people ever heard of forgiveness? What about welcoming a lost sheep into the fold? Did anyone ever ask her the real story behind those rumors? It was so unfair when people based their opinions of a person on half-truths and hearsay! I could certainly understand how Lizzy found it almost impossible to be herself when everyone already thought they knew all about her. The wisdom behind the Ninth Commandment, the one that forbade bearing false witness against thy neighbor, certainly rang true in this case.

Another thought nagged at me though. What if the townsfolk weren't bearing false witness about Lizzy? What if those things they said about her were true? She herself said she went out with Marlene's boyfriend. She alluded to loose behavior when she talked about the town's boys and 'when we do whatever.' What did that mean anyway?

Furthermore, if people told it around town that I was seen embracing Lizzy outside the laundromat, well, it wasn't an out-and-out lie. They might jump to tawdry conclusions because of who she was, though, and that made me angry—on her behalf and mine!

I grabbed a stick and took a vicious swipe across a bush, dislodging a handful of bright green leaves and leaving a sharp hiss of rushing air in its wake.

"Why you so mad at that shrub, Billy Ray?"

I jumped, whirling around to look behind me for the little voice, but there was no one there. Just when I thought I might be imagining things, I heard a contagious giggle.

"I'm up here, goofy."

I looked to the right, off the beaten path, and there was Lily Quinlan about ten feet above the ground, sitting in a tree.

"What on earth are you doing up there?"

"Sittin'."

"Well, that's obvious." I paused and changed to my best imitation of a big brother. "You'd best get down from there before you fall."

She tilted her head to the side and looked at me thoughtfully. "No."

"No?" I had to admit I was amused at her blunt reply, completely devoid of petulance.

"I like it here, and I'm not ready to go home yet."

"Why not?"

"It's sad there today."

"It is?" Concern rose up in my chest. "Is your mama all right?"

"Mm-hmm, she's fine, but Lizzy's sad."

Now my concern grew ten-fold. "She's sad, is she? Do you know why?" I dreaded the answer, but I had to know.

Lily shrugged. "She didn't tell me. She doesn't know I know."

"How's that?"

"I heard her last night after she thought I was sleeping. Well, I was asleep at first, but a noise woke me, and it was her. We share the same bed."

"What was she doing?" I asked, very softly.

"Cryin'. I don't understand it. Lizzy never cries anymore. She used to a long time ago when I was four, but not now."

"She must have been unhappy back when you were four."

Lily nodded, her expression solemn. "I don't like it when Lizzy's sad. She doesn't play with me, so I come here to my favorite spot."

"This spot is awful far away from home for such a little girl."

She grinned. "That's why I like it. They never find me—not till I want to be found."

"Lily, I would like to go see Lizzy and try to cheer her up. Would you come down and show me the way?"

"You just came from there, so you already know the way."

I sighed in exasperation. Lily wasn't as easily swayed as other children; I had to give her that.

"Would you come with me anyway?"

She thought for a minute. I really hoped she'd agree. I didn't want to leave her there, and I certainly didn't want to climb up after her. And perhaps it would be less obvious to show up at the Quinlans with a wayward little girl in tow rather than by myself—like a suitor might.

"Okay." She scampered down before I had a chance to even walk over and catch her.

"So you like to climb trees?" I asked, trying to make conversation.

"Yup, but I like playing in the creek too. I found some rocks over there," she pointed while she spoke, "so I can sit in the middle and dangle my feet in the water. Lizzy says all creeks and rivers end up at the ocean. Is that true?"

"Yes, it is."

"I think I would like the ocean. Lizzy says you can see forever there. Is *that* true?"

"I don't know."

"You never been there either?"

"I haven't, no."

"I want to go someday 'cause Lizzy says it's loverly."

I smiled at her mispronunciation. "Maybe someday you can."

As we approached the Quinlan barn, I could hear voices calling out for my errant walking companion. "Lilian!" "Lily!" I recognized Lizzy's voice in the mix, but it was Jeannie we came upon first down beside the barn.

"Lily!" She came rushing toward us. "Where have you been? I oughtta tan your hide for making us worry like this!"

"I went for a walk. Look who was walking around too—Billy Ray. He wants to see Lizzy."

Jeannie narrowed her eyes at me. "She's got chores to do."

I met Jeannie's gaze directly. "Let's let her decide if she's too busy to talk to me."

"Run on up to the house, little gal..." She turned and watched her sister scamper up the bank. Then she turned back to me, hands on her hips. "Lizzy don't need no more upset from the wagging tongues in this town."

"No, she doesn't."

"Why you want to see her anyway?"

I shrugged. I wasn't exactly sure myself, but I couldn't get the image of her crying in the middle of the night out of my head, and I just wanted to make sure she was okay. But, of course, I couldn't tell Jeannie any of that. "She asked me the name of a plant last night, and I looked it up for her." I cringed inwardly at the little white lie. Inside my head, my father's voice warned that wasn't a good sign.

Jeannie stood there a second, studying me. "Charles says you're a nice fella."

"That's quite a compliment, coming from Charlie. Given that he's such a nice fella himself."

After thinking a second, she shrugged her shoulders and sighed in resignation. "Wait here. I'll tell Lizzy you're down by the barn. She can come see you if she wants."

"No need, Jeannie. I'm already here. Afternoon, Billy Ray."

"Good afternoon."

Lizzy had approached us from the side, so I didn't see her until she was very close. Her hair was down loose and she had on a cherry print dress that crossed in the front like the blue one she had on the other day. Her lips, although still full and pink, were without her usual bright red color, and her eyes were dark and oh-so-serious. It was definitely a new look for her, one that appealed to me a great deal. My heart gave one big thump and then took several seconds to slow back down to normal.

"I'm walking over to Mrs. Gardener's if you want to come along." She turned up to the gravel drive that led to Linden Road.

I hurried to catch up to her. "Sure."

She stopped, surprised. "We'll have to walk through town."

"I know."

"People will see us together—the Bad Girl and the Preacher's Son."

I nodded.

She chuckled and resumed walking. "Well now, that's a far cry from not wanting anybody to know we went skinny-dipping out at the lake."

"It wasn't skinny-dipping, that's—"

"I know, I know. That's swimming without any clothes on."

"I'm not ashamed to be your friend, Lizzy."

"Yes, well, we'll see," she whispered. Then louder, "You ready for people to talk about you?"

"People have talked about me all my life. I'm the preacher's son, remember?"

"Not like they're going to now. But if you want to use me as your charity case to prove to everyone how Christian you are, it's no skin off my nose."

I put out my hand and caught her arm, turning her back to face me. "You are not my charity case." I stood over her, looking down into her eyes. "I know I'm a Christian, and I don't need to prove it to anyone else. That's just prideful. I do what I think is right. And no one tells me who my friends are but me."

For once, she had no smart-aleck remark to fire back.

"I have a theory about you, Lizzy Quinlan. I don't think you are what this town says you are."

She jerked her arm out of my grasp and kept walking. "Don't put me on a pedestal as a mistreated innocent, Billy Ray. You'll be sadly disappointed."

"I'm not putting you on a pedestal. I don't know what's in your past, but I do know that every day can be a brand new start."

"Maybe I don't want a new start. Maybe I like the way I am."

"Well, I think you do want a new start. And I like the way you are too."

"People don't change, you know."

"I've seen enough of the world to know people usually don't. However, just because they don't, doesn't mean they can't."

"Well, I don't want to change."

"Because it's easier to just go along with what the town gossips think? Is that why you don't fight it?"

"I said I wouldn't tease you anymore, but you're starting to annoy me."

"All I'm saying is 'to thine own self be true.' That's Shakespeare, by the way, not the Bible."

She looked back at me, glaring—and I smiled at her. Even though she tried to resist, she giggled.

"Fine, fine, be my buddy; be my friend. You'll see what they'll do to you."

I caught her hand. "I don't care what they think. I like you. Why is that so hard to believe?"

She looked down at the ground. And I decided I'd pushed hard enough for today.

"Why are you going to Mrs. Gardener's?" I kept hold of her hand while we walked.

"She altered some more clothes for me, and I'm going to pick them up."

"Did she fix this one you've got on?"

"Yep. You like it?"

"Very much. You look extra pretty, but I expect you know that already."

She grinned. "I've noticed that the less I fix up, the more you compliment me."

"I like your hair down." I reached up and ran a curl between my fingers, then tugged on it playfully. Truthfully, I didn't care if she 'fixed up' or not as long as I could make her eyes sparkle as they did right then.

It was strange, but I was starting to get used to the way the air buzzed all around us when she was near. I could actually think and talk as a rational person, even while my heart pounded in my chest. Even more odd was how bereft I felt without that adrenaline coursing through my veins. The air seemed empty without the presence of Lizzy Quinlan to fill it.

BY THE TIME WE WALKED back to Linden Road, the sun was edging down toward the horizon. In spite of her insisting I didn't have to, I offered to carry the bag of clothes Mrs. G made for Lizzy. I didn't mind in the least, and it gave my hands something to do, which was a good thing, because my palms were itching to keep Lizzy's hand in mine or put my arm around her. We approached the Quinlan's house, ambling and talking and laughing now and again—about Mrs. Gardener and her potions, and Lily and her wanderings, and anything else that popped into our heads.

As we neared the steps, I looked toward the house and saw Jeannie Quinlan sitting in the glider on the porch. She held Baby Susie against her shoulder, rocking back and forth as she covered the baby's head with one hand and patted her diapered rump with the other. Keeping her hand supporting Susie, she put her index finger against her lips, gesturing for us to hush.

"I just got her to settle down a little. Mama's about wore out with her crying. I'm afraid this one's gonna have the colic."

"Oh, I hope not," Lizzy answered. "I didn't think we'd ever make it through Lily's. We were all ready to pull our hair out before it was over."

Jeannie Quinlan's answering smile was like a cool breeze; it drifted around us, soothing and restful. It was pleasant to be around her. That was probably why Charles liked her so much. Plus, she was pretty in that traditional, blonde-haired, blue-eyed way.

"Did you get your new dresses, honey? Let's have a look," she asked, nodding toward the bag I carried.

"Wait till you see. There's a skirt or two, but there's some of those new capri pants, and couple of the prettiest tops I ever saw." She pulled them out, and held them up for her sister to cluck over. I stood by the steps, out of the way, but strangely fascinated by a feminine ritual that I never knew existed.

"That was so nice of Mrs. Gardener to think of you."

"I know." Lizzy flashed me a happy smile. "I must have thanked her a million times, right Billy Ray?"

"That you did."

"Let me go put these in my room. Be right back."

The sun went behind the line of trees, and crickets began their evening song. Jeannie started a gentle hum in response to Baby Susie as she stirred and whimpered. I sat down right where I'd been standing on the steps, afraid to talk too loud and disrupt the lullaby's effects. Lizzy came back outside, carefully easing the screen door shut. She sat down beside Jeannie, holding her arms out.

"You want me to take a turn?"

"Oh no," Jeannie answered. "If I give her to you now, she might wake." She looked in my direction, and I saw a radiant smile appear on her face. Its brilliance stunned me for a second, until I realized the smile wasn't for me. Jeannie was looking past me down the drive that led up from Linden Road.

I turned around just as Lizzy announced, "Well, well, well. Here comes Charlie-boy—right on time."

Charlie's tires crunched in the gravel as he rolled to a stop. He got out and started walking toward the house, and I saw the instant Jeannie's and Charles's gazes met, forming a ribbon of feeling between them, intertwined and strong.

Lizzy stood up and came over to the railing, gesturing for Charles to be quiet like Jeannie had gestured to us a few minutes before.

"Is she sleeping?" he asked in a stage whisper.

Jeannie leaned back to look at her baby sister's face. "I think so. Let me go try to put her down."

Charles watched her with an absorbed, awe-struck look I'd never seen on him before. Lizzy saw it too, and she smiled knowingly at me.

"Jeannie's just got a natural way with Susie, doesn't she? She can soothe her when none of the rest of us can."

Charles didn't answer, so I piped in. "Maybe—but then, you have a way with Lily. I saw it last night, when you were playing hide-and-seek with her at the laundromat."

She laughed. "I have a way with her because she's a little heathen like me. Birds of a feather, you know."

"You're not a heathen, Lizzy," Jeannie said as she opened the door and stepped back outside. "You're just…spirited." Her lips turned up into an amused little smile.

Lizzy laughed softly. "Well, that's a kind way to put it, sister mine."

Jeannie sat back down on the glider, and Charles pushed past me to join her.

"I guess I try to see the good in everyone," Jeannie teased.

"One of my favorite things about you." He nudged her with his shoulder and winked. "Hey there."

Even in the gathering dusk, I could see her blush. "Hey, yourself."

While I stared at them, Lizzy gently cleared her throat to get my attention. Then she nodded toward the driveway.

Getting the hint, I jumped up in a sudden rush. "I gotta go."

"Don't leave on my account, Billy Ray," Charlie said, putting his arm around Jeannie's shoulders.

"No, I really should get back to town. Seven thirty comes early in the morning."

"I'll walk you down to the road," Lizzy offered.

"Thanks."

"Watch out for Marlene," Charlie joked.

Lizzy froze for just a second, and Jeannie's smile dimmed. Once again, the spectre of Marlene Miller cast a pall on the most pleasant of scenes.

"I'll keep that in mind," I answered, looking carefully at Lizzy. How I wish I knew what Marlene had done to her. I was almost positive that it had something to do with the way the good folks of Orchard Hill treated her.

We walked in silence for a minute or so until I looked back at Charlie and Jeannie, sitting on the glider, their heads together.

"It's nice, isn't it? The way they fit each other," Lizzy said.

"Fit?"

"Yeah, they go together—like salt and pepper."

I smiled.

"Like strawberries and ice cream, like Jerry Lee and the piano..." She grinned mischievously and looked back at the porch. "Like hugs and kisses."

"Lizzy..." I admonished, a little embarrassed.

"What? You think he's not up there, planting one on her right this minute?"

"Good grief," I muttered, desperate to change the subject. But I turned around to look anyway.

"How lucky can a girl get?" she said in a wistful voice.

I stopped and stared at her. Was she jealous of Jeannie? I'd seen Lizzy smile at Charlie that day at the barn. I'd heard her say he was nice, like his dad. Was she carrying a torch for Charles Miller? "What do you mean lucky?"

She kept walking, kicking a stone with the toe of her shoe. "Oh, you know. Jeannie is quiet and good. Charlie's not as quiet, but just as good. And out of all the places in the world they could have been born, they both happen to land here in this little town. Jeannie found a guy who can appreciate her for what she is. Someone who looks at her like she's the best thing he's ever seen. So, she's lucky. Not everyone gets that. Hardly anyone gets that here in Orchard Hill."

"My parents had it. They really loved each other."

"That's good. It makes for good memories."

"Perhaps it's not as uncommon as you think."

"So many times, it starts out good but gets twisted along the way."

"Not every time," I insisted.

"Well, I hope that's not what happens this time." She nodded back toward the house. "'Cause love's no fun when it's all twisted up."

I had no experience with love, so I kept my mouth shut. It sounded like Lizzy knew of what she spoke. I was curious what made her say such a thing, but then again, I didn't want to discuss it or even acknowledge that she might have known love. We reached the road, and Lizzy took my hand and squeezed it in hers. "'Night, Billy Ray. Thanks for walking me home." I loved the way her voice sounded when she drawled out my name.

"'Night, Lizzy." I watched her walk away, fading into the purple ink of tree shadows until she disappeared completely. Then, I turned and started toward town, my hands in my pockets.

Chapter Eight

The next three weeks were some of the happiest I'd spent since Mama passed away.

The mornings were filled with the excitement of learning about patient care, medicines, and the inner workings of a medical office. My afternoons were spent with Lizzy, walking in the country, going to Mrs. Gardener's or to the library. After dinner, I'd go out walking again, and often I'd see her somewhere in town—sometimes with one or more of her sisters, sometimes alone.

I'd also learned some interesting things about Lizzy during those weeks: her favorite color was red, she could make a perfect lattice piecrust, and oranges were her favorite fruit. Not everything I wanted to know, of course. We never talked about her past.

I asked Charles which of the boys in town she'd dated, and he couldn't actually think of any. He said she might walk around with someone or other, but she never went places with them, never cruised the Legion building on Saturday nights with anyone, and never went out for a soda at the diner. Marlene said that's because the boys didn't have to take her out to get her to put out, but by then I knew to take everything she said with a grain of salt. According to Charles, who I considered a much more reliable source, boys would laugh about Lizzy and say she was a good time, but no one seemed to give any specifics. And guys talked to Charlie about girls. His dad was the town doctor not the town preacher.

Another thing I'd learned was that studying plants wasn't just a fun way for Lizzy to spend her time. She had plans. She had finished high school in the spring and had her heart set on being a midwife and herbalist like Mrs. Gardener.

So I wrote my Aunt Catherine and asked her to send one of my biology textbooks from college. When it arrived, I couldn't wait to show it to Lizzy.

We agreed to meet at the fountain right outside the library, and that's where I found her, fanning herself with a section of newspaper. Funny how just the sound of water made the day seem cooler, even though I knew that wasn't possible. I walked up and stood in front of her, grinning, with my book behind my back. "Hi there."

I got my own 'come hither' smile and felt my insides heat up. How did she do that with just a look? And did it work on every man the way it worked on me?

"Whatcha hidin' behind your back, handsome?"

"I have a surprise for you. Got it yesterday."

She stood up and tried to reach around me, but I backed up a step.

"Nuh-uh-uh," I teased.

"Oh, I see. I've got to earn it. I don't care what you've got there, Billy Ray. I'm not washing your underwear." She arched an eyebrow in challenge.

"I have it on good authority that there is at least one young woman in town who would wait in line outside the laundromat to wash my underwear, thank you very much."

"Hardy-har-har." She lunged toward me, reaching for the book again, but once more I eluded her.

"You're an awful tease," she said.

"I'm holding out for something."

"Playing hard to get, aren't you?" A big, dramatic sigh escaped her mouth. "What's it gonna cost me?" Her voice sounded forlorn, but she was smiling.

"Hmm, let's see. You won't do my wash."

She wrinkled her nose and shook her head.

"I'll have to think of something else."

The giant rumble of a truck drew her attention to the street behind me, and her smile faded. I turned my head and saw the Dairy Queen Pick-up Goons from the other night. The truck slowed down, but there were no catcalls this time. After a long look from the boys inside, the truck sped off down the street, and Lizzy let go a little whoosh of relief.

"They don't bother you anymore, do they?" I asked, an undercurrent of anger in my voice.

She shook her head. "Nope, not since that night they saw me with you." She stepped close and tilted her chin up to look at me. "In fact, after that night, I've hardly gotten any attention at all. Either I'm losing my touch, or escorting you around town is hurting my image."

"I've had some unexpected benefits from our friendship as well."

"Oh, really."

I nodded. "Marlene has left me alone for three weeks. She'll hardly say a word to me. It's been like heaven on earth."

"I know I always liked it when she was too mad to talk to me." She stood up on her toes. "So what's the fee to see the surprise, Billy Ray?"

I squinted off in the distance. "Mmm—guess I'll have to settle for a kiss."

She plopped back down on her bench, staring at me like a wounded animal. A long pause ensued. "I see. Anything else I can do to go with that?" Her voice was chilly, and it sent the temperature around us plummeting.

I instantly sobered too, and could have kicked myself for not realizing how that must have sounded to her ears; just one more man asking for a little piece of her. I sat down beside her in a hurry and brought the book around in front of me.

"I was teasing Lizzy, honest. I didn't mean it that way. Not that I don't want to kiss you. I mean I wouldn't mind...no, I'd like to...um...if you want..." Giving up, I shrugged helplessly and held the book out. "Here. It's my college biology textbook." I dared a look up to her face. A tremulous smile with the barest hint of amusement greeted me, which made me feel a bit bolder. "You can look up anything, read anything. I won't need it before fall anyway." I put it in her lap.

She opened the book slowly and ran her hands over the table of contents before turning through the pages. Her gaze shot up to my face, full of wonder. "It's got color photos of plants in it!"

I smiled. "Mm-hmm."

"And animals and drawings, and...oh my!" I leaned over to see what page she was on and grinned when I saw a diagram of human anatomy. She giggled and closed the book.

"Thank you, Billy Ray. It's one of the nicest things anyone's ever done for me."

"You're welcome."

"I'm sorry I acted that way before."

"It's okay. I think I understand."

"I kind of got used to not thinking like that when I'm with you." She reached over and gave my forearm a quick squeeze. "I forget that you're a fella sometimes."

"Gee, thanks." I never forgot that she was a girl—not for one second.

She laughed. "Maybe not forget. You're better than any run-of-the-mill fella. It's been sort of a relief not having to always be on my guard because of what some stupid boy told you about me. I'm not feeling sorry for myself or nothing, but—well, you wouldn't know anything about it, I guess."

"Oh, I don't know about that. It's sort of like everyone thinking I'm perfect because my father's the preacher and liking me because they like him."

She smiled at me, and all of a sudden, they appeared: fireworks—bright, hot and exciting. I saw them in her eyes, and heard them exploding in my head.

We sat there just looking at each other, and then I realized our mouths were about two inches apart. I stopped breathing, and her eyes fluttered closed as she pressed her lips to mine. They were soft like rose petals, and when she pulled back, I chased them until I was kissing her again. I trailed the backs of my fingers down the bare skin of her arm before gripping it to draw her to me.

Just then, the book clattered to the ground, and we drew apart, bumping heads leaning over to get it. We both sat up, laughing, and while she looked at the book, chattering away about the pictures, I kept my arm around her, gently guiding her head to my shoulder. I kissed the top of her hair and looked over top of it onto the street.

Straight into the eyes of my father.

Dad and I stared at each other for what seemed an eternity, but in reality was probably only a few seconds. I leapt to my feet.

"Dad!"

Lizzy looked up, first at me, and then she watched as my father approached from the sidewalk. His countenance was stern yet controlled. If he was angry, he certainly wasn't showing it.

I could feel Lizzy's eyes back on me. I cast a quick look at her and caught a vulnerability I had never seen before. As he did with many people, my father and his strong presence must have intimidated her.

"Hello, son," he said gravely, extending his hand to shake mine and putting his other arm around me in a brief hug.

"I didn't expect you till Saturday. Is something wrong?"

"No. I came early"—he cleared his throat—"to visit with you and check in with Miss Quinlan's father about her baby sister's christening." He turned a guarded eye toward Lizzy but didn't address her directly even to greet her, or ask about her family or anything. I couldn't remember a time when my father had been so dismissive of anyone—no sinner, no backslider, no recalcitrant child. He was downright rude for the first time ever in my memory of him. Shock flooded my system, and I turned to Lizzy to see if she noticed his odd behavior too.

Tears filled her eyes. She stole another quick look at Dad, who was frowning down at his shoes with his arms folded across his chest.

And then the most staggering, terrifying thing happened. As if a curtain had descended, her expression hardened like a plaster mask. The fallen woman appeared before me, conjured out of thin air; her eyes dried up and glittered cruelly, her lips curved in a garish, red smile.

"Thanks for showing me your etchings, Billy Ray," she purred, but it wasn't an alluring sound; it was almost feral. "Perhaps you'll let me show you my appreciation some time."

She met my father's shocked gaze with eyes blazing hot and angry while she shoved the book against my chest, making sure her breast dragged against the back of my hand when I reached up to hold the heavy volume.

"Keep it," I replied, not sure what was going on between the three of us. "You can give the book back when you're finished with it."

"No skin off my nose." She shrugged and stepped back, sliding her index finger down the front of my shirt till it rested on the book. Then, she let me place it in her hands.

"It's whatever you like." She strode away, swinging her hips from one side to the other.

I was left staring after her, wondering who that young woman was, and astonished at how quickly my light-hearted companion of the last month had vanished into the hot, muggy summer afternoon. Dad cleared his throat.

"I think Mrs. Miller has supper almost ready," he said without emotion. We turned simultaneously and walked toward Cavanaugh Street, completely in silence, perfectly in step.

Chapter Nine

D ad's pensive mood continued through supper. I could barely eat, anticipating a difficult conversation later in the evening. Emotion rolled off him, agitated and intense; I wasn't the only one who noticed.

"Did you have good weather for your travels, Reverend?" Mrs. Miller asked politely.

"Yes, I did, thank you for asking." He carefully cut his pork roast and paused with his fork above his plate to address Mrs. Miller again. "While I'm thinking of it, I also wanted to thank you and your family for your kindness to my son while he stayed in Orchard Hill."

Dr. Miller smiled at me. "I enjoy having him around. He's a great help to me, and he's sharp as a tack. He'll make a fine physician."

"Thank you, sir," I replied, grateful for the compliment.

Mrs. Miller replied as well. "And he's been no trouble—absolutely no trouble at all."

Marlene broke in, a smug, evil smile on her face. "In fact, he's out and about so much, we hardly even know he's here." She put a forkful of sweet potatoes in that hateful mouth of hers and looked at me with doe-eyed innocence.

She knew! Somehow, that Jezebel knew Dad had seen me with Lizzy Quinlan. I wondered how far her treachery went. Had she spread some awful tale that ran through the gossip mill and brought him to Orchard Hill unexpectedly? Did she know he was coming and hid it from me? Or did she just send Dad over to the library to find me when he arrived?

I wondered… If I'd had the chance to prepare him and myself, would it have even mattered? Or would his reaction have been the same regardless of the circumstances?

Dad bristled but kept his eyes on his plate. Doc looked at me and then to Dad, a question in his eyes, but then he deftly turned the subject, and in silence, I finished what I could of my meal.

"May I be excused, Mrs. Miller?" I asked, desperate to be out of that house and all the malevolent tension around me. I had never been so assaulted by ill will as I was by Marlene's sickly sweet smile.

"Well, of course, if you'd like, Billy Ray," Mrs. Miller replied. "But there's chocolate cake for dessert. Wouldn't you like some?"

"No thank you, ma'am."

"I'll save you a piece," Marlene volunteered. "You can come back over and get it later, or I'll bring it to you. It's whatever you like."

I ignored her and tried not to think about Lizzy using those exact words with me earlier.

"Hey, you want a game of checkers out on the front porch after while?" Poor Charlie, he could sense the uneasy undercurrents in the room, but had no idea how to help me out.

"I don't think so, thanks. I'll probably turn in early." I stood up. "Excuse me."

I walked up to the back of Doc's office, fishing my key out of my pants pocket as I went, and pulled open the screen door. A heavy thud on the doorstep and a weight on my shoe made me look down. The biology book fell open at my feet. An envelope with my name on the front lay in between the pages.

As I turned the key in the lock, I retrieved the book and then opened the letter before even bothering to sit down.

Here's your book, Billy Ray. I probably won't be seeing you anymore, so I thought I should go ahead and return it. I wrote down the title. Maybe they can get a copy in the library. That way I can look at it even after you're gone, right?

I'm sorry for the way I acted in front of your father this afternoon. It's the way I act in front of everybody around here, so I guess I just kind of slipped back into it without really thinking. But you've been nice to me, and you didn't deserve to have me embarrass you like that where he could see. I hope you can forgive me.

You don't have to visit or talk to me anymore. The Reverend seemed angry today when he saw us together, and I know he's almost the only family you have and you honor him. Like you should.

I understand.
Lizzy

As darkness approached, crickets chirped longingly outside the open window, interrupted every so often by the mournful cry of an owl. I could hear voices and intermittent male laughter coming from Doc's back porch. He and Dad were sitting out there talking, sometimes in earnest tones, sometimes in easy-going banter. Mrs. Miller's voice came and went. Part of me wanted to be out in the fresh air, talking and laughing with them, but the price—enduring awkward looks from my father—was too dear. My presence would only mar the camaraderie.

I lay down upon the bed, Lizzy's note on my chest, my hands behind my head, and stared up at the ceiling. And I waited.

Finally about ten o'clock, I heard Dad's footsteps outside the door. He knocked, and I called out, "Come in."

"I hoped you would still be up."

I sat up and turned on the lamp beside the bed. Dad sat in the chair across the room, facing me.

"You're not sick, are you, son?"

"No."

"That's good." He stood and tried to pace back and forth, but the room was so confining he gave up and sat back down. "I think we need to discuss what I saw between you and Miss Quinlan today."

"Nothing happened."

"I disagree."

Seconds ticked by while I waited for his next pronouncement. He rested his elbow on the desk and rubbed his forehead in a gesture of weariness.

"I believe I have failed you, Billy Ray."

"I disagree. Sir," I added hastily.

His head shot up in surprise, but then he looked beyond me, considering his thoughts. I could see him surveying the vast universe of his vocabulary and choosing words that would coalesce into persuasive influence. I'd seen him do this countless times before when he was trying to win a soul for the Lord.

"I am a servant of God who lives in the world, and yet I try to stay apart from it. I understand…" He stopped then started over.

"I know that you are grown. I don't know how you spent your free time at school or who you spent it with, but we have been together all during the summers. I thought I knew you pretty well."

He rested his elbows on his knees, clasped his hands together and stared at them. "Today, I was made painfully aware that I have not…instructed you properly where young women are concerned."

Good Lord, did we have to do this now? It was a bit late for the 'birds and bees' talk. After all, I was twenty-one years old. "I've had courses in biology and anatomy," I said to let him off the hook, "and I have, like you, 'lived in the world.' I know what I'm about."

Dad virtually ignored me, so intent was he on getting his point across. "I understand how powerful the call of the flesh can be. Miss Quinlan is pretty, and physical pleasure is hard to resist."

"I haven't shamed you or disrespected her with my behavior."

"I'm glad to know that."

"And I haven't asked her to marry me or anything."

He closed his eyes and sighed in relief.

"Someday, though, I might."

They snapped open again. "And it's that kind of impulsive talk that has me so worried. Lizzy Quinlan is not the right woman for you. How could you even consider tying yourself to that kind of girl for…for the rest of your life?"

"What kind of girl is she, Dad? Do you honestly know? Because I'm not even sure I know, and I've spent a lot of time with her over the last month."

"To be frank, son, I don't think spending so much time with her is a good idea."

"Why not?"

"I hear the people talk around town. They say her behavior is immoral."

"Since when do you believe small town gossip?"

"That's not fair, Billy Ray. This situation is completely different."

"How many times over the years have you told me not to cast stones? I heard you say it right next door at the Miller's dinner table! How is this any different?"

The fire and brimstone evangelist emerged and rose to his feet. Flames of righteousness blazed in his eyes, but fear lurked underneath the anger in his voice, and that kept me from quaking in my shoes.

"It's different because you're my son!" he roared and struck his hand on the desk for emphasis. "And my son does not run around fornicating with the town Magdalene!"

"How can you, of all people, say such a thing?" Rage boiled in my gut —undeniable anger toward this man who had been the center of my life for so long, I couldn't remember him any other way. "Have you no respect for her as a person? As a child of God? Have you no faith in *my* character?"

He banged his fist on the table, but more gently this time. "Billy Ray —" he began.

"Dad, listen. You don't understand what's going on here. I'm not sure I understand it all myself. But I know what I see. There is real kindness in Lizzy, and believe me, there's more to her than what the spiteful Orchard Hill gossips say."

"You're making excuses for her. Why would you do that if she hadn't dragged you down into sin yourself?"

I walked to the door, pulling it open and gesturing him out with my hand. "I have never lied to you, sir, and I certainly didn't start today. But if you won't hear the truth, then I have to end this conversation and say good night."

His expression was walled off and closed tight as he stared at me. "Sometimes, you're so like your mother. It's uncanny. After all this time without her, I never thought..." he whispered.

His words shocked me and stilled my anger for a second. "Dad...?" I began.

The strong, upright shoulders visibly stooped, and for the first time, I saw early hints of age in the lines around his eyes and his mouth. "Your mama always saw the best in people. It was one of the things I loved most about her—one of the things she taught me."

"Then why are you so set against seeing something worthwhile in Lizzy?"

He sat back down with a weary sigh. "Lord help me, I don't see it. All I see are lewd smiles, harsh red lips, and cold, glittering eyes. I see suggestive movements designed to lead men astray."

In spite of my anger, my lips twitched in amusement. "That's what I used to see when I looked at her because that's what she showed me. That's what she showed you today too. But the real Lizzy isn't cruel or harsh or immoral at all; I'm telling you."

He leaned back against chair, folding his arms across his chest. "All right then—help me see it, if you can."

I shook my head. "I'm not sure I can be the one to show you. I think she has to do it, and right now she won't. You made sure of that today when you ignored her. You made her feel worthless, and she responded just the way you expected." I paced to the other side of the room and back to the bed. "I asked you about her when you were here last month, do you remember?"

"Yes."

"You said she was like a wounded, wild creature."

"I remember that."

"I took your words to heart." I paused, trying to formulate my thoughts. "Every time I looked at her, I wondered, 'What makes her act like that? Doesn't she realize how she makes everything worse?' The more I talked to her, the more she let me see another side of her—a side that wants to help women and babies, and is interested in botany; a side that plays hide-and-seek with her little sister, and apologizes when she does wrong or hurts someone's feelings; a side that holds her head up even when men ogle her and say ugly things that no woman should have to hear from anyone. I saw a little bit of the path Lizzy has to walk in this town. I've even walked it a short way with her these past couple of weeks. And believe me, most of the people around here do not make it an easy row to hoe. You heard what Marlene said at the dinner table the night we came here."

"And if you remember, her parents and I reprimanded her for it."

"But *why* did you? Was it because it was wrong of her to say, or because it was embarrassing dinner conversation?"

"I hope you know me well enough to know the answer to that." Dad went on, keeping his voice even. "Alvin's daughter—her behavior concerns me too. Marlene has set her cap for you, and I'm not surprised she would say anything she thought would steer you clear of other young women."

Or do anything for that matter. Dad had *no* idea.

He went on. "The Bible says in Proverbs, chapter ten, verse eighteen: 'He that hideth hatred with lying lips, and he that uttereth a slander, is a fool.' Marlene is acting very foolish, and her design on you is yet another reason I've decided you should leave with me when I set out for Kingston on Monday."

"What?! No, Dad! Absolutely not. I can't leave Doc in a lurch like that. He's expecting me to stay until September. He's counting on me."

"He'll understand and might even be relieved for you to go. I know he already worries about Marlene's good sense where young men are concerned because we've discussed it before. Apparently, you're not the first boy she's made up her mind to…pursue."

"I can handle Marlene Miller, for Pete's sake. I don't want to leave Orchard Hill right now. It will look bad to leave a summer job so abruptly. And I'm learning so much—"

"I'm not sure I like what you're learning."

"You disregard my judgment."

"I don't believe your judgment is sound—at least not in regard to Miss Quinlan. She's a distraction—an enticing one, to be sure—but you have a calling, son, and a conviction. I've seen it. Alvin tells me he sees it too. God has called you to be a healer, and no woman should stand in the way of that mission.

"You may not believe this, but I'm proud that you reached out to a sinner and tried to bring her to the Lord. If you succeed, you've won a sister in Christ, a friend. But after you've done that, perhaps it's time to move on. Don't mistake friendship for a deeper kind of affection."

"I see." My voice shook with indignation. "So it's acceptable to preach to her about her faults, but don't dare get close enough to show her any real feelings; certainly don't show her any love."

Dad sighed in exasperation. "You don't love her! How could you? Her behavior is suggestive at best, immoral at worst."

"Like I said before, I have yet to see her behave in an immoral manner."

"Look at her with objective, God-fearing eyes and tell me how Lizzy Quinlan can be any sort of suitable companion for you."

"I don't know how or why. It's not like I haven't seen beautiful girls before. I can't explain it except—"I expelled a whoosh of air in frustration—"her soul calls me."

Dad snorted in derision. "Her body calls you; that's all it is."

"You demean her—and you discredit your own son." I was getting angry, with him and with Lizzy for putting me in this position. And I was starting to feel a little desperate. I couldn't refute the way Lizzy appeared to him, but why wouldn't he believe me about her? He had never disbelieved me before.

His features hardened into a stony, formidable mask. "My decision has been made. We leave together on Monday morning. Make sure you pack your things and have them ready."

He got up and crossed the room. With his hand on the doorknob, he turned back to face me. "I'm doing this for your own good, Billy Ray."

Then he left, shutting the door behind him, leaving my anger and frustration trapped and festering in my throat. I swallowed a lump that had grown there.

I had been so consumed by thoughts of Lizzy the past weeks that I had hardly thought about my work with Dr. Miller, but now, every fiber of my being told me I should stay, fulfill my commitment to him. This was bigger than Lizzy, than Marlene, than me. There was more to be done here; I could feel it in my bones, and leaving now would be taking the wrong path. I knew it as surely as I knew my own name.

My father had drawn his line in the sand. Now, I had to decide if I was strong enough to draw my own.

Chapter Ten

Marlene showed up at my doorstep Sunday morning, ostensibly to tell me breakfast was ready. Before I could even collect my key and my wallet, she barreled into my room, looking over at the Miller's house in the hopes someone saw her come inside.

"So you're leaving?" She pouted. "I overheard the reverend tell Daddy this morning."

"No," I replied. "I've been thinking, and I've decided to stay in Orchard Hill."

Her feline grin spread from ear to ear. "Perfect," she purred. "I knew you would. I told Doris as much last night on the phone."

I suppressed a shudder at the thought of Marlene discussing my comings and goings with her friends. "My father won't be pleased with my decision."

She waved her hand as if swatting at a fly. "Oh pooh, who cares? My father is always saying I should do this or do that, and I never listen to him either."

I interrupted her. "But I promised your father I'd work the whole summer, and *that's* the reason I'm staying."

She went on as if she hadn't heard me. "Daddy's told me all the things I shouldn't do as well." She stood right in front of me so her breasts brushed against my chest. She slipped her arms around my neck. "And I never listen to those either."

I took her hands down and stepped back from her. "Look, I've tried to be as plain-spoken as I can be with you—"

"You never smile anymore, Billy Ray, and it's an awful shame. You've got such a handsome smile. It just cuts a girl off at the knees."

I folded my arms across my chest and frowned to spite her.

"See how unhappy all this business with that Quinlan tramp has made you? You're arguing with your father, never smiling, and everyone in town's talking about you. Is it really worth it? Did you honestly think he would approve of you kissing her by the public library fountain?"

"How do you know about that? No one else was there."

She smiled and turned away, walking over to the desk and running her fingers back and forth, as if caressing it. "When he got into town, he asked my brother where you were, and Charlie said you were at the library. I figured you'd be with *her*. You're always panting around after her, and the little hussy is always skulking around the library for some reason I can't even fathom. So I followed your father over there." She chuckled—a low, ugly sound. "Boy, you should've seen y'all's faces. The reverend looked appalled, and you looked as if he'd caught you with your hand in the nookie cookie jar." She snorted. "I think it was the first time I'd ever seen Lizzy Quinlan look even the tiniest bit remorseful over something she'd done. She must have actually thought she had some kind of chance with you, the poor girl." She leaned against the desk and looked at me with flinty-eyed amusement. "I guess Reverend D put the old quietus on that little scenario, didn't he?"

I wasn't about to dignify that with any kind of response. "So, I'm staying here in Orchard Hill, and we"—I gestured between the two of us—"need to get some things straight."

"And what might those be?" She twirled her ponytail around her finger.

"Well, for starters, no more midnight marauding over to my room." I'd heard her try the door a couple of times, even after I bought my little dead bolt.

She smiled. "We'll see."

"I don't ever want Doc to think I'd betray his trust by sneaking around at night with his daughter. And think about your mother; she's opened her home to me, Marlene. You must think I'm some kind of lowlife to disparage their kindness like that."

She glared at me. "Oh, I wouldn't worry about your reputation now. My parents would believe you capable of almost anything. After all, you've been under the influence of the town slut."

Could it be true? Had I lost Doc's respect? I shook my head to clear it of Marlene's venom. No, Doc wanted me to stay in Orchard Hill. He said so

—told my father so. She was baiting me. I clenched my jaw against the tide of awful words that wanted to pour out and drown the malicious she-devil in front of me. "Is that the lie you've been spreading all over town? Is that what brought my father here with fear in his eyes and judgment in his mouth?"

"You're the one who lowered his opinion of you by stepping out with that loose piece of baggage. I had nothing to do with it."

And right then and there, I made up my mind to find another place to sleep at night. If I didn't get away from Marlene Miller, my days as an upstanding Christian man were numbered. Either she'd convince everyone in town she and I had done the deed—no matter what the truth was—or she would manage to make me so angry I'd shake her till her teeth rattled.

I walked around her and out the door.

"What about breakfast?" she called after me.

"Not hungry," I answered in a curt voice. "Tell my father I'll meet him at church."

I walked the four or so blocks to Adalia Street and knocked on Mrs. Gardener's blue door. She pulled it open and looked at me, surprised.

"Well, good morning, Billy Ray." She looked around. "No Lizzy with you today?"

"No, ma'am. I need to talk to you a minute. May I come in?"

"Well, of course you can." She stepped back and held the door for me, and I walked into her little foyer. She ushered me into the living room and sat on the couch. "Won't you sit down?"

"Thank you." I put myself in a chair across from her, but then I jumped up and began pacing. "I heard talk around town you have a boarding house; is that so?"

"Why yes, I do. It's across the street. It belonged to my husband's mother, and when he died, it passed to me."

"Would you happen to have a spare room I could rent—just until I go back to school in September—and if so, how much would it be?"

"Sit down, Billy Ray; you're making my head hurt."

I obliged her.

"I'm confused," she said softly. "I thought Doc was letting you stay in his office rent free. That's got to be a pretty good deal for a struggling college student."

"Yes, ma'am, he's been real nice about it too, but circumstances have changed, and I think it best I not have my sleeping quarters so close to…"

Her eyes twinkled with wry understanding. "Ah, I see. Too close to Marlene Miller for comfort, are you?"

I let out an exasperated sigh, relieved I didn't have to spell it out for her. "Yes, ma'am. I don't like to speak ill of anyone, especially one of Doc's family, but—"

"I know." She sobered. "You're wise to steer clear of her, but be careful. 'Hell hath no fury like a woman scorned.'"

"Shakespeare," I replied with a solemn nod.

"Actually, William Congreve, but yes," she said, with a vague sort of amused resignation. "Marlene can't do any real harm if you don't let her, but she can make people awfully miserable when she chooses." Her voice softened. "Lizzy learned that lesson the hard way."

That piqued my curiosity. "What happened between the two of them? Lizzy doesn't seem to hate people, even those knuckleheads that ogle her whenever she walks by, but her face puckers up like she ate a persimmon whenever Marlene is mentioned. I know it had something to do with Marlene's boyfriend…"

Mrs. Gardener watched me carefully for several seconds. Then she smiled and shook her head. "No, I believe that's Lizzy's story to tell, if she chooses to tell it. You're a nice young man and a kind person, so she may entrust you with the tale at some point. I probably shouldn't have mentioned it at all, except I didn't want you to be blindsided by Marlene's shenanigans."

"Please don't worry about me, Mrs. Gardener. I can handle Marlene Miller. But Lizzy…"

She patted her knees and stood up, cutting me off. "…is a remarkable and strong young lady. Now about the room—you're in luck. I happen to have a vacancy as of just last week."

I left five minutes later with a deposit receipt for a first floor room and a key, but no more answers about Lizzy's past.

I ARRIVED EARLY AT THE church and watched from the doorway as Dad moved about the altar, setting up the christening for little Susie Quinlan. It was a peaceful and familiar scene. I always drew strength from a church in the hours before the service. In an empty sanctuary, I had a keen sense of

God's Spirit. It was almost as if I could hear the souls that had worshipped there in the past and catch a glimpse of the ones who would follow me—a meeting of the past and the future tied together in the present. There was peace all around, yet I could perceive the anticipation and optimism of what was to come.

As he made his way over to speak with the church pianist beside the altar, I took a seat on one of the front pews. Members of the local congregations rarely sat in the front row, so it was almost always empty.

Slowly, over the next half hour, the church filled with the Orchard Hill faithful in their Sunday best: men with Brylcreem in their hair dressed in dark suits, women in pillbox hats and tailored dresses, little boys tugging at too tight shirt collars, and girls in hair ribbons and flowery summer frocks.

The Quinlans arrived about ten minutes before the service started. Mr. Quinlan had decided to attend and had at least trimmed his beard and combed his hair. Mrs. Quinlan followed him in, a wan but pleasant smile on her face, carrying Baby Susie in a yellowed christening gown. The other girls followed their mother—Jeannie looking serene as usual, Carla looking solemn, Lily jumping up and down and being restrained by a subdued Lizzy, who held her hand.

As usual, my pulse raced at the sight of Lizzy Quinlan. She had on that pretty blue sundress, her hair curled around her shoulders. It swung forward to hide her face as she bent down to whisper something in bouncing Lily's ear. I watched as the family proceeded toward the front of the church. My father had asked that they sit close to the altar because of the christening, but the front third of the church was mostly filled already. Like most churchgoers, the Orchard Hill townspeople were creatures of habit and liked to sit in their usual pews. A few of the older women smiled at Mrs. Quinlan and scooted over to make room for the new baby and her family, but there wasn't enough room for all six of them to sit in a row. Mr. Quinlan looked ready to retreat to the back of the church, and I wondered if he would leave the building altogether. Lizzy caught his elbow and spoke in his ear, gesturing toward her mother. Slowly, he nodded and sat down. Lizzy, still holding bouncy Lily's hand, scanned the nearby rows for a seat, and she was promptly ignored. Lily continued jumping up and down, and people stared at her, but nobody moved so the two girls could sit with the rest of their family.

It galled me that people who considered themselves good, upstanding Christians in every other part of their lives could actually behave this way inside the Lord's house, but I guess human beings can only carry out on Sunday what they've practiced all week long.

I watched all this happen from the empty front row, seeing Lizzy slowly move farther from her family, farther from a spot where she would be able to see Susie's christening. My blood simmered at this latest example of the town's callous treatment of her. I shot up from my seat and walked down the center aisle—slowly, so they'd all see me. I could feel my brow furrow and my mouth draw into a hard line, and from the looks on their faces, I imagined I must look like my father during one of his revival sermons. People shrank back from the aisle as I approached.

I caught Lizzy's free hand, and she startled as I tugged her gently, gesturing toward the front with my other hand. My father stood at the back of the church, his expression closed, just watching without emotion. I met his gaze with a direct stare of my own, and as I led Lizzy and Lily toward the front pew, I glared defiantly at anyone who dared to look surprised. I kept Lizzy's hand in mine as she urged her little sister to sit down. Then I sat down beside her, and just for good measure, I looked around to gather as much attention as possible and laid my arm across the back of the pew behind her shoulders.

Not until that moment did I wonder about Lizzy's reaction to what I'd done. Was she embarrassed? Angry? Would she look smug and gloat? Would she look at me with adoration? Was I her hero?

We hadn't spoken since Thursday when Dad found us in front of the library. Whenever I walked by our usual haunts, she was never there. And now?

She would hardly look at me, but she sat deathly still, her eyes darting back and forth, as if, like a scared rabbit, she might take off at any time. When I squeezed her shoulder gently, she glanced up and gave me a brief smile, but all during the service she hid behind a mask—not her bad girl mask as I had come to think of it, but a protective mask that shut out the entire world, including me. When we stood to sing, she shared my hymnal, just barely touching the side of the book. When we joined hands to pray, I could feel her pulse flutter against her wrist like the wings of a trapped bird. When she sang, her voice was so soft, I could barely hear her at all.

Her only genuine smile appeared when Susie began to wail as the water touched her head during the dedication. Dad looked over at us then, his expression full of questions as if he were trying his darnedest to figure out what was happening between me and Lizzy Quinlan.

About half-way through the service, Lily started jumping up and down again, and I leaned around Lizzy and said in a low voice, "Please sit down, gentle lady."

She rolled her eyes, but she did sit, and only the rhythmic swinging of her feet indicated that she was ready to run and play outside as soon as possible.

When church was over, I stood and escorted the two Quinlan girls to the front of the church, so they could stand with their family and greet the congregation. I shook Mr. Quinlan's hand, and he looked at me and at Lizzy, a bit confused. I congratulated Mrs. Quinlan, and she just gave me a tired smile and a thank-you. Jeannie smiled at me approvingly, but Lizzy's expression was still closed. I took her hand in mine, and she looked up at me.

"I heard you were leaving with your daddy for Kingston tomorrow." A flash of sadness appeared in her eyes.

"Not if I can help it," I answered. I squeezed her hand and turned to walk to the back of the church, leaving her standing there with a shocked look on her face.

That afternoon, I found myself back at Doc Miller's office, looking around at a room that, all of a sudden, seemed stifling. I picked up a box and methodically started piling my books and papers in it.

When he'd returned from church about an hour earlier, Dad let me know he'd changed his plans and would be traveling that very afternoon to Kingston. He expected me to leave with him, but I had other ideas, and it was time to tell him.

I'd had all morning to consider my situation. If I defied my father and stayed in Orchard Hill, it wouldn't be right to put Doc in an awkward position with Dad, who was his long-time friend. I didn't think Dad would hold it against Dr. Miller if he allowed me to stay at my job, but living under his protection in his medical office might be pushing it.

I walked over to the Millers and let myself in the back screen door after a quick knock on the frame as I'd done so many times in the last few weeks. We ate Mrs. Miller's meticulously-prepared lunch, which, unfortunately, tasted like sawdust to me. Afterwards, over coffee and dessert, I told Doc and my father about my short-term agreement with Mrs. Gardener.

"If I still have my job with you, Doc, I want to stay until September like we planned."

Doc's eyes widened in surprise, and he sat back in his chair, putting his cup in his saucer. He glanced at my father, who shrugged one shoulder.

"You're welcome to continue working at the medical office, of course, Billy Ray."

Dad picked up the sugar spoon and twirled it in his fingers for a second, frowning. Marlene's chair scraped the floor, and she stalked out of the room. Mrs. Miller, Louise and Charlie all sat there, gaping at me.

The other reason for me moving to Mrs. Gardener's boarding house remained unsaid among us out of respect for Mrs. Miller. I wasn't sure about her or Louise, but the men sitting around the table all knew that, if I was going to stay in Orchard Hill, I needed to put some distance between myself and the younger Miss Miller—especially after what Dad told me last night. If he and Doc were talking about Marlene's behavior toward me, it must be pretty obvious to everyone. And here I always thought guys were the ones who made unwelcome passes at women, not the other way around! I guess I still had a lot to learn about the world in general and about women in particular.

Late that afternoon, Dad and I stood by the 1949 Oldsmobile, not meeting each other's eyes. I dug my toe in the gravel beside Doc's driveway.

"I'll be back in Orchard Hill sometime in late August. Will you be returning to your Aunt Catherine's with me after that?"

I set my mouth in a line. "I've committed to work for Dr. Miller until school starts the week after Labor Day."

Dad let out a resigned sigh. "I'm leaving you with misgivings and a heavy heart. Alvin says he will look out for you, but—"

"I'm where I need to be, sir."

"I'm still in astonishment that my son would so blatantly disobey his father."

Remembering the words in Lizzy's note, I replied, "Your son honors his promises as his father taught him, and so honors his father."

"Then for heaven's sake, think before you make promises of any kind. Don't take an oath that will bring you to ruin." He cleared his throat. "I expect you to temper your friendship with Miss Quinlan."

I said nothing because there was nothing left to say.

"I will pray for you to see the right path, Billy Ray."

"Thank you, sir. So will I."

There was no handshake, no father and son embrace, no 'God bless you and keep you.' He simply got in the car and drove away. I had not felt this alone since the hours before my mother's funeral. But I had brought it on myself, I suppose, by calling down my father's cold judgment and his disapproval.

After he disappeared from sight, I stood for almost ten minutes, staring at the road. I was reminded of the first time he'd left me at Aunt Catherine's after Mama died. Back then, I had a strong urge to run after the car, but I didn't because he told me I had to be a man. That little boy's impulse returned like a rush of wind, but now I was a man in truth, and it was time to make my own way.

Chapter Eleven

After Dad left, I turned and walked over to the back porch of the medical office to pick up my suitcase. I'd return for the books later. Charlie came barreling down the steps with his dad's car keys in hand.

"Hey, Billy Ray! You don't think I'd let you carry all that stuff over to Adalia Street on your back, do ya? Come on; we'll load up Dad's car, and I'll drive you over."

"Thanks." Charlie Miller really was a good guy, a true friend.

He stepped up on the porch and grabbed my box of stuff. "Mom says you should still come over for meals. She'll never forgive herself if you go hungry."

"Tell her I appreciate that, and I'll be sure to let her know ahead of time if I can't be there."

"Marlene's in her room sulking because you're leaving." He shook his head. "Don't know what gets into that girl sometimes."

"I'm sorry. I wish I could say this had nothing to do with her, but—"

"Shoot, Billy Ray, you got nothing to be sorry about. It's not like you encouraged her or anything. A blind man could see how that was gonna play out in the end. She thought having you right here close meant you were hers for the taking, I suppose. She just neglected to get your consent beforehand."

I tried to think of something meaningful yet kind to say and came up with zilch.

"Hey, I'll miss having you right next door too," Charlie went on, "but we'll get to see each other. I'm at the Quinlans' most evenings anyhow."

90

I didn't answer his implied question. I certainly hoped Lizzy would still see me, but I wasn't going to speak for her. "Why don't you ever invite Jeannie over to your house?" I asked him.

"I would, but Marlene and Louise aren't very nice to her."

"It's your home too, Charlie. You should be able to invite your girl to visit."

"There's just so much upset and ill feeling when they're together. Jeannie doesn't trust Marlene because of what happened with Lizzy." He shrugged. "It's easier to go out some place in town, then back to Linden Road."

Maybe it was easier in the short run, but if Charles was serious about Jeannie Quinlan, he should set his sisters straight about how he wanted them to treat her. But I guess he would have to figure that out for himself.

We loaded up the car and turned out of the driveway.

"I heard Dad telling Mom why you were leaving. She didn't understand at first, and she was worried we'd done something to upset the Reverend."

I shook my head. "No, it wasn't like that..."

"I know. Dad told her the Reverend really wanted you to go back with him, and you were worried if you stayed in the office, it might make bad feelings between them."

"I was worried about that at first too, but Doc seemed to understand. And my father certainly doesn't hold my decision against your father. Dad is nothing if not fair-minded." Except when it came to Lizzy, I thought, but I only said, "And I think part of him is proud of me for keeping my promise. He wouldn't have given in so easy otherwise."

We pulled up in front of the boarding house, and Charlie turned off the car. Mrs. Gardener came out the front door, waving to us.

"Let's get you settled then." Charlie grinned at me and opened the car door.

THAT EVENING I WALKED EVERYWHERE searching for Lizzy: the library, the laundromat, the Dairy Queen. She seemed to be avoiding me, which hurt more than I cared to admit. She and the little buzz of excitement that surrounded her had become a welcome consternation in my life, and I was lonely without her company.

It was two more days before I finally caught up with her. I heard the gate over at Mrs. Gardener's slam shut, and my gaze went straight to the window, hoping. There she was, her stride brisk and energetic, wearing her cherry print dress, ponytail as bouncy as ever. An involuntary smile of relief accompanied the pounding of my heart, and I dashed out to the front porch.

"Hey, Lizzy!" I called, waving like a complete nerd.

She stopped in her tracks and slowly turned around. One hand was clutching a jar of her mother's tea, and the other lifted slowly to greet me. I couldn't see her expression, and that drove me crazy, so I vaulted over the porch railing and called out, "Wait up!"

She stood there, clutching the jar to her chest and looking around, while I jogged across the street. I didn't run hard or anything, but I was still out of breath when I got there. Squelching the urge to put my arms around her, I put my hands in my pockets instead. "Hi."

"Hi yourself. What are you doing here?"

"I'm staying here." I pointed to the boarding house. "Didn't Mrs. G tell you?"

"Yeah, she told you. Why aren't you at Doc's office? It's the middle of the afternoon."

"We were slow, so he let me go early."

"Oh." She turned and continued on her way.

"How've you been?" I asked, as I made to follow along behind her.

"Fine, thanks."

"And your mama? And Lily?"

A chuckle escaped her, and my stomach turned a flip.

"They're fine too."

I reached out and clasped her hand. "Lizzy, please wait. I've been looking out for you for two days."

She stopped, but she kept looking at her feet as she turned to face me. "I been busy." She huffed and narrowed her eyes at me. "I didn't come here to parade myself in front of your house, you know. I came for my mother's tea." She held it up. "I didn't think you'd be here this time of day."

My heart sank. "Are you avoiding me?"

She turned and started walking again. "Us being friends is coming between you and your father. I won't do that. It's not right."

I took her hand again to stop her. "Dad will come around eventually. He really is a good man. And besides, no one tells me who my friends are, remember?"

She looked away from me and then back, biting her bottom lip in the most enticing way. It made me want to bite her lip too, and find out what it tasted like. I forced my gaze from her mouth to her eyes. She was uncertain, her expression guarded, but she was softening; I could tell.

Then I remembered what she said melted her like a puddle on the floor. Even Marlene said it cut a girl off at the knees. *Might as well use it to my advantage.* So I smiled at her. I smiled with all the joy I felt when I saw her out the window. And I had her. I could see it in the pink stain on her cheeks and the way her eyes got all dark and round.

"Dear sweet lord," she whispered, "Turn that off, will ya? I'm 'bout to go blind."

Mischief and triumph rose up inside me and spilled over into my expression. "Not until you say you'll let me walk you home."

She huffed with an unconvincing burst of air, trying to suppress a grin. "Okay, okay, you can walk me home."

We said little as we approached the Quinlans' house. I was content to bask in her presence without any words to distract from our unspoken connection, and I was pretty sure she was feeling the same. When we got there, Lizzy opened the screen door, and I held it while she walked into the dim front room.

"Mama!" she called. "I'm back!"

"In the kitchen, honey."

Lizzy started toward the back of the room, and I waited patiently by the door. She paused in the kitchen doorway and turned to me with a questioning look on her face.

"Don't you want to come in?" Her expression was guarded, and suddenly it occurred to me that she might take my reticence as unwillingness to be in her family's home. That wasn't it at all. Aunt Catherine and Dad taught me to wait until invited to come in past the entryway, but I sensed that in this house, that might be taken as rudeness.

"I won't disturb your mother?"

She shook her head and gave me an impish smile. "You afraid of my mama, Billy Ray?" Her eyebrow lifted in another one of her compelling little challenges.

"Why no, Miss Quinlan, not in the least."

She gestured with her hand. "Come on in then."

I followed her into a kitchen with unfinished floors, a long rough-hewn table with benches up and down the sides, and scratched appliances that had to be at least twenty years old. A bare light bulb hung from the ceiling, but surprisingly clean white curtains hung from the window over the sink. Mrs. Quinlan was standing there, breaking green beans into a stockpot.

"You remember Billy Ray, don't you, Mama?" Lizzy said, leaning over and kissing her mother on the cheek.

Mrs. Quinlan turned around, surprised. I nodded my head. "Good afternoon, ma'am."

"Oh, hello." Mrs. Quinlan's soft voice sounded thin. I don't know that I had ever seen the woman healthy and strong, but then she'd just had a baby.

"Here's your tea." Lizzy set the jar on the counter. "Where is everybody?"

Mrs. Quinlan turned back to her work. "Your father's out at the barn. Jeannie took Lily outside so she wouldn't wake the baby again. I swear that child is wound up tighter than a spring. Carla's hiding somewhere with her nose in a book, as usual."

Mrs. Quinlan ran some water over her green beans and put them on the stove. "Is this young fella stayin' for supper?"

I hesitated—was that an invitation? I looked to Lizzy for a clue but her expression gave me none. I looked back at Mrs. Quinlan and realized with shock that she was counting potatoes as if she were worried there wouldn't be enough.

"Thank you for your hospitality, ma'am, but I can't stay. Maybe some other time," I added to let her know I wasn't dismissing her.

"All right." Her voice indicated a tiny bit of relief. "At least get the boy some iced tea, Lizzy honey. It's hotter than blazes this afternoon."

"Yes, ma'am." She walked to the cabinet and got out a tall glass. I watched with fascination as she drifted across the room to the refrigerator and got out a pitcher. She hummed while she filled the glass and brought it over to me.

"Let's go sit on the porch, shall we?" Her smile beckoned me, and I wondered absently if she was aware of what *her* smile did to me. The next thing I knew, we were in the glider on the front porch, sitting together, me pushing the glider back and forth with my foot and sipping on the best sweet tea I'd had in ages.

"Cat got your tongue?" she asked, a teasing lilt to her voice.

"Didn't you want any iced tea for yourself?" I asked her, determined not to sink under the spell of her flirtatious banter.

She leaned over and covered my hand, holding the glass with her own.

Keeping her eyes on me, she brought the tea to her lips and took several successive drinks. She guided the ice-cold glass to her neck and rested it against her collarbone, closing her eyes while a contented purr escaped her lips.

"Mmm. That hits the spot."

I swallowed hard.

Her eyes popped open and twinkled with affectionate amusement. Without looking away, I brought the glass to my lips, and tipped it back. I was promptly assaulted with a clunk of ice cubes. Drops splashed on my cheeks and nose. Narrowing my eyes at her, I wiped them away.

"You drank it all."

She laughed—a sweet, sultry laugh, and took the glass from me. "I'll get you some more." She started toward the door, but I caught her hand.

"No, it's okay. I've had my fill."

She shrugged and set the glass down on the porch rail. Leaning against it, she fixed me with a warm, sparkling look. I stood up, stepping almost close enough to brush her with my chest, and rested my hands on the porch rail, one on each side of her, thinking that would take that smug little smile off her face. I was learning for the first time not only how much fun it was to be teased, but also the enjoyment of teasing back.

"I should get back to town."

"Oh?" Her voice was a tad breathless, but otherwise betrayed no effect of my nearness.

"Mrs. Miller wanted me to come for supper tonight. I really couldn't have stayed here to eat with you."

She pulled a face. "Dinner with Marlene—lucky you."

I grinned and stood up straight. "The food's pretty good, so I guess I can take the company."

Her nose wrinkled in an expression of mild disgust. "The food must be to die for to put up with that shrew."

"Well, Doc and Charlie will be there too."

She pushed off the rail. "Come on then, I'll walk you to the turn off."

We ambled down to the road, swinging our joined hands as we went. The air was thick and humid, and the wispy little curls around her face and on the nape of her neck grew damp and stuck to her glowing skin.

"You wore your hair up today," I commented in an off-hand manner.

"It's too hot to wear it any other way," she replied. "I had to get it off my neck."

I caught myself staring hungrily at those darkened curls. If I kissed her there, would her skin taste salty like I imagined the ocean did? Not realizing I'd done so, I tugged on her hand to bring her closer. The two days of wandering around and thinking she didn't want to see me anymore had made me begin to ache for her in a whole new and frightening way. Right then, I only wanted to be closer to her. That was all—not take from her, just be closer.

We stopped when we reached Linden Road, and she looked up into my eyes.

"Oh, dear," she teased gently, but her voice seemed a bit wistful too. "I know that look."

"What look?"

"Never mind," she waved her hand as if to wave her comment away, but I could guess what look she meant. I tried to rearrange my expression. The last thing I wanted to do was remind her of some knuckle-dragging cretin in her past.

Her free hand came up and pushed a lock of hair off my brow. I turned my head as her fingers descended over my cheek, just in time to brush her palm with my lips. She hesitated, and I brought my other hand up to hold her fingertips against my jaw. It had been a lifetime since anyone had touched me in such a gentle way.

She looked very serious as she said to me, "This will change you, Billy Ray. It's already started."

"Is something wrong with that?"

She smiled ruefully. "No, it's inevitable, I suppose, but part of me is a little sad. I like you the way you are."

I grinned. "I like you the way you are too."

Her voice was almost inaudible. "Why?"

I drew her into my arms and whispered against her ear, "So many reasons." It was a lame response, but I couldn't seem to articulate how the world was more exciting, relaxing, bright, and interesting when I saw it with her beside me. I touched my lips to her neck and tasted, just like I'd imagined about a minute earlier. Her skin was moist and hot like the air around us and softer than a kitten's fur. She shivered as if she were cold, which surprised me, and I stepped back and rubbed my hands over her bare arms to warm the chill bumps I felt there.

She cleared her throat. "I'd better get back and help Mama start supper."

"Okay. See you tomorrow?" A blissful breeze stirred the tree limbs and cooled my skin. It did nothing for the roaring in my ears, however.

She nodded as if making some momentous decision. "Yes, tomorrow."

"I'll meet you at the library after work."

"Okay." Her smile was hesitant, almost shy, and I was utterly charmed.

"Bye, Lizzy."

"Bye." She turned and started walking.

"Bye," I called again. Walking backwards so I could see her as long as possible, I ambled toward the crossroads until I saw her disappear over the rise.

Chapter Twelve

I didn't think it was possible to be any happier than I was those weeks between the laundromat and when Dad came back to Orchard Hill for little Susie's christening. But I was wrong. Spending nearly every spare moment with Lizzy was even sweeter because of those days when I feared she had turned her back on me. We both knew we were on borrowed time because I was leaving for school in a few weeks. Somehow, though, we managed to put that eventuality aside in favor of living in the present. It did, however, lend a sense of urgency to our time together, a gray cloud that grew heavier as September drew near.

The air was heavy with a smothering expectancy as I approached Lizzy's house that third Saturday in August. When I walked up the drive, I heard the sounds of a mandolin and a whiskey-timbered voice bringing forth the strains of a familiar hymn, the lyrics declaring how we'd understand our trials and tribulations better 'by and by.'

Tom Quinlan was sitting on a stool, singing and watching me as I came up the drive. I stopped at the bottom of the porch steps, and we eyeballed each other—a mutual sizing up, I supposed. Finally, he jerked his head toward the door, indicating I should come up and knock. Although he had stopped singing, he still strummed the mandolin in a frenetic, relentless rhythm. Sensing that he didn't want to make conversation, I nodded, and he stood up and walked to the porch railing to look out over the hills and trees.

I knocked on the screen door, and Lizzy came bounding in from the kitchen. The warm light she carried around inside her stirred my senses even before I could see it shining through her eyes.

"Hello there!" she smiled, full of joy and happiness.

I gestured with my thumb toward the creek that ran along the side of the Quinlan property. "Care to take a walk, Miss Lizzy?"

"I was hoping you'd come around today. I made us a basket. Let me get it." She disappeared and then returned with an egg basket covered by a threadbare cloth.

When she reached the porch, she called over her shoulder, "Daddy, Billy Ray's taking me out walkin'."

With his back to us, he nodded but didn't stop his strumming or singing. I leaned over to take the basket with one hand and held out the other elbow in an exaggerated courtly gesture. She laughed and took my arm, and we proceeded to stroll down the hill to the other side of the barn.

"I didn't know your father was a musician."

"Mm-hmm," she replied absently.

"He was singing gospel," I commented.

"Well, usually he's singing about some kind of awful vice, like 'that good ole mountain dew,' so you must've caught him in a serious mood."

"That hymn he was singing," I persisted. "It's about faith and endurance, and that we'll understand God's purposes for our trials but perhaps not while we're here on earth."

She nodded. "It's one of his favorites. I suppose we have to believe that there's a reason for our trials, or we just wouldn't keep going. I think Daddy sometimes sings that song to keep himself going."

"I'm surprised."

"At what?"

"That he would turn to a hymn for comfort."

"Why?"

"I didn't think your father had much to do with God."

"He doesn't have much to do with church. That's different."

"The church is an embodiment of Christ. How can you live on the earth and have one without the other?"

"He had a falling out with Mr. Collins a long time ago, and he hasn't been to church since then except for Susie's christening."

"What happened?"

"I don't know. It was years ago. I wonder if even they remember it."

"Has he tried to mend his fences with his brother in Christ?"

She shrugged. "I don't know. Who knows why people do what they do, Billy Ray? I certainly can't fathom it."

I let the subject go, but it bothered me that Tom Quinlan would let a grudge keep him away from church, especially if he needed the Lord's comfort 'to keep going.'

As we meandered along the path by the creek, I slipped my arm around Lizzy and rejoiced when she put hers around my waist. We found a grassy knoll beside the creek where the tall trees reached out and formed a canopy over the sun-dappled ground. Lizzy spread out a little blanket for us and we sat a spell, watching the creek run by. She pulled out a mason jar filled with sweet tea, took a few drinks and handed the jar to me. I took a sip and set it down beside me, reaching into the basket for a blackberry tart. Lizzy leaned against me and put her chin on my shoulder.

"How about a little nibble off that tart?" she murmured in my ear. I leaned back to look at her, marveling that she somehow managed to look mischievous yet innocent as a baby bird with its beak open.

I broke off a bite-sized piece and fed it to her, feeling my blood stir as she licked my fingers. She closed her eyes and purred, "Mm, that is so good!"

I threw the tart back into the basket and whirled around on her. "That's it, you little rascal!" I rolled over her, catching her head in one of my hands to protect it before she hit the ground, and keeping my full weight off her with the other. She giggled, her eyes filled with a joyous mirth.

I laughed too, although I was trying to make my face stern. "Just for that, I'm going to kiss you senseless," I vowed.

Typically, our outings didn't lend themselves much to kissing. We were usually in town somewhere, and that little exhibition outside the library had taught me to control myself in public places. So I kept her hand in mine a lot, or my arm around her, but kisses, except for little pecks on the cheek or lips, were a rarity. But today, I felt brave. There wasn't a soul in sight and virtually no danger of being caught unawares. And we were laughing and joking and all felt right with the world, so...

I leaned down and brushed her mouth with mine, once, twice, and the third time I stayed there, while her lips slid slowly over my own. After an eternity that lay inside a moment, I raised my head and gazed down at her face. That moment froze in time, and I knew I would never forget it, that instant that I knew I loved Lizzy Quinlan.

Her eyes were closed, her curls lay soft in my hand, and her lips bloomed rosy as a result of my kisses. A little smile and a sigh told me she was happy, and a bolt of lightning came from the sky and cleaved my heart in two. One part stayed in my chest, and the other half went to her. If only I could persuade her to give me half her heart in return, then I might feel whole again.

Oblivious to my revelation, she whispered, "If this is what it's like to be senseless, I kinda like it." She opened her eyes, and immediately her expression sobered.

"Lizzy," I choked out, "Lizzy, I love..."

She pulled me back to her with surprising force, mashing her lips against mine and undulating a little farther under me.

I couldn't finish my declaration because my voice was gone, stuck somewhere in my throat. I kissed her again, trying to put all those unexpressed feelings inside her, first with my mouth and then, as her lips gave way under mine, with my tongue. Suddenly, I was no longer myself, no longer the square, the aspiring healer, the preacher's son. I was a wild man, a plunderer, a devil-may-care rake who took what he wanted, growled 'Mine, mine!' to the world and dared anyone to stand in his way. I pressed my lower body into hers, dimly realizing that she had opened her legs and I lay cradled against her. I sought comfort in her softness, mindless with lust and unrequited love. A groan laced with pain escaped me and I tore myself from her, scrambling up and walking to the creek, leaving her splayed on the ground and panting.

I knelt down at the water's edge. Reaching over and cupping my hands, I splashed cold water on my face and ran my fingers through my hair. With a determined sigh, I stood up, fists clenched, and stared across the creek. A hand touched my shoulder, and I turned to face her. Her eyes were round, her expression unsure.

"Are you angry at me? You look angry."

"I'm angry at myself because I got carried away. I didn't mean to disrespect you with my behavior."

To my surprise, she chuckled. "Billy Ray, I don't think you could disrespect a woman if you tried."

"But...I acted wrongly toward you."

She sighed in exasperation. "You acted like a man—nothing more, nothing less."

I pressed my lips in a thin line. I wanted to be special to her, not just any old fella who thought only of himself.

She tugged on my arm. "Hold on a second, will ya? And stop frowning. I'm not trying to insult you. What I mean is, whatever else you are—and you're many incredible things, things you haven't even discovered about yourself yet—while you live on this earth, you are a man. And that means the urge for a woman's body is part of you. There's no escaping it and no way to just shunt it aside. A powerful yearning drives a man and woman to be together and compels them to create life."

"So I've been told. I'm not an idiot, Lizzy."

"Of course you aren't. It's a sign of your non-idiotness that you even think about what's on the other side of this…"—she gestured back and forth —"this thing between us." She laid her hand against my jaw and turned me toward her. "But fighting that impulse is like fighting the tide—and just as pointless."

When I looked down, embarrassed and ashamed, she lowered her hand and sat down on the bank of the creek. She patted the ground beside her, and I plopped down on the soft grass. "Tell me," she asked, "have you ever been to the ocean?"

I shook my head.

"When I was a little girl, my daddy was in the Navy, and we lived on the coast." She leaned back on her elbows, staring off across the creek. I knew she was seeing the seashore in her mind's eye.

"I love the ocean; it makes you feel tiny and beautifully invisible. It can swallow you whole, but if you can rise far enough above the water, you can see forever. You could float to the ends of the earth with no one to stop you.

"On Sundays after church, Daddy would take Jeannie and me to the shore. We would build sand castles and play in the waves all afternoon until supper time. As the waves came in, no matter how hard I tried to stand against them, they knocked me over. It made me so angry, and it hurt too when they drove me into the sand. Finally, one afternoon after a particularly rough one slobber-knocked me, I went to Daddy bawling. And you know what he told me?"

"No, what?" I wanted to lean back on my elbows too, but my flesh was still too proud, and I didn't want her to see.

"He said, 'Lizzy honey, you can't fight the tide. If you try to defy it, it will knock you on your keester, but if you watch out for it and just dive in, well, then it will pass right through you. Sometimes it will even carry you back to shore.'

"So, years later, when Mrs. Gardener explained the birds and the bees to me, she told me it was a natural force like the tide, and then it all made sense to me. Love has power we disregard at our peril. But if we let the mighty waves pass over and through us, it's true we might lose control for a bit, but then we can regain our footing and learn to enjoy it—like I learned to enjoy the water."

I looked at her in wonder. Never had I thought about physical love in that particular way, but over the summer, I had learned that Lizzy's perspective on the world was unique.

Unbidden, some questions needled the back of my mind. How much did she actually know about physical love? Was this Mrs. Gardener's influence? Or did someone else give her that perspective? Was it something she'd gleaned from experience? That last question unsettled me, and before I could stop it, my skeptical side had to ask, "But did you ever consider how dangerous the waves can be? The destruction they can cause? How they can harm a person?"

"I have considered it." She nodded sagely. "You're right, and there's no doubt about it."

We sat there in silence for a long time. I listened to water flowing over rocks and birds chirping in trees, and felt myself calming down.

Lizzy reached over and took my hand in hers. She brought it to her lips and kissed my fingers. Then she held it against her cheek. When she spoke, her voice was soft and gentle.

"I can ease you, if you want me to."

"Pardon?" It was hard to pay attention when she touched me, especially when she talked in riddles at the same time.

"I can ease you, make it so you don't feel so—desperate, so frustrated."

My eyes widened as I suddenly realized what she offered me. "No, we can't do that—not until we're married."

She smiled patiently. "I don't mean intercourse," she held onto my hand when I tried to pull away from her. "No, now, don't get all embarrassed. It's just a word."

My face flamed hot. "It's a word that means something—something..."

"Shameful?" she asked softly.

"Momentous," I looked at her, fighting through my embarrassment. "Life-changing. Significant."

"Yes," she answered, holding my gaze with a fierce burst of emotion. "Fateful. Important." She shook her head, grinning. "You understand. Without ever experiencing it, you still understand. How do you do that?" she asked, a touch of awe in her voice.

"I have no idea what you're talking about," I admitted.

She laughed and put her head on my shoulder. I chuckled in bewildered response.

After a minute of turning that over in my mind, my inquisitiveness resurfaced. "Do girls ever feel—desperate?" I asked in cautious tones. "Like guys do sometimes?"

"I'm not sure it's exactly the same, but yes, they do. I think it's worse for you fellas because you're such physical creatures. It's the way you're made. You men go out in the world and you do things, seek adventures, build things up and tear them down. Mrs. G says women are the ones who really rule hearts and homes. They're the center of families. It's an important job, and they should be mindful of their responsibility to men and not take selfish advantage of a man's nature."

"Mrs. G has some interesting ideas."

"Yes, she does."

"My father would say the man is head of the household."

Lizzy smiled a smug little grin. "Mm-hmm. I thought he might."

"But I haven't really seen him be the head of our household since Mama died. I think it's because there was no household left, just two separate people—him and me."

Lizzy's voice was sympathetic and kind when she replied. "See? Your mama was the center. The head isn't the center of the body"—she touched my temple with her delicate yet strong fingers, and then moved them to my chest—"...the heart is."

"Hmm." I sat and pondered that a minute or two.

"So, what does Mrs. G say men are in charge of?"

She leaned over and kissed my cheek. "She says they are the light and fire of the world. They can burn and destroy, but through that flame, they can also push the world from one thing into the next." She giggled. "She also says they keep us girls warm on cold nights."

"Mrs. Gardener is important to you, isn't she?"

Lizzy nodded, a sudden solemnity in her expression. "Very important. I don't know where or what I'd be without her. She probably saved my life. I know she saved my soul."

I tucked a strand of hair behind her ear. "Will you tell me what happened, Lizzy? Can you?"

She threw her arms around me and pulled me close. I felt the tension in her body and stroked my hands down her back, trying to soothe her.

"Maybe someday I can," she whispered into my neck.

I didn't push her to answer any further. One couldn't push Lizzy Quinlan anyway, not when the burden she carried seemed so intertwined with her very self. If she rid herself of that heavy load, would any part of the actual Lizzy be left? I didn't know. So I just kissed her hair and held her close, and as the sun began to sink in the sky, I stood and held out my hand to her. And then I led her home.

Chapter Thirteen

The day my father was due back in town, there was a terrible storm. All that afternoon, dark clouds threatened overhead, rolling around in the sky like a maimed serpent might writhe on the ground. Heat lightning flashed and thunder rumbled, but the clouds stubbornly refused to open and give their water to the earth.

Dad arrived at Cavanaugh Street about three in the afternoon, right about the same time as the rain did, but I didn't see him because Doc and I were stuck in the office. It had been dry for almost two weeks, but when the rain finally came, it didn't come in gentle showers that gradually filled the streams and dampened the ground; it fell violently in sheets. The discombobulated weather seemed to rattle the townsfolk as well, and we saw many little complaints and injuries, making us late for dinner. Although it was only just past eight o'clock, the sky was dark as night. Dad, Charlie and the Miller women were gathered around the table, just about to begin eating as we blew in the front door, shaking rain from our shoes and shoulders. Doc set his umbrella in the stand, took off his hat and tossed it up on the hook at the top of the coat rack.

"Martha?" he called.

She hurried in from the dining room. "There you are! We were just about to start without you."

"I'm sorry, dear." He leaned over and kissed her cheek. "It was wild over there today."

Doc's demonstrative gesture made her cast a quick, self-conscious glance at me, and I looked away, trying not to grin at her embarrassment.

"Well, I understand, of course, Alvin, but the food was getting cold and we have company so..." She brushed at the raindrops on his shirt.

"I'm glad you went ahead and started."

Dad stood as we came in the dining room and shook Doc's hand. "Alvin!" he boomed, smiling.

"Should we build an ark, Reverend?"

My father laughed at Dr. Miller's joke, and then he turned to me. I waited, wondering what he would say and how he would greet me after the way we left things last month. It startled me to realize he seemed almost as apprehensive as I felt. He reached out a hand to shake mine, and when I took it, he patted me awkwardly on the arm.

"How are you, son?"

"I'm well."

He took a step back and looked me over. "You look well," he replied, a note of surprise in his voice. "A little damp though."

"Yes, sir. How about you? Are you well?"

"Can't complain."

We all sat down to a meal of buttermilk fried chicken, zucchini and summer squash, and sliced tomatoes. I was starving, and I ate like I hadn't had a meal in a week. Of all of us, Dad talked the most at supper. After he said the blessing, he entertained us with stories from his travels around the state while we listened and laughed, then refilled our plates. In record time, it seemed, the meal was over, and Louise and Marlene were clearing the table when a knock sounded at the front door.

Doc frowned. "I wonder who that could be on a night like this?"

Mrs. Miller disappeared into the front foyer and returned a minute later with the visitor in tow. My back was to the door, so I didn't see right away who it was, but when Mrs. Miller spoke her name, I whirled around.

"Alvin, Miss Quinlan insists that she needs to speak to you right away."

I sat, stunned for a second at the sight of Lizzy in the doorway of the Millers' dining room. Before I could get up and go to her, Marlene came over to get my plate and put a polished claw on my shoulder. I shrugged her off and stood just as Doc reached Lizzy.

"I'm sorry, Doc, Mrs. Miller, to interrupt your supper." She looked at the rest of us, apparently not noticing or caring that Marlene had tried to stake her claim on me. "I wouldn't have come, except—"

"Why don't we step into the parlor, Lizzy?" Doc gently took her elbow and escorted her out of the room. I moved to follow them, but Dad touched my arm.

I pulled against him. "Dad, it's Lizzy."

He restrained me with his hand and the soft, commanding tone of his voice. "It might be a private matter, son."

I stood indecisively, looking from my father to the door, to Marlene's churlish smile. Doc returned just a few seconds later.

"It seems that little Lily Quinlan is missing."

There were murmurs around the table, and Marlene rolled her eyes. Lizzy had come to stand just inside the room, and I immediately went to her and took her hand. She was soaked to the skin and ghostly pale, her lips a bluish sort of pink from being chilled.

Doc was still speaking. "She's been gone—how long now, Lizzy?"

"We're not sure, but at least since about two or so. She didn't come home for dinner, or when it started storming. And that's how we knew she must be in trouble. Lily's always home by mealtime."

There was an annoyed sigh from one of the Miller girls that we all ignored —except for Mrs. Miller, who shot a glare of shame in their direction.

"I was hoping maybe Doc could use his phone to call people, see if they'd seen her."

"We can certainly make calls," Doc answered. "But really, how likely is it that she's in town? Isn't it more likely she's out somewhere around Linden Road?"

Lizzy's eyes filled with tears. "I suppose. I just didn't know what else to do. We've been looking for hours, and there's no sign of her anywhere…"

I put my arm around her. "Why didn't you come get me?"

"I thought we'd find her. I know she wanders around a lot, but she's never been gone after dark like this. And she's afraid of lightning and thunder, so I know she must be out there, scared and—" Her voice broke.

"Well, here's what we're going to do," Doc said in a calm, firm voice. "Charlie, Marlene and Louise will start looking in town. I'll call some friends and neighbors, and then we'll all split up and search for her."

Lizzy nodded. "I don't want to put anyone out, but I have to admit I'll gladly accept any help."

"Nonsense, honey. Your neighbors will be happy to help find your sister." Doc gestured toward the phone in the front hall. "Martha, can you make Lizzy some hot tea? I'll get started on the phone calls."

Two hours later, though, there was still no sign of Lily. Lizzy and I were part of the group scouring the roads between town and Linden Road with no luck at all.

Lizzy's silent sobs were almost constant now. I tried to hold her hand in mine, but she drew it away, retreating behind the mask that shut out the whole world. Her tears brought a protective rage up from somewhere inside me. I wanted to hit something, pick up a big stick and just—

I stopped in mid-stride. "Lizzy..."

She turned to me. "What is it?"

"I think I have an idea where she might be." It struck me out of the blue —a vision of myself taking out anger on a poor defenseless plant.

"Why you so mad at that shrub, Billy Ray?"

I tried to look around in my mind's eye, to go back to that sunny day in the woods. Were there any landmarks I could remember? How far away was it? Could I even find the spot again?

"Dad, can I use your car to go out to the Quinlan place?"

"I'll drive you." He fished in his pocket for his keys.

Dad, Lizzy and I piled into the Oldsmobile and headed out. The rain fell from the sky in torrents. Sheets of water were thrown from the windshield as the wipers tried in vain to clear our view of the road ahead. Every once in a while, a flash of lightning illuminated the road, the woods, and everyone in the car.

Dad was frowning, concentrating on the road, his lips moving swiftly in what I was sure was a prayer to help us find Lily.

Lizzy stared straight ahead, her eyes dark and deadened, as if the light that shone from her had been extinguished. She was retreating into herself, I knew, because the reality of what might be happening was too awful for her to contemplate. I leaned over the seat and reached for her hand.

"Lizzy? You remember that first day I came up to Linden Road? And you and Jeannie were looking for Lily?"

She looked at me in solemn silence and nodded.

"I was walking by the creek, and she was hiding in a tree. She said it was her favorite hiding spot, and that you all never could find her there."

"You think she's there?"

"It's worth a try."

"It's by the creek, you say," my father interrupted. He looked at me, and a knowing anxiety passed between the two of us. "The creek will have risen very fast with all the rain from this storm."

"Yessir." I looked back at Lizzy and squeezed her hand. "We'll find her. I know it."

We got to the Quinlans', and Dad went up to the house to tell Mrs. Quinlan where we were going. Lizzy and I started toward the barn, and it was a couple of minutes before he came jogging to catch up to us.

"Mrs. Quinlan is beside herself. I almost didn't want to leave her, but we need every spare pair of eyes to help look. The middle girl, Carla, is with her, and I guess that will have to do."

Dad and I each took a flashlight. He scanned one way, and I scanned the other, and the three of us took turns calling out for Lily into the night. I grasped Lizzy's hand tightly and led her as near as I could remember along the path I'd taken that day. Sometimes, something felt familiar, but it was maddening how everything looked so different in the dark. I couldn't tell for sure if we were even going the right way. After about twenty minutes, I saw a shrub very like the one I'd swiped with the stick. I looked off to the right, my heart beating with wild hope.

"I think this is it." I went a few paces to the right and ran my flashlight up the trunk of the tree. No Lily. As I brought the light back down though, it rested on a little piece of fabric caught on one of the branches. An anguished cry escaped Lizzy's lips.

"That's her dress!" She began to sob. "That's her dress. Oh God!" Her voice lifted into an almost hysterical scream. "Lily! Answer me! Lillian!"

My light was frantically scanning all the surrounding brush. Dad was several feet ahead of me when I heard him shout above the wind and rain. We ran up ahead to meet him.

His flashlight was trained on something near the other side of the creek —a little figure, sitting on a rock next to the opposite bank, huddled against the elements. Her arms wound around her knees, her head was hidden and her shoulders were shaking—with cold, fear or shock, or maybe with all three.

"Lily!" Lizzy called, running toward the bank. I put out a hand and yanked her back.

"Wait! You can't see without a light, and the creek's overrun its banks. I don't want you to fall in."

Lizzy fought me for a second, but then she realized I was right. "We're gonna get you, Lily!" she called. "Just hang on."

Lily's dark head popped up at the sound of her sister's voice. "Lizzy?" She screamed and held her arms out. "Lizzy, help me!" She started to get to her feet. All three of us shouted, "No!" all at once.

"We're going to help you, child," my father called. "Just don't move, all right?"

Her voice was full of frightened tears. "There was rocks across the creek, but after I got here it started to rain real hard and now the rocks is gone, and I can't get back."

"I could wade across," I mused to myself. "It's not that deep."

"No!" Dad's voice was harsh, his anger a thin veneer over a deep-seated panic. "We'll go back for help."

He and I walked a few feet downstream to figure out how we might get to her.

Lizzy called, "No, Lily, stay where you are!" There was a splash, followed by Lizzy's frantic cry.

Before I could think straight, I waded in. Water, that was usually around mid-thigh deep, swirled up around my hips and rushed past at an alarming speed. I held my light aloft and looked, heedless of the cries from Lizzy and my father. I scanned back and forth, saw a brief flash of arm, lunged for it...

And promptly lost my footing.

Down under the water's surface I went, and the creek stole my breath. All around me I heard the crashing water. It carried me I don't know how many yards downstream before I was able to feel the creek bed and stand up again. I planted my feet firmly into the sandy bottom and tried to get my bearings.

My flashlight was gone, of course, but I could see Dad's light upstream and that helped me orient myself and put the earth and sky back in their rightful places. A long flash of lightning illuminated the water around me for several seconds, just as Lily passed me, her arms flailing above the water. I grabbed her and held on, willing my legs to be as immovable as tree trunks.

I almost lost my balance again as I pulled her to me but managed to clutch her to my chest as she sobbed and sputtered against my shoulder.

"I've got her! We're down here!"

Lizzy and Dad were there in a matter of seconds, she holding a long branch and he searching the creek with his light. Dad took the branch from Lizzy, and while she held the light on us, he took a couple of careful steps into the creek. He held the branch out, and I grabbed hold of it with one hand, while the other kept Lily against my side. Dad pulled, and I walked, and we came out of the water with a rush. Dad fell backward, sitting on the soggy bank, but keeping hold of the branch. The two of us climbed the slope, until we were well out of the way of the rushing water. I collapsed on the ground, and Lizzy pulled her unresponsive sister from my arms, crying and calling her name.

We laid her down on the grass, the two of us. I checked, and thankfully, she was still breathing on her own.

"Hold the light," I commanded, and Lizzy complied, shining it on her sister's face. When I heard the gasp, I looked up and saw the deep gash on Lily's forehead. It was bleeding, and Dad handed me a handkerchief from his pocket to staunch it.

Lizzy and I crouched on either side of her, Dad standing behind me looking on. Finally, he spoke. "We need to get her back so Doc can look at her. Can you walk, Billy Ray? Are you hurt anywhere?"

I stood. "My ankle feels a little sore, but I believe I can walk just fine."

Dad and I took turns carrying Lily the mile or so back to the Quinlans. When we got there, Mrs. Quinlan let out a keening cry and rushed toward us. Dad put out an arm to shield me from her, afraid, I guess, that she'd knock me over.

"She lives, Frances. She's hit her head. Where's Tom?"

"Still looking. He checks back every thirty minutes or so for news."

"I'll take my car then and go fetch the doctor. Billy Ray, you come with me; maybe I can help you wrap that ankle."

"But…" I looked to Lizzy. She was holding the cloth to Lily's head, but at the hesitation in my voice, she turned.

"Yes, Reverend, please take care of him." She took her mother's hand and placed it on the cloth covering Lily's forehead. She stood up and came to me, standing on tiptoes and kissing my cheek.

"There are no words for what you've done for us tonight. Only thank you." Her voice was choked. She kissed me again. "I'm going to stay here with

Mama and wait for Doc. I'll see you soon."

"Okay."

Dad and I left the house and drove in silence to Doc's office. Doc met us at the door, took a very quick look at my foot to ascertain it wasn't a serious injury, and he was gone. I sat on one of the patient gurneys, wrapping my ankle and washing up the best I could. When I finished and looked over at Dad, he was sitting on a chair, his head bent in fervent prayer. I walked over, limping only slightly, and put my hand on his shoulder to comfort him. He looked up at me, stood, and reached up to take my head in his hands. In a rush, he pulled me into his embrace, holding me in an iron grip as if he was afraid to turn loose. An agonized cry tore from his throat, and then I heard the terrifying sound of my father, who was proud, strong and brave beyond belief, sobbing into my shoulder.

Chapter Fourteen

D ad and I waited at Doc's office for him to come back with the news about Lily. I got up and paced a few times but finally had to sit down on the waiting room couch because my ankle was throbbing. I lay down, elevating my foot on the arm of the sofa and turned to look surreptitiously at my father.

Dad sat on a chair, hunched over, resting his elbows on his knees. He dried his tears by running his fingers over his eyelids, then leaned back and looked at me across the room. The low light from the lamp cast shadows on his face, making him look tired and haggard.

"I'm sorry I lost my composure—sorry that you had to see my weakness," he began.

"Dad—"

"No, a boy should be able to count on his father to keep his head."

"It was a tough night for all of us."

"I pray that the little Quinlan gal is all right."

"Me too."

"Should we pray together? For where two or three are gathered in His name, there He is also."

I sat up and nodded. Dad led us in a fervent prayer for Lily and her family, and for Doc and the good Lord to heal her.

"How's your foot, son?"

"It may swell a bit; think I might have strained a ligament, but wrapping it helped."

"It's excruciating to watch one's child in pain or danger, but I'm proud of you, Billy Ray. You saved that little girl's life tonight; I'm sure of it."

I shrugged, not sure how to answer.

"How proud your mother would be, too, if she were here."

I looked up at him, surprised. Mama was rarely discussed between us —at least, not at any length.

"When you went into the water tonight, I was terrified. I'm sure you know why. But I called on the Lord to help you, and He answered by telling me to give you into His care. 'Give him to me,' I heard Him say, just like I heard Him say on the night you were born and the night before I left you with your aunt and started the traveling ministry. Back then, he told me, 'You are the steward of this child, yet you should give him to me, and I will set him on the path he should go. I know the plans I have for him.' But that's been so hard for me to accept, especially after your mother died. See, Billy Ray, I wanted to keep you to myself: to be my son, my pride and joy. You are the last part of your mother I have on this earth. But you don't belong to me; you belong to God, and He reminded me of that tonight by letting me see how easily you could be snatched away."

I sat, stunned at Dad's words and wondering what to say when the front door slammed and Dr. Miller walked in.

He greeted us with a nod and walked into his office. With a mighty sigh, he dropped his medical bag on the floor beside his desk. We watched as he came back into the room where we sat waiting for news of Lily Quinlan.

"I called an ambulance because of her head wound, and she's on her way to the hospital in London. They'll stitch her forehead and cast the arm that she broke when she fell into the creek. She must have hit one of the rocks under the surface as she went downstream. Probably has a concussion." He sat down on one of the waiting room chairs and ran his hand through his rain-soaked hair. All three of us looked like drowned rats after being out in the storm. "She did come to for a little bit, crying and calling for her mama."

"Did Frances go in the ambulance with her?" Dad asked.

"No, she had to stay on account of the baby."

"The little gal must be awfully frightened to be all alone at the hospital."

"Tom rode with her. He'll come back tomorrow with news. Gene Lucas is going to drive up and fetch him." Doc looked over at me. "How's your ankle, Billy Ray?"

"It's fine," I replied.

He walked over and put his hand out. "Just wanted to shake your hand, son. Who knew, when you came here in June, that you'd end up being a hero?"

"Indeed," my father said in a pensive voice. "Who knew?"

"Lizzy sang your praises the whole time I was there. If you hadn't happened upon Lily's favorite hiding place a few weeks ago, or remembered it earlier tonight, we might not have found her—not before she tried to make it back across the creek. Oh, and Tom Quinlan said to tell you he is 'much obliged.'"

Dad let out a noise that was a cross between a snort and a chuckle. Dr. Miller grinned. "Yes, Reverend, it's an understatement, but the gratitude is there. You can see it in his eyes even if it doesn't come out of his mouth."

"Well"—Dad stood and reached to help me stand up—"think I'll take the town's latest hero to get some rest. I'll be back in a few minutes, Alvin."

"Yes, of course. Good night, Billy Ray."

"Good night."

He turned back as if a thought had suddenly occurred to him. "Oh, and Billy Ray?"

"Yes sir?"

He grinned just like Charlie. "Take tomorrow off."

I smiled back. "Thank you sir."

While we drove to Adalia Street, Dad said nothing else about Mama, giving me to God, or his 'weakness' as he called it. I knew the look on his face, although I didn't see it often. He was struggling to come to grips with something—struggling to accept. I was silent so he could do it in peace all the way to the boarding house.

"You need some help to get to the door?"

"I'll be all right." I dug for my key. It was a miracle I still had the thing, but there it was, lodged in the front pocket of my jeans. Slowly, I made my way up to the boarding house. Dad waited until I got the door unlocked, and then I turned, lifting my hand in farewell, and he drove off, the rumble of the 1949 Oldsmobile fading into the now quiet recesses of the night.

I walked into my room and turned on a lamp. I knew sleep wouldn't come for quite a while, so I flopped on my bed and opened the novel I'd picked up last week from the library. *Dr. Zhivago* had looked interesting on the shelf—and the librarian said it was about a physician—but honestly, the story was just depressing. After a few minutes, I tossed it into a chair and lay there on the bed, wondering if I should get up and dig L'Amour out of my box of books, when I heard a rap on the window.

I considered ignoring the knock, but then I decided Marlene Miller would never venture out in this weather. She had already spent most of the evening complaining about looking for Lily in the rain.

I raised the blind, and there stood Lizzy, her curls damp and a man's shirt clinging to her, although the rain had gentled considerably over the last hour or so. I lifted the window.

"Lizzy! What are you doing outside in this?"

She rubbed her hands up and down her arms. "I came to check on you. How's your ankle?"

"It's fine." We stood looking at each other for a second, and then I shook my head to clear the fog. "Umm—you should come in. It's wetter than sop out there."

Before I could tell her I'd open the front door, she'd put both hands on the windowsill and hoisted herself up, swinging her legs into the room.

"I thought you'd never ask. I know it's not proper, but…" She closed her eyes and took a deep breath. "I can't sleep. It's so strange, lying in bed and no Lily beside me." She gave me a wan smile. "She kicks, you know. She moves all the time, even in her sleep, and I can't settle down when the bed is so still." Her voice had started to wobble a little, and as I pulled her tight, her arms went around and held me close. She rested her head on my chest, and then the tears came.

Sob after sob emanated from right below my chin, and we stood there for a good five minutes, while I rubbed her back and let her cling to me. When she stepped back and wiped her eyes, I took her hand and led her to the bed, the only place in my room where two people could sit together. I drew her into my lap, and she sat there with her head on my shoulder, hiccupping. The sobs gradually grew farther and farther apart. Still, neither of us said anything. What we'd been through that night was too raw for words, and I wondered if we would ever be able to talk about it.

Finally, though, I managed a query. "How is she?"

"She was crying when she left in the ambulance, wanting Mama. But Mama's not fit to travel, and the baby can't go into the hospital anyhow. And Mama can't be away from the baby while she's nursing her."

"Doc told me your father went with Lily."

She nodded. "The medic said her crying and talking was a good sign that her head's not muddled too much. But that arm will hurt something fierce. We got our work cut out for us when she comes home. How we gonna keep her out of trees and away from the creek?"

I smiled and stroked her face with the backs of my fingers. "You'll manage. She'll do anything for you."

"You mean she'll do anything for *you*. When she came to, she kept telling Doc, 'Billy Ray saved me from the water. Billy Ray caught me. Billy Ray this and Billy Ray that…'"

I blushed and ducked my head, a sheepish grin on my face.

She leaned over and said softly in my ear, "You couldn't be any more her hero if you'd rode in on a white horse and plucked her right from the rock." Her lips found my cheek, my jaw, my mouth. And then we both caught fire, all the pent-up emotions—fear, anxiety, anger, pain, despair—rushing between us as we devoured each other with lips and hands. Before I knew it, I was lying on the bed with Lizzy pulled tight on top of me. Her legs were open, one on each side of my hips. She pressed herself against me, and I thought I was going to lose my mind. Then she sat up, still moving against me, eyes closed, lips parted, her arms folded over her head. She bit her lip and made the most incredible noise in the back of her throat, which I answered with a wild, untamed sound of my own.

So this was lust—true, tempting, drag-you-down-to-the-gates-of-Hell lust. I understood the power of it now. But this was much more dangerous than lust, I realized, because hidden in my heart and driving me onward was my love for her. I knew in that instant I would follow her anywhere, give her anything—promise her anything. I couldn't disengage myself, couldn't even move, except for meeting those hip movements of hers with my own.

"My skin's on fire," she said in a hoarse whisper, and her hands eased down her neck and over her breasts, her waist, to the place between her legs. I watched her in fascination, helpless to do anything as she reached down for my hands and put them on her thighs, guiding them up her hips to her waist, under her shirt.

"Touch me. Make me forget it all."

Yes, forget, my mind answered her. *Forget, forget, forget.* I tried to keep the memories at bay by chanting that word in my thoughts—memories like the cold fingers of the water and the bright spots behind my eyelids as

I held my breath.

Forget, forget!

I watched my hands as if they belonged to someone else. They moved up her body to her breasts, cupped and kneaded the fabric-covered softness in my hands. Lizzy was my light in the dark, and I clung to that light while I pushed away a long-faded image of a car, overturned, the door hanging open. I gasped for air.

I'm alive! The words burst inside my head.

All too late, I realized what was happening to my body, too late to stop it. "Oh God, no," I groaned. Lizzy's eyes popped open, and their dark beauty was the last thing I saw before my own eyes slid shut and I was lost to oblivion. From far away I heard her voice cry out my name, and then I felt her weight on my chest. I was breathing hard and fast, as if I'd run for hours. She lifted up slightly and then rested heavily on me, still rocking back and forth in rhythmic, gentle waves.

That's when the reality of the last few minutes came roaring back, and mortification washed over me, a burning in my gut.

"Lizzy," I mumbled as I tried to push her off. "Let me up."

She hardly budged. "No, no, not yet."

"I have to get up," I urged her again. "I—spent myself."

"Mmm," she purred. "Of course you did." She rose up and stroked my face. "You looked amazing while you did it too." She chuckled. "What did you call it? Spend? What an old-fashioned sounding word. I spent myself too, the girl version of it anyway."

I finally got her off me and sat on the edge of the bed, my head in my hands. Without speaking, I got up and pulled some clean clothes out of the drawer. Then I disappeared down the hall into the bathroom.

What had I just done? Besides lead myself into complete and utter humiliation. How could I have lost control like that? When she touched herself, I was mesmerized, and that must have been the point of no return. I couldn't do anything but watch her. The picture of her pleasuring herself would be burned on my retinas for the rest of my life. Girls did that? I felt my body respond again to the memory. "Good grief," I muttered, washing up in the sink and changing my clothes.

When I got back to the room, Lizzy was dressed in my university gym class sweatpants and a t-shirt. She had to roll down the waist and roll up the pants legs to make them fit, and the shirt was so big she had it knotted at her waist.

"I hope you don't mind," she said, looking down at the pants. "Mine were all wet from the rain and—"

My face grew hot, and I looked away. "I'm sorry."

"Don't be."

I threw my clothes in the corner and turned my back to her. Suddenly, I felt her behind me, pulling on my arm.

"But you are, aren't you? Why?"

"I shouldn't have..."

She tugged on my hand. "Hey, it's my fault if it's anyone's—which I don't think it is, by the way." She led me to sit on the bed and knelt beside me, her chin on my shoulder, arms around me. I had to admit it was comforting.

"I kinda lost myself," she went on. "I dove into the wave before it could knock me over. I couldn't help it. I was aching inside. I just wanted to forget about that ache, not hurt you or embarrass you."

"I know," I whispered. "I wanted to forget too."

"Danger makes people aroused. Did you know that?"

"No."

"It does. I guess it's normal to want to create life after life's been threatened."

She made the most bizarre ideas sound completely logical.

"Here." She sat back, legs folded, took my hands and tugged so I was facing her. She kissed my hand and cuddled it against her face. "Are you all right, Billy Ray?"

"I'm fine. I wrapped the ankle, and it—"

"I wasn't talking about the ankle. Are you all right? In here?" She touched my chest.

I shrugged. I didn't want to acknowledge what I suspected was truly bothering me.

"That sure didn't make us forget for long did it?" she said in a wry tone of voice.

"I'll never forget."

"No, I won't either."

"I don't mean tonight."

She tilted her head to ask an unspoken question.

"The night my mother died..." I began.

Her eyes widened and filled with tears. "I'd forgotten; she drowned, didn't she? Oh, Billy Ray!" She put her arms around my neck. "I'm so sorry."

I pushed her back. The story was coming out, like water rushing over a burst dam. I had never told anyone about that night, but I couldn't stop myself now.

"My mother was forever traveling around the county where we lived, taking sick people food, visiting invalids, giving clothes to the poor. My father used to talk with pride about how they were a team for the Lord. He made the sermons, and she tended the flock. He was proud of her, and that was probably one reason she did it, but it also really made her happy to help people.

"That night she had gone out to visit a family who lived way out in the country. Dad asked her to wait until the next day, but she didn't want to for some reason—some other plans or maybe they needed something in particular; I don't know.

"It stormed after the sun went down, like it did tonight. Torrents of rain fell and fell from the sky. When she didn't return, Dad borrowed the neighbor's truck, and we went looking for her. He thought maybe she'd had a flat or something, and he was grousing good-naturedly about having to fix it in that awful weather. About a mile from the turn off to the family's house, there was one of those old rickety one-lane bridges that crossed a river. A ways downstream we saw her car when the lightning flashed. The door was open, but she was gone."

I turned my hand over to grip hers tightly. A tear or two dropped on our entwined fingers, and dimly I realized they were from my eyes. I didn't feel sad though, just numb.

"They found her the next morning. The sheriff figured that she had tried to cross the bridge even though there was water on it, and the flooding carried her car off the bridge and into the river. When she tried to get out and wade to shore, the rushing water must have taken her. Or perhaps she was injured and unconscious and fell out of the car.

"My father was nearly crazy with grief. The morning before the funeral, he locked himself in the chapel with her casket, and for hours I could hear him in there—crying, yelling at her, alternately praying and calling to God, asking why He took her from us. I tried to get in there to him. I banged on the door, even tried to break in with my shoulder, but he just shouted at me to leave him be. I was terrified of what he might try, so I stayed right outside the door. I don't know what I thought I could do, but I couldn't bear to leave him. I'd never seen him be anything but strong until that day."

I looked up and saw tears running down Lizzy's face. "How old were you?"

"Eleven.

"About an hour before the funeral was to start, he finally came out of the chapel. He embraced me, apologized for showing such 'weakness' as he called it, and said he had asked the Lord to forgive him for questioning His will. He put his hand on my shoulder and said, 'At least I still have you, Billy Ray, and I do thank God for that.' After that, we rarely spoke about Mama, except in very general terms. We'd say, 'Mama would have liked that song' or 'Wasn't it great when Mama made thus and so for Sunday dinner?' He didn't want me to forget her, and it wasn't like I *couldn't* have talked to him about her. It was more that I was afraid I'd lose him to whatever demon took him that morning if I let him remember too much or too often." I wiped my eyes with the back of my hand. "Anyway, after that, I never strayed too far from what Dad wanted from me and for me. You see, he'd suffered so much already, and I didn't want to cause him any more pain. Nothing mattered more to me than that—until he tried to convince me to leave Orchard Hill last month. I didn't want to leave my job, or leave you, and for the first time, there was something that meant more to me than what he wanted. I'm starting to think I was supposed to be here tonight, so I could help you find Lily." I shook my head, marveling for the first time at the truth behind the old cliché: "The Lord works in mysterious ways."

"I'm beginning to believe you," Lizzy whispered.

We sat there, holding each other for what seemed like hours. Gradually, exhaustion finally took my body and my mind. I leaned back against the pillows, wincing slightly as I stretched out my legs. That ankle was starting to stiffen up a bit.

Lizzy nudged me a little and reached up under my shoulders to pull down the blanket. She tucked me in like I was a child and sat down on the edge of the bed, resting a hand on each side of me and studying my face. Her eyes closed, and she leaned down to kiss me. It was a tender kiss, full of soft lips and sweet movements. I felt a stirring low in my body and racing up to my chest, but I lacked the energy to do anything but let it wash over me. She rose up and stroked my hair. "You are something else, Billy Ray Davenport, something special." Her gaze gentled from a vague amusement to a vulnerable look I'd seen only once or twice. She started to speak and then stopped, snapping her lips shut abruptly.

"Don't leave," I urged her.

"What?"

"Stay."

She grinned. "That's not exactly proper."

"I won't make a habit of it," I replied, yawning. "And we'll keep our clothes on."

"That doesn't seem to make much of a difference for us, now does it?"

I couldn't even work up enough energy for a good embarrassed blush. "I don't want to be alone."

She crawled under the blanket beside me. "Neither do I," she whispered. "I'll stay. You go to sleep now."

I was already dozing, and in my dreams I could have sworn I heard the words I longed for fall from her lips.

"I do love you, Billy Ray."

Chapter Fifteen

I awoke to thin, morning sunlight peeking through the curtains in my room. At first, I was surprised to feel a living, breathing presence beside me. Little by little, I recalled the previous night's events—only scattered images at first, but then the entire evening cascaded from my memory, ending with the unbelievable intimacy of sleeping next to the girl I loved.

I eased onto my side, facing her, and a thousand thoughts turned over in my mind as I took in every detail of her face. She slept soundly, her shoulder moving up and down in rhythm with her breath, an occasional twitch or sigh escaping her. I smiled at those endearing little movements, plans spinning in my head as I thought through the next set of necessary steps. It would not be an easy road, but it had to be done, and the sooner, the better. Finally, when I could hold my thoughts in no longer, I gently stroked her cheek and spoke her name.

"Lizzy, darlin'? Wake up, sweetheart."

"Hmm?" She stirred, her eyes blinking at the light streaming through the window.

"It's morning," I murmured in a soft, deep voice.

She tried to sit up. "What time is it?"

I glanced over at the clock. "Ten after seven."

"Oh!" She bolted upright, running her fingers through her curls and looking around for her shirt and pants. She felt of them, checking they were dry before she began stripping out of my gym clothes. I started to look away, but then I forced my gaze back to her. What did it matter if I saw her in her underthings? I'd seen them before—that day I first came back to Orchard Hill two months ago. Besides, soon enough it wouldn't matter anyway.

"I've got to get home before Mama misses me." She sat on the edge of the bed, pulling on her shoes.

"Wait, Lizzy." I tugged on her hand, pulling her toward me.

"I don't have time for no kissin' right now. Hopefully, Daddy will be back with some news today." She started to leave, and I bolted out of bed. Standing in front of the door with my arms blocking her exit, I almost shouted at her in my desperation to get her attention.

"No! We have to talk about what we're going to do."

"What we're going to do? I told you. I'm going home to see if there's any word on Lily. And you have to go to work."

"Doc gave me the day off."

"Oh, well then I guess you don't." She grinned.

I shook my head to try and clear it. Somehow, I'd started off on a tangent, and we had to make plans. We had a rough day ahead of us. Dad was not going to be pleased. I ran my hand through my hair and began pacing back and forth in front of the door. "Can you just sit down a second and let me think how we're going to do this?"

"Do what?"

"Tell my dad and your parents we're getting married."

That stopped her dead in her tracks. She plopped back down on the bed. "Getting married?"

"Yes, we spent the night together. Now we have to do the right thing."

"That's a joke, right? If so, it isn't very funny. Why on earth would we get married?"

I frowned at her. She was going to make me admit how wrong I'd acted. Well, so be it; I was man enough to admit when I made a mistake. "Because we've been...you know"—I gestured back and forth between us—"...intimate, in a way that husbands and wives are. And we slept in the same bed. I want to do the right thing by you."

"Well, lordy, lordy," she replied with a heavy dose of sarcasm in her voice, "if I'd known this was all I had to do to get married..." She folded her arms across her chest. "Hey, if I remember right, you were the one who asked me to stay with you."

I looked down in embarrassment. "I know, and I'm sorry. I was weak and—"

125

"You're sorry! Well, isn't that reassuring? Don't worry about it, Billy Ray; I wasn't after no marriage proposal. Now let me by. I have to get home." She stood up again.

"Dad may be upset at first, but he'll see reason once I tell him why we have to do this."

Her eyes got round as saucers. "You will NOT tell him anything of the sort! He can hardly look at me now. Just imagine how he'll feel about me if he thinks I Delilah'ed Sampson right out of his virtue!"

We stared at each other a full minute, before she let out an incredulous, humorless chuckle. "You're serious, aren't you?"

I couldn't believe she asked me that—of course I was serious—but I nodded anyway.

"Billy Ray," she said, "I can't marry you. You're going away to medical school in a few days. You can't have a wife lashed to your side!"

"There's university housing for married students. We'll get an apartment, and I can get a job of some kind. You might have to find work too, at first."

She put her fingers over her eyes in frustration. "We're not getting married. You've never even said you love me."

Well, it wasn't like I hadn't tried to say it, and more than once, but every time I worked up the nerve, she stopped me.

"We have to get married," was all I said.

She snorted. "Don't get yourself all in a self-righteous tizzy. It's not like I could be pregnant or anything."

I stared at her, deeply offended. "I have an obligation to you and to God."

"As much as it would thrill me to have a man marry me with a spiritual gun to his head, I think I have to say, 'No thanks.'"

It took a minute for me to hear what she was saying, and then it felt like all the air was sucked out of the room. As impossible as it was to believe, she was turning me down.

She shook her head. "I know you believe in this obligation of yours, but you needn't worry. I release you from it if that will make it easier."

I felt anger rising up—fury and humiliation so intense I couldn't speak.

Lizzy closed her eyes and took a deep breath before she pinned me with a sad look. "You have to be realistic here. You are going to medical school. That's going to take all your time, all your attention, all your money. There will be nothing left over for a wife. And what if a baby comes along?" She

126

shook her head. "No, I won't do that to you. You'll end up hating me."

I found my voice, but it sounded bitter as it came out of my mouth. "Any normal girl would jump at the chance to be a doctor's wife."

Her eyes flashed in immediate anger, and their heat stirred my emotions and aroused my body. I wanted to grab her and shake her, and then kiss her —hard. I even moved a little toward her before she spoke, throwing words that stopped me in my tracks.

"Normal? You mean if I wanted to be one of those twits like Marlene Miller who tries to sink her claws into a guy and lead him around on a string? If that's what normal is, then I'm perfectly happy being abnormal. You think that's what I want? To be a doctor's wife? Sit around the house and make meals that my husband may or may not be home to eat? Have babies and raise 'em by myself? Sit around at the coffee klatch and talk about fifty ways to roast a chicken?" She shook her head, deep inside her own thoughts. "Oh no, I seen that scenario all my life. Man saddles a woman with a house and some babies, and twenty years later she realizes she's living with someone she don't even know and nothing to talk to him about. I swore I'd never be the wife who turns around one day and sees her man toss hungry looks at some other woman, the way I seen Doc cast them longing glances at Mrs. G!"

The room went deathly quiet. Reeling from the shock of that last statement, I stood there with my mouth hanging open. Doc was unfaithful? With Mrs. Gardener? How could Lizzy talk about them like that? Doc was a good man—I'd heard her say it herself. And she almost worshipped Mrs. G.

"What are you saying? Doc wouldn't—"

She put her hands over her mouth. "I shouldn't have said... Oh! You infuriating man! You got me all riled up and loosed my tongue!" She paced back and forth wringing her hands. "Look, I know he'd never act on it. I'm sure he's fond of Mrs. Miller in his own way. And Mrs. G would never consent to adultery anyway, no matter what."

"Did Mrs. Gardener tell you this about Doc?"

"No." She sighed in resignation. "If she knows, she don't let on." The anger in her voice returned. "I wish I'd never seen it, and I sure as shootin' wish I'd never told you. Talk about hurting people with gossip. Dear Lord!"

"I don't believe it."

Lizzy was on a roll now. "I can't figure out what men and women expect from each other anyway! The Millers seem like two strangers living in the same house. I don't ever want to live like that. I'd rather have no man at all than live with one who doesn't want me anymore. I couldn't turn a blind eye and not see it."

"Wait a minute—this is what you think of *me*? You think *I'd* feel that way? That I'd commit adultery, even in my heart? That I'd put you aside for someone else?"

"Well, you're a man, aren't ya? They all do it eventually," she said in exasperation.

And that's when I remembered my father's words from earlier in the summer, and I felt the wounded creature in front of me bite the hand that wanted to feed her, to heal her, to care for her and keep her safe till the end of her days. I winced as my heart burned and bled—as Lizzy Quinlan tore it to shreds. I hardly knew what I was saying as I nearly choked on my frenzied temper. "I should have expected this from a girl like you. I suppose sharing a bed with a man means nothing at all, as long as we didn't have—"

"Yeah, you tell yourself that, Billy Ray, if it helps you sleep at night. You narrowly escaped being hog-tied to a girl like me. Thank your lucky stars."

"All I wanted was to do the right thing. How am I supposed to live with myself after this?"

"Well now, that's *your* problem, isn't it?"

She pushed past me and went out the door, slamming it behind her. It probably woke everybody in the boarding house, but at that moment, I didn't care what they thought.

Lizzy was gone.

I PACED FOR A FULL ten minutes, throwing books and clothes and banging drawers. I was desperate to get out of that room and walk around the town to clear my head, but my ankle had stiffened up and hurt pretty bad, so long walks weren't an option. About eight-thirty, Dad came by to get me for breakfast and have Doc take another look at me. I wasn't in a mood for company, so I begged off supper at the Millers and asked Dad to take me back to the boarding house, pretending I wanted to take a nap. If he saw my misery, he didn't call any attention to it.

When I got back to the room, I discovered a fat envelope with my name on it just inside the threshold, like it had been slid under the door.

Lizzy, I thought. Anger filled my heart and I seriously considered ripping the letter to shreds, but then curiosity got the better of me. I ran my letter opener across the top of the envelope, and pulled out a stack of pages that held the promise of a good long explanation of Lizzy's inexplicable behavior that morning. I sat on the bed, propped my leg up, and began to read.

Billy Ray,

First of all, don't worry. I'm not going to use this letter to lash out at you. I know I said some awful things to you this morning, but you said some pretty mean things yourself. I also know I deserve some of what you dished out. But I have to say, you've got some strange notions about women in general and about me in particular. I can understand that you wouldn't understand much about girls, growing up without your mama around. Plus, if you've ever had a ten-minute conversation with Marlene Miller, I'm sure you know every rumor that's ever been told about me. I can only imagine what you must think.

After you and I became friends, I never wanted to taint your view of me with the truth. That's my pride, I guess—thinking you saw something in me that I wanted to see in myself. But that something you saw isn't the real Lizzy, and believing in it is hurting you. So now I suppose I don't have any choice but to tell you why this town treats me like they do. I remember once you asked me about it, and I said maybe someday I could tell you. I guess that day is today. I cautioned you not to put me on a pedestal—now you're about to find out why.

My curiosity spiked, temporarily overshadowing my anger. Finally, I would have some real answers about Lizzy Quinlan, straight from the source.

I know I told you about Marlene's boyfriend dumping her and asking me out. That was two summers ago. What you don't know was that Seth Corbett was just about the baddest guy around these parts. Marlene's parents had forbidden her to see him, but you know Marlene. She does what she wants, regardless of the consequences or who suffers for it.

Well, after she'd been seeing him on the sly for a while, he got tired of her. Maybe he realized he'd never get what he wanted. Maybe he decided he didn't really want it after all. Anyhow, he then turned his eye on me, and,

God help me, I was flattered. He was a handsome guy, a real smooth-talker. I had blossomed the year before and started getting looks from the boys at school. But I was still a backward girl from the sticks, a dumpy-looking kid in my hand-me-down clothes. So, nothing ever came of those looks.

Seth changed all that. I thought he could see through the tattered dresses to someone worth loving, that he saw something Marlene didn't have. It made him even more appealing. I'd been chafing under her scorn ever since we moved here. Now, finally, I'd have a chance to one-up the girl who I thought had everything—to steal something she wanted, as it were.

Well, that sure explained Marlene's animosity toward Lizzy.

So, yeah, going steady with Seth was a spiteful, childish decision on my part, a decision that I've paid for ever since and will pay for the rest of my life. I know that decision cost me any chance with a man like you. It's sad when the choices made when you don't know any better affect you forever, but that's the hard truth, Billy Ray. Sometimes, they do just that.

Anyway, my parents didn't forbid me to see Seth. I'm not even sure they knew. He never drove his motorcycle up to our house. Never took me for a walk by the creek like you did. Just took me over to that redneck honky-tonk he liked to frequent and to his apartment above the garage where he worked. I'm sure you know what happened there.

I felt my stomach begin a vicious roll, twisting and writhing as I was forced to face what I hadn't permitted myself to imagine.

Seth charmed me, and I trusted him. He told me he loved me so he could talk me into going all the way with him—which I did, and more than once. After the first time, I even enjoyed it some. Are you shocked yet, Billy Ray? Are you disgusted with me?

No! I couldn't reconcile that girl with the Lizzy I knew, the Lizzy who cared about her sisters, who sat quiet as a mouse in church, who laughed in a way that sent joyful music through the air.

But Seth lied to me, like he probably did to all the girls, at least the ones who didn't have vigilant parents like Marlene Miller. Or maybe Marlene was actually smart this time, smarter than me at any rate. It's an old, old story. He seduced me and then left town. I begged him not to go, even threatened to tell everyone he ruined me, but he just laughed. He said he'd told enough of his friends in Orchard Hill about me, and no one would believe he was the only guy I'd been with. Then he abandoned me, moved on to some other place, some other woman.

The writhing in my stomach turned into red-hot anger, its flames shooting high enough to singe the back of my throat.

After he was gone, I started thinking about what I'd done and what it meant. I remembered what happened to Mama when Jeremiah was born, and the possibility I might be pregnant terrified me. I was ashamed to tell Doc, and I remembered what Mrs. Gardener had done for my mother, so I went to the little house on Adalia Street—threw up three times on the way over there, I was so nervous. I thought maybe Mrs. G knew something that would get a baby out of me if there was one in there. I was so stupid.

My heart broke for that terrified girl, adding pain to the raging inferno of anger, and pushing me closer to hatred than I had ever been. All I could think was someone should make that Corbett guy pay for what he'd done to her!

Well, you know how kind and good Mrs. Gardener is—she let me in, sat me down, and held my hand while I told her the whole story. She asked me some questions and insisted I let her make me an appointment with Doc. She even went to his office with me. I cried during the whole examination. She and Doc talked in hushed voices for a long while, and I was too distraught to even remember what all they said. He took some blood and patted my hand while he explained all he needed to do. He was so calm and patient, Billy Ray, so kind. I will love him forever for that. And he never told a soul.

I had always wondered why Doc was okay in Lizzy's book, given how horrid Marlene acted toward her. And why, in turn, she accepted Charlie being with Jeannie. I'm sure some people thought Lizzy liked them just because they were men, but now I knew the real reason. And it wasn't only because Mrs. Gardener had a high opinion of Doc. Lizzy formed her own judgment, from her own experience, and that was why Doc and Charlie got real smiles from her while other men only got taunting, provocative stares.

Afterward, Mrs. Gardener took me to her house and made me hot tea while I cried it all out and got enough control of myself to go home. That day, we had the first of what would be many long talks. She told me exactly what happens when babies grow and what happens to the mama when they're born. She said she was sorry that I had been taken advantage of, and she helped me see that I had to make my own decisions—not based on flattery, pride, or spite, but on what would be right for me in the long run. It seemed like she told me a million things about love and about life, and she helped me see a glimmer of hope on the other side of my humiliation. I needed to see that too because Seth's buddies were the fuse that lit up the Orchard Hill gossip ring, and I had to be stronger than I ever imagined in order to beat back the flames.

A shower of gratitude rained over me for Mrs. Gardener, giving me a moment's respite from my temper. Mrs. G was a virtuous woman, and as the Bible said in Proverbs 31:10, her price was far above rubies.

When all the tests came back, I was fine—fit as a fiddle. You know, it was odd: in everyone else's eyes I was ruined, but I didn't feel any different —maybe sadder or wiser.

After that, I spent a lot of afternoons helping Mrs. Gardener, to learn from her and to thank her for everything. That's when I started thinking about being a midwife and studying about plants and herbs as medicines. I knew no decent man around here would have me, so I had to figure out another means of making my way in the world. Mrs. Gardener was doing just fine without a man around, so I figured I could too.

And that leads me to the other thing I said today, the thing I let slip. I beg you, please don't ever say a word to anyone about it. It's what I saw, and while I think it was accurate, to the people in this town, it wouldn't matter if it were true or not. And that kind of gossip would hurt some good people. You and I know how gossip hurts.

Yes, now we both knew how gossip hurt.

If Mrs. G knows how he feels, she doesn't let on. She would never violate marriage vows, no matter what, and I'm sure he feels the same. But you know, the person I feel sorry for is his wife. She's put her whole life into doing all a wife is supposed to do, and still, even a good man like him wants something more, someone else.

And my parents aren't much better. All Daddy wants is a son to replace the ones he lost, so he keeps giving Mama baby after baby. When will it stop? When he finally kills her? And what about the children he already has? Don't we mean anything to him?

That's my opinion of the holy estate of matrimony. So it's like I told you, you'll be disappointed if you put me on a pedestal. I'm not an innocent, and I can't give you my chastity. I can't ever be a good wife, not the way you expect. Furthermore, your father would never accept me. And because you're his son, he formed your mind as surely as my parents formed mine. Eventually, you'd grow to despise me for my past, no matter how you feel right now. Once the new shine is off the penny, you'd go back to thinking of me as the town slut. I can't change that, and there are no fresh starts, regardless of what you'd like to believe. I barely survived Seth Corbett with my soul intact, and I'll never survive the abandonment of another man.

I can't choose a life where I'm only tolerated, living with the constant oppression of shame for something that happened before I met you. As the years go past, the urge to change me or wish that I was someone I'm not will be too great a temptation, even for a man like you. I can't marry you, Billy Ray, and that's that.

My anger surged back with a vengeance. That's that, huh? She wasn't even going to give me a chance. I wanted to rail at the unfairness of it all, but there was no one to hear me. My only comfort was that the torture was almost over; I'd reached the letter's final lines.

I do wish you every happiness though and hope someday you find a woman who will be a good wife. I know that woman can't be me.

I will only add, God bless you.
Lizzy

I lay on my bed until dusk, steaming and fuming as anger and hatred boiled up inside me—hatred for the monster who hurt Lizzy and anger at her for never even giving me an opportunity to prove myself.

A knock startled me out of my red haze, and I heard Charlie's voice on the other side of the door.

"Hey, Billy Ray! I brought you some supper. Mom was fit to be tied when you weren't there so she could feed you."

I lumbered up to the door and opened it.

He stuck the plate in my chest, and I took it while he barged into my room.

"I'm supposed to sit here and make sure you eat it, too, so you might as well get started." He pulled out an apple and sat down at my desk, smiling and chomping, seemingly oblivious to my fit of temper.

I sighed in resignation and sat down on the bed, using my nightstand as a table. It did make me feel better to eat, I realized, as I worked my way through ham, scalloped potatoes and greens—good enough that, after a little while, I started to talk a bit about Lily and the storm. He teased me about being a town hero, and I said he should tell Doc I was coming in to work the next day.

I looked up and caught him watching me carefully.

"Hey buddy," he said, "you seem down for someone who just became the man of the hour."

I set my fork on my now-empty plate. "Can I ask you something in confidence, Charlie?"

"Sure thing."

"You know where I might find a guy by the name of Seth Corbett?"

Charlie looked surprised, but after a second, he answered, "You mean that hoodlum that used to date my sister a couple years back?"

"Yeah."

He paused, and realization dawned. "And the guy who messed around with Lizzy. Oh no, Billy Ray, that's a no-good, no-win situation for you."

"I just want to know where to find him."

"What for?"

Inside, I envisioned beating Corbett to a pulp, but outwardly, I just shrugged.

Charlie looked at me with pity in his eyes. "I'm sorry, but you're never going to get any satisfaction out of beatin' the tar out of Seth Corbett."

"Why not?"

"'Cause he died—knifed in a bar fight about a year ago."

I felt a savage kind of satisfaction that made me ashamed of myself. "Who did it?"

Charlie shrugged. "Some other hoodlum."

"Was it one of those cavemen that dated Lizzy after he did? Was it a fight over her?"

"No, it was some ex-con, over a lost game of pool or cards, or something. And I told you before: I'm not so sure there actually were any guys who dated Lizzy after him. I never saw 'em anyway—heard lots o' stuff, but you know how that goes."

"Yeah, I know how that goes," I said in a voice as cold and hard as steel.

Charles sat in silence, brows knitted, the chomp-chomp of his apple the only noise in the room. Finally, he spoke. "'Vengeance is mine; I will repay, sayeth the Lord.'"

My expression must have shown my surprise, because he chuckled.

"Romans twelve—" he began.

"Nineteen," I finished along with him.

"I guess I learned a little something in Sunday school." Then he grew serious. "If I remember right, the first part of the verse says, 'Dearly beloved, avenge not yourselves, but rather give place unto wrath…'"

"Is this your way of telling me it would be wrong to tear Corbett limb from limb, even if I could?"

Charlie pitched his apple core in the trash and leaned his chair back on two legs. "You wanna know why I think vengeance is the Lord's?"

"Why?"

"Well, it's not to make us feel all vindicated, like the Lord is on our side, and it's not because scumbags don't deserve a reckoning. It's because of what revenge does to the avenger. The burden of doing violence is heavy on the soul, even for the best of men. I've seen it myself—in the World War II vets up at the VA hospital. I go up there sometimes with my dad."

I turned my eyes to him and said in a cool voice, "Easy for you to say since you've had it easy all your life. You've never suffered under anyone's cruelty."

I thought that would make him angry or defensive, but he just nodded his head. "Or had to go to war. You're right. I think maybe that's why it's possible for me to imagine a world without so much violence. Victims can't imagine that; it's a luxury, and it was taken from them. No, I don't blame people for *wanting* revenge or condemn them when they seek revenge, I just don't think it's necessarily good for them to take it. And that's the reason the Bible says so in Romans. How can the cycle of cruelty ever be broken otherwise?"

It was a good question—and sounded very much like something my father might say. At the moment, however, I was all wound up inside my feelings of anger and loss, and it was hard to think straight.

"It burns me up that I don't get a chance to make him suffer for what he did to her."

"I know, but in a way, you're protected by the fact that revenge on him is impossible. You've been saved from hate—maybe saved so you can do better things," Charlie said, his voice quiet and sure.

"That low-life—he hurt Lizzy. Maybe he messed up your sister too, even if it was just hurting her feelings; maybe that made her the way she is. He was cruel to other women too, Lizzy says, and he'll never have to pay for it."

"He's dead, Billy Ray. How much more do you want him to pay?"

"Well, all I know is Lizzy's still alive, and she thinks she'll never get past what he did to her."

"I thought maybe you two had a fight. Did you break up?"

I barked out a humorless laugh. "I guess you could say that, yeah."

"Maybe she'll come around."

"She won't; she thinks he ruined her life forever and believes he ruined her for me."

Charlie looked at me earnestly. "Did he? Ruin her in your eyes, I mean."

The question stopped me short and made me think a minute. "Good grief, Charlie, I don't know. This isn't what I expected for my first love, that's for sure."

"You love her then." He rubbed his chin, considering. Charlie thought it was a reasonable conclusion. Most likely, everyone could see inside my heart—except the girl who needed to see it, of course.

"Love her? Well, I thought I did. But I don't seem to know anything anymore. I've got some 'strange notions' about women, according to Miss Quinlan." I hated the sarcasm in my voice.

Charles grinned. "That sounds like something Lizzy would say."

"If I have 'strange notions' about women, then the whole world has 'em."

"You know, that's a statement that could actually be a truth. I suppose everybody has to get rid of their strange notions along the way. Maybe that's what living is, in the long run—getting rid of all our strange notions."

"I don't know how I'm going to do that."

"Me neither."

After a minute, Charlie stood up. "Guess I'll head home. Maybe I'll see you tomorrow." He paused, his hand on the doorknob and then turned back, a thoughtful look on his face. "Has Lizzy forgiven him, do you think?"

I stopped, surprised. "Who? Corbett? I don't know."

"You might ask her about it."

"Why?"

"Forgiving him might be the only way she can get herself back, now that he's dead. And it might be the start of you getting past it too. 'Night, Billy Ray."

"'Night. Thanks for bringing me supper."

"Not a problem." He smiled, and then he was gone, leaving me to my thoughts.

Chapter Sixteen

I was mighty lonely those last days I spent in Orchard Hill. Lizzy had pulled her vanishing act again; she was nowhere to be found, but then I didn't go looking for her either. I buried myself in work and basked in the hero's glow that surrounded me after the news of Lily's rescue got around town. Inside, I carried my broken heart around with me, a weight that made me look a bit more somber and move a bit more slowly. I'm sure people noticed that I wasn't with Lizzy. After all, people in Orchard Hill noticed everything, but no one said a word. Behind my back, they probably talked about how it was just like her to be ungrateful for what I did. It didn't matter if they said it behind my back or to my face. I couldn't forget her anyway.

In a way, I wished I could. I was almost desperate to forget Lizzy. I had offered her the rest of my life, and she had thrown it back in my face. Every time I thought about it, I was mad all over again—furious and humiliated.

A few days after that disastrous marriage proposal, I helped Charles pack his things into the back of Doc's car after church. He was heading back to the state university for his senior year, and after finishing the hot work of carrying trunks and boxes, we sat on the porch, enjoying a glass of Mrs. Miller's lemonade.

We looked out over Cavanaugh Street, taking in the quiet Sunday afternoon. A couple of stalwart souls braved the heat and strolled by, calling out greetings as they passed us. A gentle wind stirred the fern baskets hanging from the beams overhead. Charlie was often a pensive guy, but he'd added a tinge of wistfulness to his expression.

"You know, I'm going to miss this place."

That wasn't what I expected him to say. After all, he wasn't leaving home for the first time. This was his senior year of college. "You'll be back at Thanksgiving and Christmas."

"Yeah, I guess."

"And next summer after you graduate."

He was silent. Then he took another sip of lemonade. I watched Mr. Hopkins next door step around the corner of his house with a water hose in hand. He looked up at the window, listening to the thin, nagging voice coming at him from inside. The old man nodded, the window closed, and then he shook his head. I could almost hear him grumbling.

Charlie looked around, and leaned forward. "I haven't told Mom and Dad this yet," he said in a low voice. "But I'm planning to ask Jeannie to marry me at Christmas."

"So, you think she will say yes?"

"Yeah, I do. Why?"

"I don't know. Sometimes things don't work out like you plan."

He looked at me curiously, but then he shrugged.

"We've talked about it a little. I won't be able to get a job until I graduate, so we'll wait to tie the knot until then."

"Where are you going to work?" I asked, running through the various banks and stores in Orchard Hill and the surrounding towns in my head.

"Don't know yet. But not here. Jeannie and me, we've talked about it. After Christmas I'm going to start looking: New York, Chicago, maybe even California. We want to move far away to some big city somewhere."

"Really? I can't imagine Jeannie leaving her family." What a blow that would be for Lizzy, to be left behind by one of the few people she could count on. I was angry all over again that she wouldn't go with me, wouldn't let me take her away from Orchard Hill.

"It will be sad of course, and she'll miss them. But honestly, Billy Ray? There's nothing for us here—no opportunities. Orchard Hill expects me to be like Dad and will always see her as the poor girl I took pity on. We wanna be ourselves, and I just don't think we can do that here."

I was beginning to see the wisdom in that.

"So this time next year, I'll be heading off to some big city with a new job and a new wife. Wish me luck?"

"Sure I will. Good luck, Charlie." I tried not to think about how, if I'd had my way, I would have been taking a new wife with me to med school in just a few days.

AS THE FINAL DAYS OF summer passed, though, I got used to the idea of going on alone, and I adapted to the mind-numbing world that now surrounded me—a world that just a few weeks ago had hummed and sparkled all around. I couldn't believe I had defied my dad to stay in the hot, stifling town of Orchard Hill. Now, I couldn't wait to leave it behind.

On Labor Day weekend, Dad came into town to drive me back to Aunt Catherine's. I'd be at my aunt's for a couple of days before orientation at Sumner University. It was going to be a rigorous first year of classes, but it was a beginning that would lead me to my profession—to my mission, my life's work.

On the Sunday I left Orchard Hill—and telling myself I at least owed her a civil goodbye no matter what had transpired between us—I went to Linden Road in search of Lizzy. What I found instead was Mrs. Quinlan sitting on a rocking chair on the front porch, baby Susie sleeping in her arms.

"Hello, Billy Ray," she called. "Surprised to see you here."

A little embarrassed that I had basically stopped calling on her daughter without a word, and having no idea what Lizzy told her about that, I shuffled my feet a bit and rubbed the back of my neck. "Yes ma'am, um...well...I've been busy at the doctor's office and—" I stopped.

"I s'pose you come to see how Lily fares."

"Yes, of course. How is she?"

"On the mend. Tom took her up to that doctor today, the one that stitched her head and set her arm. They'll be home before sundown, but I guess you'll be gone by then."

"Actually, I'm on my way out of town, starting back to school, and I thought I might say bye to Lizzy. Is she home?"

Mrs. Quinlan stared at me for a full ten seconds before little Susie started wailing and took her attention away. She brought the baby up to her shoulder and patted her back. "Lizzy's gone, Billy Ray. I thought you knew that."

"Gone?"

"Gone last week—to that midwife school up in Hyden. She didn't tell you?"

I was stunned. Why would she keep that from me? "No ma'am, she didn't."

"Well, I guess it was kind of sudden-like. I didn't even know she was thinking about going, but Mary Gardener came out here and talked to Lizzy, and next thing I know, she's packing her things, and off she goes." She went on, musing to herself, "Don't know how I'll keep Lily outta trouble now. She always listens to Lizzy better than anybody." Then to me, she said, "You want some iced tea?"

"No thank you, ma'am." My brain was whirring with this new information, and I was itching to get over to Mrs. G's place and find out what happened.

"I'm glad Lily is on the mend. You take care, Mrs. Quinlan." I turned on my heel and almost ran into town, not stopping until I reached 212 Adalia Street. I banged on the door, a little louder than was strictly polite.

"Coming!" I heard Mrs. G's pleasant voice from inside the house and footsteps coming near. The door opened, and she smiled brightly at me.

"Hello, Billy Ray. How are you today?"

"Good afternoon." I nodded at her with brusque impatience.

"You're packing up your things, I hear, and back to school with you. We sure are going to miss you around here—Doc especially. I think he likes having someone to work with."

"Mrs. Gardener, can you tell me where Lizzy is?"

Her shoulders slumped a little, and she pursed her lips. "She didn't tell you."

"No, ma'am."

"I told her she should, but sometimes she's a little stubborn." Mrs. G stepped back and held the door open for me. "Come in, then."

I stepped past and waited for her. She led me past the front room and into the kitchen, pulling out two glasses and a pitcher of lemonade. She filled the glasses, handed one to me, and indicated the kitchen table. A warm breeze blew the blue gingham curtains at the window and settled around us, giving the illusion of a calm, late summer afternoon. I felt anything but calm, however.

I pulled out her chair, and she thanked me as she sat down.

"Now," she began briskly, "about Lizzy."

"Her mother said she left for midwife school last week. I didn't even know she was going."

"It did come up unexpectedly," Mrs. G conceded. "She applied to the school back in the spring, and although she was accepted, there weren't any scholarship spots available. The administration told her to apply anyway, and there would probably be a spot next year. With her grades and my recommendation, she would be at the top of the list."

Mrs. Gardener sipped her lemonade and eyed me with curiosity as she set the glass on the table in front of her. "About a week ago, I got a call. One of the girls on scholarship had relinquished her spot because she was getting married, and the school offered the place to Lizzy. There wasn't much time to deliberate over a decision, but then, she didn't need any time, really. She took the opportunity without hesitation. Two days later, I put her on the bus."

This was the best vanishing act Lizzy had pulled yet.

"Do you want the address? You could write to her."

"I doubt she'd want to hear from me," I replied.

Mrs. Gardener nodded. "I wondered why the two of you hadn't been by in a while. You had a spat." It was a statement, not a question, so I didn't reply. She studied my expression, considering, before she spoke again.

"All right then, I won't pry, but I feel obligated to help you understand something."

"What do you mean?"

"Lizzy is a special girl, wouldn't you agree?"

"Yes, ma'am."

"She has great potential—as a healer, as a woman—but in order to realize that potential, she also has to be healed herself."

"She told me what happened with that...that..." I couldn't think of what to call him, and I didn't want to even utter his name.

"Ah, so she did trust you with her story. You should feel honored. She must have great faith in you to have done that. What did you say?"

"She told me in a letter, so I didn't have a chance to respond. And then she just ran off without saying good-bye."

"I see." Mrs. Gardener knit her brows and thought for a second. "That's unfortunate."

"How so?"

"Because she has no idea what your reaction is. For all she knows, you've turned your back on her."

"*She* turned her back on *me*."

"And you're angry."

I frowned, and she patted my hand.

"A special woman needs a special kind of man to love her." Mrs. Gardener lifted her shoulders in a nonchalant shrug. "Maybe a girl like that isn't for you. Perhaps you don't want to take on Lizzy Quinlan for the long haul."

"I told her I did."

Mrs. Gardener smiled. "But she didn't believe you, did she?" She sighed. "That girl—so much anger and hurt bubbling around inside her. She thinks all words are cheap. If you know her story, you know why."

"All I know is she's throwing away a good life with both hands. I can give her better than she's ever known—if she would just let me."

"Could you really give her everything she wanted?"

"Yes." Although, I had to admit that moment I sounded more confident than I felt.

"I bet Lizzy isn't always an easy girl to love."

"It isn't easy right now, I tell you."

"No, I guess not." She paused, taking another sip of lemonade. "You know, if you truly wanted her for a lifetime, you'd have to be prepared for any number of strange journeys."

"Journeys?"

"Yes. Detours through your well-planned life that might not be what you expect. For example, on one path, like when a woman has a baby, she leans on you, and you'd be strong for her. At another time, perhaps the tragedies of the world that you see in your line of work will trouble you, and you might lean on her. There are many times, all kinds of little journeys, where you walk hand-in-hand as lovers, enjoying each other's company, excluding everyone and everything else around you. And then there are times when you'll just be friends, walking side by side."

"'But from the beginning of the creation, God made them male and female. For this cause shall a man leave his father and mother, and cleave to his wife. And they twain shall be one flesh...'"

"Mark, chapter ten. Yes, that's a succinct way to put it," she said with a bright smile. "Lately," she went on, "especially since the war, it seems the TV and the magazines are telling us that once young people marry, their lives are smooth sailing. Every husband tows the line and every wife knows her place at home. There's this idea floating around that marriages like that are 'traditional,' but actually, they're a pretty modern notion, in my opinion —one I'm not sure is strong enough to last a lifetime. But regardless of all that, Billy Ray—do you honestly think Lizzy is the kind of girl who will live her life like everyone expects her to, just because they expect it?"

"No. In fact, I'm sure she wouldn't."

"Too right. Moreover, would you be so fond of her if she were that kind of girl?"

"It sure would make things easier, but maybe you're right. Maybe I wouldn't like it."

Her lips twitched in amusement. "If you want a woman like Lizzy, you have to ask yourself: are you ready to accept all those little journeys I talked about? And wait for the cycle to begin all over again? Could you accept her as she truly is, and allow her to become what she will be in the future? Because that is the honest-to-goodness truth of a woman and a man living together for all their days. That's what I had with my Ed. We just didn't have as many journeys as I hoped."

Mrs. Gardener's smile had a dreamy yet sad quality, and it occurred to me that, no matter what Doc thought he wanted with her, he was the kind of man that would be hard pressed to walk a path like the one she described—not with her, not with Mrs. Miller, not with any woman. He was too set in his ways.

She shook herself out of her reverie and pinned me with an earnest look. "Lizzy's soul needs healing, no doubt. Love will certainly help, but love alone won't do it. You alone can't do it. This drive she has to nurture other people, to help women and babies, it is essential to her well-being that she carry it out. She must allow that part of her to flourish, so she can be a whole person. Surely, you can relate to that. You're called to be a healer too."

"I suppose."

"You may not want my advice, but…" She moved her glass around in a little circle, drawing on the table with the condensation pooled around the bottom of it. "I think I'll give it to you anyway. Maybe it will take root—if not now, maybe later on."

I didn't want to hear advice. I just wanted someone to say I was right to love Lizzy—that I was right to want her for my own—but Mrs. G's next words gave me pause.

"Don't ever try to take her mission away from her or make her choose between that calling and you, because if she chose the mission, you would lose her companionship, and if she chose you, you would eventually lose her love. And be patient, young man, because maybe all she needs is some time." She went over to the counter and pulled out a pencil and paper. "Here's her address. After you're through being angry, you might want to write her a line. I know it seems like she's closed the door, but you may be able to re-open it someday—if you want."

She put the paper in my hand and enclosed it in both of hers. "You know, you're the real deal, Billy Ray, and a rarity in this day and age—a truly good man." She squeezed my hand and gave me an amused wink. "And there's something very pleasant about your smile." She let me go and stepped back, retrieving her apron from the back of her chair and tying it around her waist. "Now, I've got to get out in that garden, and I'm sure you've got to get back to packing."

"Yes, ma'am."

"Good luck to you, young man."

"Thank you." I turned to walk away but paused as I reached the door. I looked over my shoulder at her, stray wisps of hair around her face, her sad but graceful smile. "God bless and keep you, Mrs. Gardener."

"And you," she said, her smile growing broader.

I WALKED ACROSS THE STREET just as Doc and Marlene pulled up in front of the boarding house.

"We came to help you move out," Marlene said brightly, adjusting her ponytail and smoothing the oversized shirt that dwarfed her figure.

"Marlene insisted we would need an extra pair of hands," Doc added.

"Is my father at your house already?" I asked him, ignoring Marlene as best I could.

"He wasn't there when we left, but I'm sure it won't be long."

"He'll definitely be there for Mrs. Miller's dinner." I just barely grinned, and Doc laughed.

"Yes, Martha knows how to put a good meal on the table." He rubbed his belly and winked at Marlene. "As y'all can tell by looking at me."

She rolled her eyes. "Daddy!"

"I've got most everything packed up already," I said as I led the way into my room. "I appreciate the help." Reaching into my pocket for the room key, I unlocked the door and went inside to survey my things. I also pulled out the piece of paper Mrs. G had given me with Lizzy's school address. I stared at it, wadded it up, hesitated, and opened it again. When I looked up, Marlene was watching me, a curious expression on her face. I reached over, drew my biology book off the top of the stack in the box and stuck the paper inside.

"Decided to keep that?" she asked.

"What? Oh, yeah. It's just some notes that fell out earlier," I lied.

She opened the door, and I carried the box of books down to the car, putting them in the back seat.

"Are we ready?" Doc asked.

"Yes sir, I think so. I'll just go take one last look around the room and run the key over to Mrs. Gardener.

When I returned, Marlene was sitting in the back seat with the door open. She turned toward me, trying to draw me in with a brassy smile.

"Hop in, Billy Ray."

I ought to be annoyed with her, I thought, but after everything that had happened, her attempts to get my attention just made me tired—and maybe a little sorry for her too. I shut the back door and opened the front passenger side for myself. She pouted, but I pretended not to see. Doc pulled away from the curb and crept down the street away from my first real home away from home. I was headed toward my new life as a med student—by way of Mrs. Miller's dinner table.

Chapter Seventeen

I n early September, 1959, I left the town of Orchard Hill without looking back and started my studies at Sumner University's Medical School. That first month was a blur: learning my way around the campus, organizing my books and notes—and the reading! It seemed to never end. There were three very specific subjects of study—gross anatomy, histology, and biochemistry—where it was a challenge to read the chapters before they were covered in class, but it was necessary in order to grasp even half of the professors' lectures. There was no time to think, no time to be homesick, no time to pine over the girl who had just run out of my life for good.

The second month was even crazier than the first, and I gloomily wondered what I had gotten myself into. For the third night in a row, I found myself at a table in the library, head in my hands, words blurring together even though I'd had plenty of coffee with my dinner. The letters swam in front of my eyes, and in a faint moment of clarity, I realized that frogs, femurs and ferns did not belong together in the same sentence. That's when I felt the nudge on my shoulder that almost sent my face crashing into the tabletop.

"Hey, Daddy-o. Wake up. You look like a nerd with your mouth hanging open and drooling on your anatomy book."

I shot up straight in my seat, almost falling out of it, and squinted at the guy standing over me. The overhead lights obscured his face, but then he sat down across the table from me, grinning from ear to ear.

"I thought that was you. Dr. Robbins' anatomy class, right? You sit in the front row."

"Yeah." I scrubbed my hands over my face, trying to clear my head. "I guess I fell asleep."

"I guess so."

"Do I know you?"

He grinned even wider and stuck out his hand. "Now you do." He shook my hand with three vigorous moves. "Richard Donovan."

"Billy Ray Davenport," I replied.

"Billy Ray, my man, you are a serious med student now, and you need a serious name to go with it. From now on, you're Bill."

I chuckled. "If you say so."

"Me and the guys over there were having a ball watching your head sink lower and lower toward the table. They started taking bets on how long it would take you to plant your nose in that book. But I'm a good guy, so I took pity and came over to roust you. You have a rough night last night?"

"Hmm? Oh...yeah. I was up until almost two in the morning reading that histology chapter."

Donovan laughed. "That is *not* what I meant by rough night. I meant being out on the town, maybe playing a little back seat bingo with some dolly, but making out with your school book till 2:00 a.m.—that's just sad, man."

"I can't afford to get behind in my classes."

"Sure you can't, but running yourself in the ground is cruisin' for a bruisin'. There's plenty of time for staying up all hours when we start the clinical stuff. You should study with us. It's a lot easier in a group. We meet up around eight o'clock most weeknights here on the second floor. We read the chapters on our own, but then we divvy up the material and make study cards, quiz each other. So far, it's working." He clapped my shoulder. "And we don't end up using our books as pillows."

"Thanks, I'll be here. It sounds like a good idea."

"Come on over, and I'll introduce you to the guys. We're getting ready to head out for the evening, go grab a brew before heading home."

I followed him to the table where the other guys were packing up their books and papers.

"Hey guys, this is Bill. He's joining our study group tomorrow. Bill, this is John, Ed, Dan and Tony."

We shook hands all around, and Tony asked me, "You wanna come out to Barney's with us? Get a beer?"

"Thanks, but I don't drink."

"You don't drink beer?" Dan asked.

"I don't drink anything," I answered, ready for the chortles and smirks. I'd gotten those from time to time back in college.

"Not even a Coke? They do sell Cokes there. Just ask Ed—that's what he gets every time," John answered.

Ed gave him a playful punch in the arm. "Hey, I don't like beer. Sue me."

"Well…"

"Or maybe Bill can get some coffee," Richard joked to the others, "so he can stay awake till he gets home."

They all laughed, but it wasn't mean-spirited. I decided I'd go and get to know these guys better. After all, we were going to be in a lot of the same classes over the next couple of years, and if the first month was any indication, I couldn't keep up the pace on my own.

The first thing I learned that night was that Richard Donovan could put away some beer.

"Another round, honey." He winked at the waitress, indicating our table with a circle gesture of his index finger.

Dan shook his head. "Not for me, big guy."

"But it's Friday night! It's the Irish way, Danny Boy!" Rich declared in a fake accent that had the whole table laughing.

"And the German way!" John lifted his own glass.

"Long live Coca-Cola!" Ed chimed in with his Georgia drawl, and I felt my lips twitch into a smile.

THEY WERE ALL GOOD EGGS, those guys, but Richard and I in particular became good friends that first year. He was different from most of my fellow students, and different from my church friends like Charlie. At college, I knew straight-laced squares, like myself, and the party guys, whom I avoided, but Richard was the first guy I'd met who played as hard as he worked. He was from a large family in New Orleans, the second of seven boys, and from his description, he and his brothers were as wild as rabbits. His father was, in Richard's words, 'a tough old sonofabitch' who helped build the Higgins boats used at Normandy. Apparently, Mr. Donovan considered his son's choice of profession, obstetrics, a 'ninnified' way to make a living. That was a pretty stark contrast to my own father's reverence for medicine.

Dad always considered it a calling, a life's mission.

Sometimes Richard lived it up a bit too much in my opinion, but he studied hard too. He was easygoing and didn't seem to take life too seriously. At first I wondered if he had the dedication it took to study medicine, but every night I was up cramming for a test, he was right beside me with a cuppa joe instead of a beer mug. He had a quick wit and a way with people that carried him a long way—with professors, with other students, and also with the ladies. He went through about half a dozen of them that year: a pretty one, a smart one, a giggly one, an older one. I don't know how he had time for girls. My spare time was next to nothing, and if he talked me into double dating with him, we always dropped my date off by ten o'clock. I went home to my books long before he did.

Although I was busy, I didn't spend all my time in the library or at my studio apartment. If there was some school-related social event, I'd find a date and go—always with a different girl, however. I never let any of them think there was more to it than a friendly outing. Growing up, I thought being the preacher's son put me under a microscope, but being a medical student was even worse. I made sure I escaped any female entanglements. And scowling—I became very practiced at that. I certainly didn't dare smile at any of them. To be honest, I wasn't too interested in dating anyway, and the frenetic pace of first-year med school made it easy to put Lizzy Quinlan out of my mind. Those first few months, I stayed angry. As the year wore on though, that anger began to lose its intensity, and curiosity began to take root. I actually began to contemplate writing to her, just to see how she was doing, of course.

FUNNY ENOUGH, IT WAS ONE of those double dates Richard set up that planted the seed of curiosity about Lizzy's new life. The girl he'd fixed me up with was, according to him, 'perfect' for me.

"She's just as serious as you are. You should get along like tea and honey, and if you don't, you can talk all about how the world should be but isn't."

"What's her name?"

"Jo Anne. She's majoring in sociology over at Derby College."

"I don't know. Those Derby College girls are a different sort."

"Intellectual. Not really my taste, but you two should hit it off. You're just alike." He grinned. "But she's a helluva lot prettier."

He wasn't wrong about that. Jo Anne *was* a pretty girl. She had sandy brown hair and eyes that were like ice, the lightest shade of gray I'd ever seen. She was shortish, about Lizzy's height but not as curvy. And she smelled nice—like soap, not that cloying, heavy perfume that girls sometimes wore.

We went to dinner and then to see a movie that Richard thought was hilarious, I thought was silly, and Jo Anne thought demonstrated everything that was wrong with society. Richard's date had no comment. She just watched in disappointment as Richard and Jo Anne argued themselves into a tug of war that became laden more and more with sexual tension as the night went on. At one point, I thought he was going to grab her and 'plant one on her,' as Lizzy used to say.

"She was an idiot," Jo Anne insisted, referring to the female lead. "And he was the worst sort of misogynist."

I made a mental note to look up *misogynist* when I got home that night.

"Of course he is—he's a caricature of the lecherous businessman. It's a *comedy*, Jo Anne. It pokes fun at life."

"I think that film made some dramatic points—the emptiness of the American corporate ladder, suicide attempts, adultery."

Richard rolled his eyes. "Okay, okay, so it isn't comedy, it's *satire*. Happy now?"

"The purpose of satire is to criticize, not just ridicule," she replied, lifting her soda glass to her lips. For all her tiny, delicate-looking stature, she sure had a powerhouse of opinions.

"Adultery is immoral," I chimed in.

"It so happens I agree with you, but why do you say that?" she asked.

"It's one of the Big Ten."

"Big Ten?"

"Commandments."

Richard suddenly seemed to remember I was there. He grinned. "Bill is a P.K."

"P.K.?" his date asked.

"Preacher's Kid."

"Ohhh." That seemed to make a lot of things fall into place for Jo Anne.

"Adultery breaks a promise. When people start believing they can break their promises, all of society breaks down."

"I don't think Moses had the corporate ladder in mind when he wrote down the Ten Commandments."

"'Thou shalt have no other gods before me.' Exodus 20:3. I think that applies to—what did you call it?—the emptiness of the American corporate ladder."

Richard smiled. "He does that Bible-quoting thing a lot, Jo Anne. I hope it doesn't annoy you."

"Oh, I'm not bothered at all."

She *did* look annoyed though. Whether it was because I brought up the Bible while we were on a date, or interrupted her discussion with Richard, or just because I didn't agree with her, I didn't know.

"See, I think the schmuck on the corporate ladder is the idiot," Richard volunteered.

"You would," Jo Anne replied, but she smiled—and they were at it again.

AT THE END OF THE evening, I walked her to her door. A biting, February wind stirred the dry, cracked leaves around our feet and seemed to draw the blood from our bones.

"Thank you for dinner," she offered politely.

"You're welcome."

"And the movie. I'm sorry you didn't enjoy it more."

"I think you and Richard enjoyed it enough for all of us."

Before we were compelled to give the obligatory goodnight kiss that neither of us wanted, I stuck out my hand. "It was good to meet you."

She let out a little sigh of relief and shook my hand. "You too."

"Better get inside—it's cold out here. Good night."

"Good night, Bill." She cast a quick look over my shoulder at the running car, where Richard and his date had their heads together, taking advantage of a private moment. Then she hurried into the house.

I walked back to the car and tapped on the driver's side window.

"No good night kiss, Daddy-o?" Richard asked.

"No, not tonight. Hey, I think I'll walk from here. It's only a few blocks to my place."

"Nah, Bill, get in. It's too cold to walk."

"I think I'd like a walk. It'll clear my head. I like that at the end of the day."

"You sure?"

I nodded.

"Okay then. I'll see you Monday."

"'Night."

He drove off, the red taillights disappearing around the corner.

It was cold, but I needed to breathe a little, and Richard would be happier to continue his date without me.

FOR THE THIRD TIME IN as many weeks, my thoughts turned to Lizzy. I missed her smiles, her kisses, her hand in mine, but the evening's lively discussion forced me to realize I missed our talks and her teasing just as much. And then, a little piece of my anger blew away with the frigid wind. I wondered what Lizzy was doing in Hyden. Did she like school? Was she curled up with a botany book, learning about herbs and medicines? I imagined her sitting on a gently worn sofa in a dormitory common room, or lying on a narrow bed under a comfortable quilt—and reading, always reading. I smiled.

When I got back to my apartment, I made myself a cup of instant coffee and sat down to my own books.

Instead of concentrating on anatomy, however, my mind returned to Orchard Hill, to Lizzy, and to the last time I'd seen her. I regretted so many things about that day.

Mrs. Gardener was right. It *was* unfortunate that Lizzy told me her story in a letter, because I never got to tell her that she wasn't ruined in my eyes. My anger had taken a turn over the last six months, and with some distance, it took a more proper direction. I didn't blame Lizzy, but I still hated Seth Corbett, regardless of whether or not he was dead.

Without thinking too much about it, I took out some paper and wrote:

Dear Lizzy,

It seems trite to ask how you are doing, as if nothing happened between us the last time we saw each other. But I honestly want to know, how are you?

I've thought about you so many times these last months. Little things will remind me of you—a couple of months ago, I ran across that old biology book we shared. Last summer, I saw feverfew on a hillside on the outskirts of town. Tonight it was a spirited discussion between my date and Richard. You'll have to meet Richard sometime. And the date? Well...

And here I flattered myself that she would care…

Don't worry about her. She's a nice enough girl, but we didn't have too much to talk about.

This may surprise you, but I still have the letter you wrote. I must have read it a dozen times at least. In it, you asked if I was disgusted with you. Well, I'm not. I never was. I was angry though, and embarrassed, and I said things I wish I could take back. You once said you weren't a mistreated innocent, but I disagree. I know you take responsibility for your own decisions, and I've always admired that. But in that situation, you made a mistake, a very human mistake, to trust someone you shouldn't have. People have been making those kinds of mistakes since the dawn of man, and they will continue to make them until the sun sets for good.

Thinking of Charlie's advice about forgiveness, I added: *I think it's time you forgive yourself for that mistake.*

But enough about that. I want to talk about now.

There is one thing I know for sure. You were right about medical school taking all my time. I study every weeknight with a group of guys from my classes and spend most of my weekends reading. It was a wise decision not to get married last summer. There. You were right. I can admit it.

I went on and on for about three pages, telling her all about school, and the guys in my classes, and my dad. I asked her about her school and her family. About Jeannie and Charlie. About Doc Miller.

When I finished, I hunted down an envelope, thinking maybe I'd send it. But when I searched through my book box for her address, the piece of paper Mrs. Gardener gave me was missing. I looked in every book I had without success. Remembering her smug smile in the back of her dad's car gave me a sneaking suspicion that Marlene had taken the paper out of my book the day I moved out. Should I write to Mrs. G and get the school address? I didn't even remember the name of the place. Or maybe losing the paper was a sign to move on with my life.

Besides, I thought as some of the hurt resurfaced, I had offered my heart to Lizzy Quinlan, and she turned me down and left without a single word.

I'd had no indication that she'd changed her mind about me, so why should I have to be the one to make the big gesture?

I went round and round about it that night, and finally, I tucked the letter in my sock drawer. I'd think for a while about whether or not to seek out Lizzy's address. Maybe it was the right thing to do, but then again, almost six months had passed and everything was different now for both us. Maybe it wasn't such a good idea after all.

The end of that first year of medical school was approaching fast. Unlike the summers when I was in college, I had classes to attend over the summer months, so I wouldn't be traveling with my father for the first time in many years. I'd done well in med school after I found my study group—or as Richard called it, 'The Studly Group.'

Richard sure had an interesting way of looking at things, and the name of our group was only one example. Actually, I don't know where he got the idea to call us that, because, Richard excepted, it wasn't an accurate description of the rest of us at all.

We were sitting in the library on a rainy afternoon, cramming for final exams during that May of 1960. Richard came strolling into the library, medical journal volume in hand.

"Oh, what a beautiful morning! Oh what a beautiful day!" he sang, tossing the paper on the table. "Everything's going my way."

"Look," he said, pointing to the article title on the front.

I read aloud, "FDA approves oral contraceptive pill." Then I squirmed and blushed. I was trying to stop my automatic reaction to subjects like that —after all, I was going to be a physician, and I needed not to get embarrassed so easily—but old habits were hard to break.

"Big deal." Tony turned back to his book.

"It is a *very* big deal," Richard insisted, tapping the paper to emphasize his point. "That little pill's going to change everything—for the ladies, sure, but for us too. Imagine, all those college co-eds no longer afraid of getting knocked up." He shot us all a wicked grin. "It's a guy's dream come true."

We were used to his irreverent comments, so we ignored that last part. Tony answered him, eyes still on his book. "College girls won't even be able to get them. I read that doctors will only give them to married women."

Richard turned on Tony, amusement all over his face. "Yeah, right. But in a few years, we'll be the doctors, and we can give them to anybody who asks." Then his smile dimmed. "I happen to know for a fact that the college girls will ask for them."

I was sure Jo Anne had told him that. After we had our double date in February, he cornered me at the next study group, wanting to know if I minded him asking her out, and they'd been dating on and off ever since. It was a tumultuous relationship. Richard confided once that he liked the making up enough that the arguments were worth the trouble. Jo Anne was leaving after graduation to get her master's degree in social work, and though he tried to pretend that it didn't bother him, I think on some level, it did.

He closed the journal and left it on the table. "And if married women get them, single girls *should* get them too. Maybe if they aren't getting pregnant to begin with, they aren't going into back alleys to get rid of the consequences."

We all sobered at that. We'd heard the stories from the university hospital. Just last month, an undergraduate student died from complications of one of those illegal procedures. It was those kinds of stories that made me realize I was in the real world where real tragedies happened all the time. Becoming cognizant of both the glorious and depraved sides of humanity had altered me in ways I'd only begun to understand. I'd never realized how sheltered I was under the protective wings of my father and Dr. Miller, but over the last year, it had become very clear to me.

Richard spoke up again. "I'm telling you guys, it's all going to be different for our generation, in the way we practice medicine and in our own lives. Imagine, after a guy and a gal get circled, they can decide how many kids they want, and when—or if they want them at all."

"You make it sound like birth control didn't exist before now," John put in.

"But it's never been as easy and reliable as this pill will be."

"The church is against it," Tony added. Like Richard, he was Catholic.

"God should decide when a child comes into the world," I heard myself saying.

Richard rounded on me next. "Tell that to the woman who's getting ready to have her seventh child when she can only afford to feed five. You ever seen that, Davenport?"

"Actually, I have," I replied, remembering the Quinlans.

"Well, so have I, all over Louisiana, and I think people should decide for themselves how many ankle-biters they can manage."

"Perhaps," I conceded. He had a point. I remembered how Lizzy felt about her father giving her mother baby after baby. Yet I knew Lizzy was crazy about Lily and baby Susie too.

"All I know is, when I'm in my ob-gyn practice in a few years, I'll be doling out these prescriptions like they were candy. You wait and see. And on the whole, I think it'll be a shining example of medical progress."

"Science marches forward," John replied, gathering up his books and papers.

"Yeah." Tony followed suit. "We're meeting Ed at the cafeteria—you guys coming?"

"I'm in," Richard said.

"I'll be along in a few minutes." I turned back to my book. "I want to finish this section."

"Suit yourself," Richard replied. He set the journal in front of me, his index finger drilling a hole over the article title. He pointed at me and the journal, as if to say, 'Read it, P.K.' and followed the other two out.

Richard's idealistic vision of this brave new world made possible by science and technology reminded me of what my father said about me glorifying the old West. Dad would always shake his head, smiling at my naiveté, and say:

"But here's the thing, Billy Ray. People thought the West was the land of milk and honey, and sometimes it was, but it was a hard, brutal place back then. You don't read about that in your Western novels, and you don't often hear about the people who didn't make it through, even in your history books."

Richard thought this pill would solve a lot of problems, for doctors, for men and women, and for society. I guessed it could, but change was hard, no matter how things turned out in the end. And I had a feeling something like this pill would instigate a lot more changes than just how many babies women had.

I wondered what Lizzy Quinlan would think about this news. She'd probably have an opinion like Richard's. How would her own life have been different if that little pill had been around in 1956? Would she even have been able to get a prescription as a teen-aged girl in Orchard Hill? I couldn't imagine Doc Miller giving her such a thing. But if he had, she at least would not have had the strain of worrying about being pregnant. I reminded myself, though, that she still would have been used and abandoned by Seth Corbett. No pill could have prevented that.

But it would have been one less trauma, and surely, that was better, right?

Although, if she knew she wasn't pregnant, she wouldn't have gone to Mrs. G for help. Would they have become friends even without Lizzy imagining herself in trouble? And if Lizzy hadn't become Mrs. G's protégé, would she have ever been able to go away to school? Or would she have been stuck in Orchard Hill, even now?

During my college days, I took a survey course of the world's religions. Dad tried to talk me out of it. He wanted me to take Old Testament instead, but to be honest, I already knew the Old Testament pretty well. I'd heard it from the time I was old enough to talk, and I was curious about what other people around the world believed. One of the concepts that I found interesting was the Taoist idea of yin and yang, the complementary forces that bent and shaped the world. According to that world view, shadow accompanied light, choice also produced confinement, good outcomes occurred along with bad.

It sounded a lot like Newton's third law of motion to me: To every action, there is always an equal and opposite reaction. Then I thought—if Eastern and Western philosophies both came up with this concept, didn't that make it a universal idea? And, could I not apply this Eastern concept to Western medicine? What would be the consequences of this little pill? Changing if and when babies came into the world? I couldn't think of anything that would affect humanity more than that, in good ways and in bad. The endless possibilities made my head swim. But perhaps I, Billy Ray Davenport, wasn't smart enough or wise enough to make sense of it. Was it foolish to try? Because if God could create the Earth and part the Red Sea and transcend death, surely He had control of twentieth century medicine too—as much control as He wanted anyway.

"He hath made every thing beautiful in his time: also he hath set the world in their heart, so that no man can find out the work that God maketh from the beginning to the end," I muttered. Could it be that He chose this time and this place for this particular change in people's lives?

My mind raced along the chapter of Ecclesiastes to the last verse: "Wherefore I perceive that there is nothing better, than that a man should rejoice in his own works; for that is his portion: for who shall bring him to see what shall be after him?" Those used to be just words to me, words I'd heard many times, that I'd memorized. But now I began to see how they fit—in medicine, with people, in the world. They told me to rejoice in the time I'd been born. I should claim the works of my world, for they were my right as the Good Book said. But I couldn't see God's plan for it all, and I would have to accept that. Because He was God, and I was not.

But I didn't see Him being angry at me for asking the tough questions, or not forgiving me when I didn't understand.

The gentle spring shower turned into a brief deluge outside the library's open window. The librarian came over and smiled at me, saying, "I'm going to close this window, son. All that moisture isn't good for the books."

Maybe it wasn't good for the books, but rain *was* good for the landscaping in front of the building and for the crops just outside of town. Action and reaction. Yin and yang. Every thing beautiful in His time.

Chapter Eighteen

As luck would have it, Dad was scheduled to preach in Orchard Hill on Easter Sunday, 1961, and I was home for a well-deserved four-day weekend that year. The second year of med school was just as demanding as the first, and although I was holding my own, the mini-vacation was a welcome respite. Easter had always been a big holiday in our house, as big as Christmas, if not more so. So on Saturday, I made the three-hour drive with my father from Aunt Catherine's house in Kent to the Millers' in Orchard Hill.

The Miller household had changed in the two years since I'd been there. Louise had married some local yokel and was living in a house in town. Just like he promised, as soon as he graduated, Charlie married Jeannie and took her to California. Marlene was still living with her parents, working as a teller at the local bank. Doc and Mrs. Miller seemed just the same, however. Mrs. Miller was quiet and busy, and Doc's easy-going kindness, thankfully, had never wavered at all.

Just as they had that fateful summer in 1959, Doc and Marlene were waiting on the porch for us to arrive. It wasn't a hot sultry day this time. A spring wind, heavy with moisture and the smell of the warming earth, stirred the unsettled feeling I harbored in the pit of my stomach.

Marlene was immaculately put together, as always. The blond ponytail was gone, replaced with a teased up do that a lot of the young women were wearing then. But her syrupy perfume was the same, as well as that unpleasant glint in her eye when she smiled at me.

160

"Hi there, Billy Ray. Long time, no see."

"How are you?" I replied in a solemn voice.

Her smile faltered a little, but after a second or two, she rearranged her features and dredged up a cheerful veneer. "I would offer to carry your bag, but you never let me before, so I guess it won't be any different this time."

"You'd be right about that."

"Billy Ray!" Doc turned from greeting my father, shaking my hand and clapping me on the shoulder. "Good to see you, my boy! You look all grown up. Doesn't he look all grown up, Marlene?"

Her eyes slid up and down my person in a way that still felt slimy. "Yes, he does."

"Come on in then. It's too bad Charlie isn't here, but he and Jeannie don't get back on this side of the country too often."

"Too often? Daddy, they haven't been back at all since the wedding last summer." She looked at me. "Mama always said that Jeannie Quinlan would take him away from us, and I guess she was right."

"I thought Charlie had a job waiting in California before he married Jeannie."

"Well…" Marlene looked surprised, as if she wasn't aware I knew that. "I'm sure it was Jeannie's idea."

I was sure it wasn't, but I wasn't going to argue the point.

After a quick lunch, I left Dad and Doc chatting in the living room, and slipped out to take a walk around Orchard Hill. I passed the library, the Dairy Queen, the laundromat—replaying each event from Lizzy's and my past. I could sense her there, feel and hear her, but my image of her kept shifting and shimmering like a spirit. How odd it was to be in a place that felt familiar, but see it with eyes that had absorbed so much else of the world. It unnerved me to be in the town that initially sparked so many changes in my thinking.

Lizzy's town.

With no Lizzy in it.

She was gone, at school of course. I knew that. I had carried a tiny hope that she might be home for the holiday, but there was no sign of her. I even walked past Mrs. G's house, but there was no one home.

When I got back to the Millers', Marlene was waiting on the porch, a scarf over her hair in an attempt to preserve it from the windy day.

161

"Where you been?"

"Here and there."

"Well, you missed Lizzy Quinlan," she replied, her eyes glittering with a sharp, cruel light that I now recognized as jealousy tinged with bitterness.

"She was here?" I couldn't help the tremor in my voice as I tried to speak around the lump in my throat.

A derisive chuckle escaped her. "No, you dope. She'd never come here —not in a million years, not even to get a glimpse of you. But she was in town last month when your dad came to preach. Sat all by herself in the back pew."

"She did?" Curiosity made me tamp down my anger at Marlene's cruel joke, even though I knew better than to trust her to tell the complete truth.

"See? I knew that's where you'd gone today. You were looking for her."

"I was not. I only went for a walk." It wasn't a lie—I hadn't gone looking for her specifically. I was just sort of hoping.

"You know, I pity you, Billy Ray."

I leaned back against the porch post and crossed my arms over my chest. The wind whipped up and left me with a distinct chill in my bones. "Why's that?"

"For all your high and mighty morals and principles, you're no better than any other guy."

"I never said I was."

"You let that cheap little tart tie you up in knots, just like she did to every boy in Orchard Hill. You're still letting her do it. And she's probably been with a dozen other guys since you."

"And you know this how? She doesn't even live around here."

"I know the type."

"You know the type."

"Yep."

"The type of girl that uses guys."

"Uh-huh."

"Marlene Miller, you *are* the type."

Her eyes got round with shock and anger. "How dare you? I have never—"

"In all the time I knew Lizzy, she never treated me like a trophy or a possession or—"

"The Lizzy Quinlans of the world just want to pull a guy's strings."

Lizzy had said that same thing about boys at one time, but... "Lizzy didn't want to do that to *me*," I insisted, knowing I sounded hopelessly naive, even defensive. But even if I couldn't convince Marlene of the truth, I knew it in the bottom of my soul. Lizzy and I had too much happen between us for me to doubt her. She had turned me down because she didn't want to trap me. I knew for a fact that if Marlene ever got her hooks into me, she'd never let me go.

"I wish I knew how she does it," Marlene shook her head. She looked genuinely puzzled.

"You want to know how she does it?" My voice was dangerously low, even cruel sounding. "If you really want to know, I'll tell you. I'd walk to the moon and back for Lizzy because she let me be myself—not who she might have wanted me to be. *That's* why I liked her so much. That's why I still care what happens to her and why I wish her well. She was honest, even when it hurt or embarrassed me. She didn't think she could own me. And never would she have done anything so sneaky as to let herself into my bedroom uninvited. Or steal an address out of my schoolbook."

Marlene sniffed. "That last bit sounds like an accusation."

"If the shoe fits..."

"I don't know what you're talking about." She got up and put her hand on the door.

"You're just sorry that Dad and I are staying in the same guest room, and you can't try any midnight marauding under my blankets." I had never spoken such ugly words to any woman, but they just kept tumbling out of me. I wanted to hurt Marlene's vanity, since it was impossible to touch her heart.

Her eyes glittered with malice. "Lizzy Quinlan is gone. You'll never see her again. You should be thanking me and God and your lucky stars that you're rid of her. She never had a thing to offer you but a reputation and estrangement from your father."

She went inside, and I stayed there for twenty minutes or more, letting the wind lash me until the clouds finally succumbed to their tears.

On Sunday evening, we arrived back at Aunt Catherine's. She had Easter ham, green beans, mashed sweet potatoes and walnut bread waiting for us. We ate in virtual silence as was typical for her table, although Dad tried to engage me in conversation. I just wasn't up for small talk.

"You been working hard at school, son?" he asked, his eyes resting on me in what appeared to be a casual manner. I, of course, knew that he was observing me carefully.

"Yessir." I pretended to be very interested in cutting my ham.

"One of my parishioners here in Kent has a son who is currently in medical residency. He says that second year is awfully tough, academic-wise."

"It's difficult, but I'm holding my own with the help of my study group."

"That's good." There was another stretch of silence; then Dad spoke again. "Maybe you could talk to him—my parishioner's son, I mean. It would be good to talk to someone who's been in your shoes. He could give you some pointers, introduce you to some people."

"I appreciate you thinking about me, Dad, but, really, everything's going fine." I didn't want to put up with some cocky resident giving me advice at my father's request. I knew the pecking order, and I was right near the bottom of it.

"If you say so," he replied, clearly wanting to say more, but knowing he couldn't convince me.

After supper, I returned to my room to pack up the few things I'd brought with me. I had to leave bright and early the next morning, before breakfast even, and it would help to have everything ready to go as soon as I woke.

I wasn't surprised at the knock on my door. Dad asked to come in, and when I said sure, he sat down on the bed next to my suitcase.

"You okay, Billy Ray?"

"Fine."

"You're not sick or anything, are you?"

"No."

"You seem...subdued. If you're not sick in your body, are you sick in your soul? Are you fighting the blues? I never had much trouble that way, but sometimes your mama did, and my father did as well."

How could I tell him that this thing I had wanted so much, this desire to be a doctor, was starting to wear on me? Even just a little.

"I'm just tired, Dad. It's nothing that a good night's sleep won't cure."

"Are you able to get yourself to church on Sundays?"

Annoyance bubbled up in me that once again, that was his solution to everything. Church couldn't give me the sleep I needed. Church couldn't make time for me to eat a real dinner instead of instant coffee and take out over the sink.

"I go when I can. Sometimes I can't."

"You—"

"And starting in June," I said over him, "it will be even more sporadic. I'll start doing clinical work, and I'll have to work on Sundays sometimes. People still get hurt and sick on the Sabbath."

"I know that, son, I do. I'm proud of you for taking on this calling. Medical school is a challenge. Just make sure you keep the Lord in your life."

I looked down, resigned, and not willing to really talk about what was bothering me because it was all about Lizzy, and he wouldn't want to hear. Most of the time I could put her out of my mind, but going to Orchard Hill and listening to Marlene's venomous words had dredged it all up again.

"I'll try to make sure I get to church on Sundays."

"Good." He stood up and looked around the room, his hands in his pockets. "You'll call if you need me, right?"

"Sure, Dad." I knew the chances that he would be around when I called were not very good. He still traveled a lot, and if I phoned, I'd be more likely to get my aunt or Zelda, the housekeeper.

He patted my shoulder a little awkwardly, and I read a helpless kind of bewilderment in his expression. He looked as if he might say something else, but apparently he changed his mind because he turned around and left the room.

Chapter Nineteen

Back at school, I was restless and unsettled. By the time the week ended, I thought I would go crazy in that little apartment, so I grabbed my books, strapped a spare belt around them and headed to the library. A couple of hours studying made me even more antsy, so I took off toward Barney's. Maybe some of the guys were there. After all, it was a Saturday night. I was in desperate need of something to get my mind off my past.

Barney's was an old hole-in-the-wall place decorated with pictures from the Thirties and a gleaming showcase of bottles behind the bar. Wine and pilsner glasses hung upside down under cabinets that held every variety of old fashioned and highball glass within. The Studly Group usually sat at one of the tables, but I didn't feel like sitting all alone, so I chose the bar instead. At least there, I could talk to Big Theo about the World Trade Center that New York's governor had just authorized, or current goings-on with the Cubans and the Russians. Theo always loved to talk about the news. I couldn't very well sit at a bar and drink a Coke, or at least that's what I told myself, and I was feeling reckless anyway, so I ordered a glass of that Scotch whiskey Ed sometimes drank. Theo raised his eyebrows a little when I asked for it, but he served it to me in a glass with a little ice.

The first drink was like the bitterest medicine, but I told myself I'd drink it slowly and then walk back home. Funny, but after about the third sip, it really wasn't so bad, and that's when I noticed the woman at the other end of the bar. She was watching me, so I smiled at her, and she stubbed out her cigarette and hopped off her bar stool. She walked over to the chair beside me and made herself at home.

"Hey, I know you."

"You do?"

"Yeah, I'm the secretary in Dr. Griggs's office."

Dr. Griggs was my histology professor last year, and it felt like I was in there about once a week during his office hours, trying to make sense of the notes I'd taken in his class.

"Oh." My eyelids were starting to feel heavy, but at least I didn't feel like the walls were closing in on me anymore.

She stuck out her hand. "I'm Marian Baker."

"Nice to meet you, Marian Baker. I'm Billy R… I mean, I'm Bill Davenport." I didn't want to hear her say Billy Ray. It always sounded odd coming off strangers' lips these days. And tonight, I didn't want to be Billy Ray anyhow.

"Buy you a drink?" she asked.

"Oh no, I got plenty left…" I looked down in my glass and realized it was empty. "Oh."

She giggled, and I laughed too. Finally, my heart was starting to feel warmer. I held up a finger the way I'd seen Richard do.

Big Theo came over, drying a glass as he walked. "Another whiskey, Bill?"

"Yep." I looked at Marian. "What would you like?"

"I'll have the same." She gave me an open, friendly smile. "You're second year, aren't you?"

"Yep."

"I thought so. You're one of the serious ones. I'm surprised to see you here on Saturday night."

"Me too."

"Woman trouble?"

"Who me? No. I'd have to have a woman to have woman trouble."

"Ah." She scooted her bar stool a little closer. "That's good to know."

"What are you doing here on a Saturday night by yourself? It's probably not a good idea for a girl to be here all alone, you know."

"Oh-ho. We got us a knight in shining armor here, Big Theo."

He laughed as he brought the drinks and set them down in front of us. I noticed mine had a lot more ice than the last time, but I didn't mind. It seemed to go down better cold anyway.

Marian told me about growing up in a little town just south of the university and coming to Sumner to work right out of high school. She wanted to go to school to be a nurse, but she just had to save up a little money first, and that's why she got a job in an office at the medical school. She didn't particularly care for Dr. Griggs, but at least he wasn't a skirt-chaser like the last boss she had.

Before I knew it, I'd finished off that second glass and ordered another, and the room was beginning to spin. I could hear every clink of a glass and a cacophony of voices swirling all around me, and I shook my head to clear it. My lack of experience with alcohol was showing, and instead of charming that pretty girl, I was going to have to sit on the bar stool and wait out my inebriation so I could walk back home. And it was too bad, because I wanted to charm a pretty girl, and I was fairly certain I could do it too. I remembered how. I was sure I did.

"Hey, Bill," Marian's voice came through my tipsy haze. "You okay?" She took my arm and righted me on the stool, and I laughed—first at my drunkenness and then at the tingle on my arm where she'd touched me.

"I'm fine," I slurred, ever so slightly, which embarrassed me further. "But I should probably call it a night."

"My car's just outside. I don't know if you should be walking around in your state. I'll drive you—anywhere you want to go. How 'bout that?" Her smile was charming and eager, and I found myself leaning toward her, about to say yes, when I felt a strong hand on my shoulder. I winced at the grip and turned around to see Richard wedged right next to me in front of a big hulk of a man who looked none too happy.

"There you are, you son of a gun. We got to get you back home."

"Huh?"

"Poor guy. That flu really put you under the table, didn't it? I told you one whiskey toddy would help. I didn't expect you to drink three."

"Toddy?"

He tossed a bill down on the bar and heaved me up off the barstool. "Thanks, Theo. I'll take it from here."

Without another word, Richard led me out to his 1956 Ford Fairlane, double-parked in front of the bar.

"I can't leave Marian in there."

"Oh yes you can."

"She's all alone. Someone needs to escort her home." I tried to turn around, but Richard turned me back toward the street and opened the car door.

"Watch your head there, Sir Lancelot." He pushed me in and shut the door in my face.

"I can't believe it of you, Richard," I slurred at him when he had climbed in the driver's side and pulled away from the curb. "You would leave a young lady at a bar by herself at this time of night?"

"No, I wouldn't. But I'm pretty sure her husband wouldn't appreciate you escorting her anywhere, especially back to your apartment—or theirs, or any cheap motel in between."

A sick feeling rolled in my stomach. "Her husband?"

"Yeah, that troll standing behind me? The one I barely kept off your drunken ass? That's Avery Baker, little Marian's ball and chain."

"What?"

"You 'bout did yourself in tonight, Slick."

"Good Lord, I almost let her drive me home."

Richard barked out a laugh that hurt my ears. "Well, don't feel too bad, my friend. You certainly wouldn't have been the first."

"What?"

"Old Avery likes to play cards in the back room of Barney's. Sometimes Marian gets to feeling a little left out, so she shows up at the place and zeroes in on some poor schmuck to help her get his attention."

I leaned back and closed my eyes. "And tonight I was the schmuck."

"Like I said, you aren't the first."

"Lucky for me you showed up when you did."

"Not luck, exactly." I could hear his grin, even though I couldn't see it in the dark.

"Then how...?"

"Big Theo called me at my place. Said you were about to dig yourself a deep hole with the help of the lovely Mrs. Baker. I got there just in time to keep Mr. Baker from putting you in it."

"Good grief!" I groaned.

"Even trashed you can't spew decent profanity."

"You're a real clown, Donovan."

"I almost didn't believe Theo—thought it must have been some kind of joke. You don't drink whiskey, P.K. What gives?"

"I don't know. I'm an idiot."

"Yeah, but you've been an idiot before, and you've never done this. Something happen when you went home last weekend?"

I closed my eyes and saw orange sparks in front of them. My stomach rolled again, and I tried to push the image of pretty dark curls and sundresses, and laundromats and hot days by a cool creek out of my head.

"No. I'm fine."

"I know woman trouble when I see it, and this smacks of woman trouble."

"I'm not thinking about Lizzy."

"And her name's Lizzy."

"No!" I almost yelled it, but then my body rebelled at the foreign substance that I'd subjected it to, and I said in a panic, "Pull over. Right now. Please."

"Yes sir," Richard answered cheerfully, and swung over to the curb. I opened the door and leaned over to empty the contents of my stomach on the sidewalk.

He waited patiently, even handed me his handkerchief to wipe my mouth. I actually felt better afterward, and drew myself back in the car and shut the door. Thankfully, I had avoided my shoes. I handed back the handkerchief, and he grimaced.

"You keep it, Daddy-o."

When we got to my apartment, Richard took my key and opened the door for me. "You gonna be okay?"

"Yes, just don't ever let me drink whiskey again. How do people stand it?"

"That's why I drink beer. It's easier on your system. How bad off are you? You need me to hang around a while?"

"No, I'm fine—better now that I emptied my stomach."

"That's the way."

"Richard," I began, leaning against the counter for support. "Thank you."

"What are friends for? Just don't make a habit of it."

"I'm never touching the stuff again."

"You know, I don't typically believe guys when they say that, but in your case, I think I do. Recommend two aspirin and a glass of water before you hit the sack, though. 'Night, Bill."

"'Night."

I shut the door and locked it behind him. Then, I stumbled to the bathroom, took the aspirin and drank the water, and fell on my bed, not even bothering to undress. The room began to spin again, and in the dark, I saw Lizzy, shaking her head and laughing at me.

"What were you thinking, Billy Ray?" her voice echoed in my head.

"I wanted to forget you."

"But you can't, can you?"

"No. What am I going to do? I still miss you."

Her voice faded into the darkness of my room until it was only an echo. "I know. I'm real sorry about that."

I slipped into a fitful sleep, full of unpleasant dreams that I had no memory of when I awoke the next day, my mouth like cotton and my head on fire.

THAT WAS MY ONE AND only experience with whiskey. Much later in my life, I learned to enjoy an occasional glass of wine with dinner, but I had no desire to ever lose control of myself like I did that night at Barney's. That was the danger of excessive drink—what it could do to people—and I'd learned my lesson well with little embarrassment and no lasting damage. To his credit, Richard never mentioned it again, and he never told the other guys what a fool I'd been, letting Mrs. Baker's pretty face dupe me that way.

I dragged myself to church that morning, even though I felt terrible. I had to get rid of the chafing in my soul with something well worn and familiar—something that reminded me who I really was. Afterward, I sat down, and like I had a few times over the last year and a half, I penned a letter to Lizzy—a letter that I'd never send. A letter of longing that was to be my very last as it turned out.

Dear Lizzy,

You would probably laugh at me if you knew about the scrape that I almost got myself into last night at Barney's. You remember me telling you about Barney's, don't you? Well, yesterday I was feeling reckless and like I wanted to step outside my own skin for a while. I think you might understand that feeling because I believe there have been times when you felt that way yourself.

I won't bore you with the details—mostly because I would embarrass myself—but suffice it to say, whiskey and I parted company last night on a sidewalk in Glenwood, never to be intimate with each other again. I know you'll agree with me when I say, thank goodness for friends who watch out for us, and for God, who sends our friends at just the right moment.

What, you might ask, would put me in a state that I'd do something so unlike me? Well, I've thought about it all day and decided it must have been you, or rather, this empty hole in my heart that opens up when I miss you.

I went back to Orchard Hill last weekend with my father, and everywhere I looked, I could see you and me in my mind's eye. I know Orchard Hill must be a place you want to forget, but I will never forget how I felt when I was there, when we were together. I guess last night was an attempt to do just that, but I've discovered that I'm not very good at forgetting. Even whiskey didn't do the trick.

After I got back from church this afternoon, I sat down to get some reading done. But there was no chance of me concentrating on schoolwork today—my head hurt, and my stomach kept rolling.

There are some things in this world that are right and true just because they are, and the affection I have for you is one of those basic truths. I've never been as happy I was that summer I spent in Orchard Hill. You made that happen—you're one of kind, Lizzy, God's own miracle.

If I could see you—just talk to you—I know I could overcome the harsh words I said that last day we were together, and open your heart again. I could melt your anger with my smile and wash it away with my kisses.

When I was in Orchard Hill last weekend, Marlene Miller told me you had been to church one Sunday to hear Dad preach. Why were you there, my darling? Were you hoping to see me? Were you looking for solace in the words of my father? And if so, did you find them? I find that his words give me less solace these days than the church rituals do. And I'm starting to realize I'm only human, that I can only understand what mortal men can understand. Is that what it really means to 'live a life of faith?' To accept what you can never comprehend?

And it always returns to one inevitable question for me. How I will face the rest of my life without you to splash color all over it? I don't know. Maybe in time, I will learn, but it doesn't seem likely. I do know that if I ever see you again, I've promised myself I won't let you get away without a fight. Not again.

I have to figure out a way to get through the days until I can sort this out. So I'm making myself a promise to put my doubts and my broken heart aside for a while. I will throw myself into being the best doctor I can be. After that, maybe there will be an answer, I don't know. But I do know a part of my heart will be—

Yours forever,
Billy Ray

I tucked the letter in the shoebox with the others. There weren't many, maybe half a dozen or so. I wasn't obsessed with her or anything. But sometimes it helped to talk over what was happening to me with the only person I'd ever met who just let me think out loud, who let me be myself. I don't know why I kept the letters, except that I imagined that they were chapters detailing how I was evolving into the man I'd be for the rest of my life. I wanted to share that story, even if it was only with pen and paper —and through them, with a girl from my past who had changed my future.

Chapter Twenty

Two years before, I had left Orchard Hill full of angry determination and started my medical training at Sumner. Of course, I had no idea what was in store for me—one rarely does—but I had adapted and learned, and I was slowly making my way. I still held to my faith during this time, but it became an underpinning of my new life rather than its focus—almost secondary to my immediate earthly needs and those of the people I was trying to heal. Those were liberating and yet frightening years for me. With a few exceptions, I had little inclination to worry about anything besides school during that time. My daily life plodded along, was almost dull in some ways, but all that was about to change. In October, 1961, during my third year, a seemingly trivial decision altered my life's path in a most profound way.

On a cool, crisp autumn evening, Richard managed to convince me to attend a college mixer down at the Glenwood Community Center. I went reluctantly, dragging my feet like a sullen ten-year-old, only half-believing I'd let him talk me into it.

The center's multi-purpose room was decorated with crepe paper streamers hung from the ceiling. A glittering dance ball twirled around and around, casting little beams of light on the linoleum floor.

"I don't want to be here," I muttered.

"Come on, Bill. You need to have some fun. You work all the time."

"We're supposed to work all the time—we're med students."

"No one is supposed to work all the time, no matter what Dr. Jenkins tries to tell you. Besides, I hear there are going to be some mighty pretty girls here tonight."

"Please, not college coeds."

"Much better. It's a group of girls from that specialized nursing program down south of here." He waggled his eyebrows. "Girls who know the birds and the bees."

I reversed course again, heading toward the door.

"No, hey, I'm just kidding about that. They're nice girls. One in particular —she's something else. A real looker too. She just started a training rotation at our hospital. We met in the cafeteria the other day and…" He clutched his chest and rolled his eyes like he was having a heart attack. "I'm thinking about asking her out, so you have to give me your opinion since you're so particular about the ladies. She said she'd be here tonight with some friends." He stuck his hands in his pockets and grinned. "And maybe, if you're a good boy, she'll find a friend for you. Oh wait; you're always a good boy, aren't ya?"

"You're a real clown, Donovan." Most people still considered me a consummate 'square.' Perhaps they always would. But Richard had seen my foibles first hand, and every once in a while, he couldn't resist teasing me about them when the others weren't around.

He looked all around the gym until his eyes landed on a clique of young women standing over by the edge of the dance floor. He ambled in their direction and half-turned to me, jerking his head toward his quarry. "You coming?"

"I'm going to get some punch."

"Chicken."

I dipped out a cup of some kind of slushy orange sherbet concoction, and standing beside the table, I let my gaze wander over the room. There were scattered groups of people, some couples, all talking and having a good time. Richard stood in the middle of the new girls, female laughter swirling around him like smoke. Nothing unusual about that. He had every nurse and candy striper in the hospital under his spell, even the cynical veterans like Nurse Fulton. I'd actually seen her crack a smile at him the other day.

I told myself I was too busy for much of a social life. The first two years of medical school had been grueling, and now, we were beginning to do rounds and see patients at a small-town hospital located near the university. There was a lot to keep me occupied, but I had to admit, I *was* starting to feel lonely. Ed had gotten married last summer, and Tony was engaged. Sure,

Richard was still a carefree bachelor, but even he was looking at women with a more serious eye. When Jo Anne left town only six months after he started dating her, I could tell it shook him up for a while. He recovered though. He always did.

While Richard mesmerized women with his devil-may-care Irish charisma, I held any charm I'd ever possessed hidden under a reserved, arid demeanor. I took some flak for it, but I hadn't met a woman in the last two years who could tempt me out from behind my shell. I hadn't let my smile loose on any girl since Lizzy. Sometimes at night, she invaded my dreams, all heat and curves and softness. I saw young women all the time who were pretty, or smart, or nice, but Lizzy Quinlan, who had left Orchard Hill in a cloud of dust, was the only girl I dreamed about.

After I drained my punch cup, I turned to set it on the tray and heard Richard approaching from behind. His voice was so loud I could hear him from ten yards away, and this time was no exception.

"Elizabeth, you have to find a girl for my two-headed friend here. It's a miracle I managed to drag him out of the hospital tonight. Bill, turn around would ya? And meet Elizabeth."

I obliged him, and felt my lungs robbed of breath as the air crackled and buzzed all around me. "Lizzy?"

Her eyes were round with shock. "Billy Ray?"

Richard looked from one of us to the other and back again while we stared at each other. "Well, I'll be damned," he muttered.

"How…how are you?"

"I'm fine." She laughed and shook her head, obviously as shocked and surprised as I was.

"You-you look wonderful," I stammered.

She blushed. "Thanks. So do you."

"That's because he's smiling for a change," Richard cut in.

It was rude, ignoring Richard that way, but I couldn't keep my eyes off Lizzy. She was striking, just beautiful. Her lips were still red as roses, but the color was softer, like velvet. She wore a party dress that hugged her figure without being too tight, and the sparks that sputtered and flared within her two summers ago had steadied into a glowing, soothing flame. She'd grown up. And she was stunning.

"You cut your hair," I murmured, itching to reach out and touch it. Her

176

curls just barely struck her shoulder, and she looked like a brunette Marilyn Monroe.

She put her hand up and touched her shiny dark locks in a self-conscious manner. "Yes, it's easier—with work and all."

"I like it."

She just stared at me, and I realized I was grinning from ear to ear for the first time in months.

"So, I guess you two know each other," Richard said.

Lizzy nodded. "We're old friends." She gazed up at me, looking unsure and with a million questions in her eyes. I wanted to whisk her off into a corner and answer them all.

"Billy Ray's daddy was the preacher in my hometown."

"You don't say," Richard answered with a slight sarcasm. "I guess it's 'old home night.'"

"Is your family well?" I interrupted. "How's Lily?"

"Everybody's fine. Lily's growin' like a weed. Don't get to see her as much as I'd like. Jeannie's expecting a baby, or did you already know that?"

"No, I hadn't heard. It's been a while since I talked to Charlie."

"They just found out a few weeks ago," she replied. "And your dad —how's he?"

"Same as always. Still traveling around the state, spreading the Good News."

"That's good…good for him." She cast a surreptitious look at Richard, and I remembered what he'd said about asking out one of the nursing students. I could only assume he had chosen Lizzy 'Light up the World' Quinlan. After all, she was the most beautiful girl in the room. But Donovan was up a creek without a paddle this time. Seeing her out of the blue like that had sealed my fate. I was the only one who was going to keep company with Miss Quinlan now—that is, if she'd keep company with me.

He sighed. "Okay, cats and kittens, I get the picture. Why don't you two catch up? And I'll go ask one of these other lovely ladies to dance." He walked away, shaking his head, but I knew he'd regain his good-natured charm soon enough, probably before the evening was out.

Lizzy smiled up at me, and her voice was soft. "It sure warms my heart to see you, Billy Ray Davenport."

"Would you like to dance?" I asked, holding out my hand, even though I almost never danced and wasn't too good at it.

"Always the perfect gentleman." She took the offered hand, and I led her to the dance floor. The song had changed to a slow, sad tune and my body hummed with excitement as I took her in my arms. We danced for a minute or two before I could speak. All over again, I had to get used to the startling effect she had on me.

"So, you go by Elizabeth now?"

She looked down, smiling. "Elizabeth was on all the class rosters. I guess it just kind of stuck after a while."

"It's pretty—all grown up sounding."

"How's medical school?"

"Well, it's…" I hesitated for a second and then chuckled. "It's downright difficult, EE-lizabeth."

She laughed.

"But I'm holding my own. So you're in midwife school?"

"I am," she answered proudly. "But how did you know that?"

"Mrs. Gardener told me the day I left Orchard Hill. She said a spot opened up, so you took it."

"It happened really fast." She looked a little sheepish, a little embarrassed, and I remembered that I'd never gotten a chance to respond to her letter. I wasn't going to talk about that on a dance floor at the Glenwood Community Center though.

"Is it what you expected? Going to midwife school?"

"Oh, it's better!" Excitement warmed her voice. "This is my first hospital rotation. I've only been in the clinic before, so I've learned a lot in the last couple weeks."

The music changed to a more upbeat song about tequila, and she had to almost shout the last answer over the increased volume of the music. I stopped dancing, pulled her close, and leaned down to speak into her ear. "You want to go get a cup of coffee or something? I can't yell over this music, and I want to hear all about you."

She nodded. "Let me tell my friends where I'm going."

"Tell them I'll drive you home."

"I have to be home by midnight. My landlady doesn't like her girls coming in late."

"I'll get you home on time," I said, grinning. "I'm the preacher's son, remember?"

"I do remember at that. Be right back."

She left the dance floor and I watched as she joined a cluster of young women at the side of the room. She glanced over my way and pointed, a shy smile on her face as she talked. The girls looked me up and down and turned back to her, giggling. They seemed genuinely to like her, and it struck me that, back in Orchard Hill, I'd never seen Lizzy with a girlfriend —with anyone, really, except Jeannie, Lily or Mrs. Gardener. What a lonely existence that must have been for her! And how much things had changed! With a sudden shock, it occurred to me that those changes might include a new boyfriend. Surely, she wouldn't have agreed to go for coffee with me if she had a man in her life, but it seemed impossible that such a remarkable woman wouldn't have a steady guy.

At any rate, I had to find out. She met me at the door, struggling to get her arm through her sweater sleeve behind her back. I held it up for her, and she smiled and thanked me. Then we walked out into the cool, starlit night.

Since I'd moved to Glenwood, the Broadway Diner had quickly become my favorite place to grab a quick bite to eat. It was a casual joint—part of the seating was at a counter with red leather and stainless steel barstools that ran the length of the place. An aisle separated the bar from booths that lined the glass front of the restaurant. I preferred a booth because it allowed me to watch the townsfolk hurrying by.

It was fully dark when Lizzy and I arrived. I parallel-parked on the street, fed the meter, and opened her door, extending my hand to help her out of the car.

"Nice chariot," she commented, looking back and running her hand over the rooftop.

"Thanks."

"It's odd to see you driving a car. I always think of you walking up and down Cavanaugh Street. We walked everywhere together in Orchard Hill."

"My Aunt Catherine gave me this when I moved here. It's her old one —she replaced it with a rag top a couple of years ago."

"I've never met your aunt, but I have this funny image of a very proper spinster in a very hip car."

"That's a pretty accurate image."

I pushed open the glass door of the diner, and the short order cook,

Eugene, turned at the sound of the chime.

"Hello, Bill." He turned back to scrubbing the grill with a wire brush. "Here for a late supper, are ya? You put in a long day over to the hospital?"

"We thought we'd just get some coffee and a piece of pie if that's all right with you."

"It's been slow around here tonight, and we'll take any business we can get. Paula!" he bellowed. "Put down that trashy novel and come take Bill's order."

Paula appeared out of the back room, smoothing her uniform and rear-ranging her hair as she walked. She reached in the pocket of her apron for her pad and paper, and stopped short when she saw us sliding into a booth. Her face fell, just slightly, and then she recovered and approached us.

"Would you rather we sit at the bar and not mess up your table?" I asked, trying to be polite.

"You just sit wherever you want, Bill honey," she replied, giving Lizzy a curious, assessing stare. "What can I get you, miss?"

Lizzy made an attempt to win her over with a gracious smile. "I'd like a cup of coffee, please."

"You too, Bill?"

"Yes, that sounds good. Thank you."

From across the table, Lizzy gazed at me, amused. "I can't get used to people calling you Bill. It sounds so strange."

"It would sound strange to me if you called me anything but Billy Ray, drawing out the 'ay' the way you do."

Paula brought our coffee and some cream. Fixing it up helped fill the awkward first moments of Lizzy and me being alone together, face-to-face.

"So, tell me about medical school." It appeared she wanted to put the focus on school, rather than on us. I supposed I could start with that.

"I'm really busy. There's so much to learn, and now that I'm doing some clinical work, there's even more. It's been a pretty intense couple of years."

"Are you going to specialize?"

"I haven't decided for sure, but I'm leaning against it. I think I'd enjoy general practice. Like Doc Miller. What about you? How has life been treating you?"

She paused, looking down at her hands holding the cup. "I'm happy, I guess. This is what I always wanted, and when I moved away from home, I promised myself I'd do things right this time."

"What do you mean?"

"At school, I started off on the right foot with people—tried to blend in a bit at first, asked a lot of questions, worked really hard. I had a lot of catching up to do."

"Catching up?"

"Mm-hmm. A lot of the girls at Hyden went to better high schools than me. I was really glad I'd done the outside reading in biology and botany, but I still had to work almost twice as hard that first year just to keep up. Some of the girls helped me out a whole bunch. That's another thing I did right. I tried to make friends up front. I was too shy to do that back when we moved from Norfolk to Orchard Hill, and it cost me…later on." She looked down at the table for a second, and then back up at me. "It was easier to make friends in Hyden than in Orchard Hill though."

"How so?"

"The girls at Hyden and me—we have something in common, something we all want but don't have to compete for—an education. It's there for all of us to take if we want it bad enough. We only compete against ourselves, and it's easier to succeed if we work together rather than against each other. In Orchard Hill, there were only things to divide us girls, like who had nicer clothes or a better house." She grinned at me. "Or the best-looking guy."

I watched my fingers pick up a sugar packet and worry it around. "And how about now? You have a guy these days?"

She put her hand over mine to still my fingers. I felt a zing of pleasure race up my arm at her touch. "That's another thing I did right."

"What?" I asked, jealous uncertainty surging through my stomach.

"I stayed away from handsome things like you, Billy Ray." She drawled out the last 'ay', and the air seemed to lighten up and fill my lungs again.

"Although, there aren't too many men around a midwife program anyway," she went on. "That was a big switch for us when we started doing rotations. Now, we're working with men all the time."

"Like Richard Donovan?"

"He's quite the charmer, isn't he? Real ladies' man. Sue Ann thinks he's a dreamboat."

It sounded like Lizzy had Donovan pegged just right. I breathed a sigh of relief.

"You left Orchard Hill all of a sudden Lizzy, without even saying goodbye."

"I know. Out of all the things I did that summer, that's the one thing I regret. It was all so overwhelming. I just…" She waved her hand in a helpless little gesture. "I don't know." Trembling fingers played with her napkin and betrayed her apparent composure. "Did you get the letter I left you?"

"Mm-hmm."

"Did it make you think better of me?" She looked away. "Or worse?"

I reached out to cover her hand with mine this time. "It made me understand you better, I think. I read it over and over. It gave me a lot to think about."

"I was feeling a bit sorry for myself when I wrote it. Do you still have the thing?"

I nodded.

"I wish you'd tear it up. I was in a bitter place then—angry and full of self-pity. I'd like to think I've grown up a little by now."

"It wasn't a bitter letter. You were trying to think what would be best for both of us. It was unselfish of you."

For just a second, a glimpse of raw, exposed feeling flashed in her eyes, but it disappeared as quickly as it came.

I squeezed her hand briefly and let it go. "I thought about writing to you…later on. Mrs. Gardener gave me your address."

"Really? She never told me she did that."

"I guess she didn't want to say anything in case I never mailed any letters. I should have. I wanted to."

"Why didn't you?" she asked, genuinely curious.

"Well, you left, and at first I was angry. And I thought maybe you didn't want to talk to me ever again, after..." I paused, considering whether I should tell her of my suspicions about Marlene taking the address from my book, but then I decided against it. I didn't know for sure what had happened to the paper, and regardless, Lizzy didn't need any more suffering at the hands of Marlene Miller. I remembered what Mrs. Gardener said to me when I went to her about a room at her boarding house. *Marlene can't do any real harm if you don't let her.* I'd used Marlene's antics as an excuse, letting them keep me from finding Lizzy again. If I'd wanted to, I could have gotten the address from Mrs. G. So I had to own some responsibility for the two years of loneliness.

"I lost the paper with your address. I wish I'd asked Mrs. G again, but I was embarrassed I guess, and unsure."

"I understand."

"I didn't stop thinking about you though, or wondering how you were doing."

Her voice was soft. "Me neither."

We each smiled, and a glimmer of understanding settled between us. No matter what happened two summers ago, we had let go of our anger toward each other, realizing how young we were back then. It was a freeing and exhilarating realization.

THAT NIGHT, WE SPENT ALMOST two hours in the diner catching up. I think Paula was a little annoyed that we sat there so long without ordering a dinner, but I tipped her extra to make up for it.

It was almost ten-thirty when we left, but I had been without this Lizzy-induced warmth in my veins for over two years, and I was abruptly conscious of how cold I'd been all that time without her. I didn't want to take her home right away. I didn't want to ever let her go. My feelings came rushing back as if I'd seen her only yesterday.

So we walked for a bit, and we sat in the car outside her boarding house and talked and talked until we were both hoarse from talking.

Finally, a little before midnight, we said goodnight.

"I should get inside." She gathered her sweater from her lap and draped it over one forearm.

"And I should go home."

"I've got a class early in the morning."

"And I've got rounds at seven a.m."

She turned to lift the door handle, and before she could vanish, I ran my forefinger down her arm and took her hand in mine. She stilled.

"Lizzy?" I murmured, my voice hoarse and rough.

She cleared her throat. "Mm-hmm?" Her lips were pressed tight together, and I could sense an odd sort of tension rolling off her. I didn't understand it. We'd been so comfortable together after that initial shock of seeing each other again.

"Can I call on you?"

Her beautiful grin and a soft chuckle broke the tension into a thousand little pieces. "Billy Ray, the way you talk sometimes—it's so old-fashioned."

I frowned. That wasn't the answer I was expecting.

Her laugh faded into a gentle smile that made my heart beat faster. "Old-fashioned and charming. I think I'd like it very much if you called on me." She leaned in close, and those red velvet lips brushed my cheek like a whisper. She was half-way up the walk before I realized her seat was empty. Casting an enticing look over her shoulder, she sent me an older version of her come-hither smile—more mature, subtle, elegant—and a hundred times more enchanting.

That night I dreamed wild, sweet dreams about Lizzy Quinlan.

Chapter Twenty-One

I had to work the next day, but on the day after that, Sunday afternoon, I drove back to Lizzy's boarding house, marched up bold as brass, and knocked on her door as early as would be considered polite.

A stern-looking woman answered. "May I help you, young man?"

"I'm here to see Liz…I mean, Elizabeth. Quinlan," I added, in case there was more than one Elizabeth. "I'm Bill Davenport."

"Does she know you?" she asked, before she pursed her lips in maternal disapproval and looked me up and down.

"Yes, ma'am. We're old friends."

She still looked unimpressed, so I decided to play the son of a preacher man card. "My daddy was the preacher in her home town," I said, echoing her words from the other night.

"The girls are supposed to let me know when they're expecting visitors." Still not mollified, she crossed her arms in front her, pointedly not inviting me in. I wondered how many other guys had dropped in to see my Lizzy, and if that was why this woman was so unfriendly.

Well, I was different from any of the others, so she might as well get used to me showing up at her place. It was time to turn on the charm. I let her have one of my best smiles.

"Don't blame Elizabeth, ma'am. She didn't know I was going to drop by." I leaned on the door frame and lowered my voice. "I wanted to surprise her."

She let out a little 'hmmph,' but then she stepped aside and let me in.

There was a rhythmic sound of footsteps at the staircase, and I looked up to see Lizzy bounding down the stairs.

"Sue Ann said I had a visitor, Mrs. Ainsley," she began, then stopped on a dime when she saw me. After a brief second of shock, a delighted smile spread over her face. "Billy Ray! What're you doing here?"

"Calling on you, of course." I wondered why she was surprised. "Would you like to take in a movie? Get some lunch?" I asked, hands in my pockets. I felt almost giddy.

She looked down at her jeans and oversized man's dress shirt. "I look a mess."

I didn't think I'd ever seen anyone look any better, but if I said that, Mrs. Ainsley might push me right back out the door. "I'll wait, if you'd like."

"Just give me a couple minutes." She turned and hurried back up the stairs.

I smiled at Mrs. Ainsley and took a seat.

I BOUGHT US TICKETS TO see *West Side Story* at the theater and root beer floats at the drugstore soda fountain. The afternoon flew by in a series of snapshot images of Lizzy laughing, talking, and walking that would give me enough good memories and sweet dreams for a month. Afterward, she wanted to see where I lived, so I took her to my studio apartment near the hospital.

Lizzy walked around the small room, looking at the books, and running her fingers along the countertop of the kitchenette. I sat down on the couch and watched as she made a quick circuit around the place. I drank in the sight of her, like a man parched from a long trek across a seemingly endless stretch of desert.

She looked over her shoulder and smiled at me, eliciting an answering grin from my own lips.

"Nice place."

"Thanks."

"Quieter than a boarding house full of girls, that's for sure."

"I imagine."

"We're all in school though, so when it's test time, everybody settles down."

I laid my arm across the back of the sofa and crossed my ankle over my knee. She turned back to the shelf under the only window, and studied the family pictures I had arranged there.

"I recognize the Reverend, but is this your mother standing with him?"

"That one? Oh no, that's my Aunt Catherine. She's his sister."

"The one you stayed with during school, after—"

"Yes, after my mother passed away."

"Is that your aunt's house in the background?"

"Mm-hmm."

"Nice."

"That was taken right after my high school graduation."

She moved to another frame—a portrait in colorized sepia tones.

"That's my mother."

She picked up the frame and studied the face. "You look like her—same eyes, nose, same mouth."

"I have dad's wavy hair though."

"And his stubborn, chiseled jaw," she said, smiling at me with a twinkle of mischief in her eyes. She held the picture up so she could see Mama and me together.

"And those eyelashes of yours—pretty as a girl's. You got those from your mama." She paused, lowered the picture. "She was beautiful—like you."

We stared at each other across the room, while in my mind I imagined striding over and pulling her against me. I hardly knew myself. I hadn't seen her in two years, and though I had gone out with half-a-dozen other women since I left Orchard Hill, I'd lived like a monk all that time. And within one day, eighteen hours and forty-five minutes of laying eyes on Lizzy Quinlan again, all I could think about was laying hands on her too. That visceral pull between us—it was still there. If we didn't see each other for another forty years, I knew it would be there when we met again.

Lizzy was the first to look away, putting Mama's picture back on the shelf and clearing her throat. "You didn't have pictures of your family when you stayed in Orchard Hill, did you? I don't remember any."

"I was there such a short time; it didn't seem that important to bring more permanent things, like pictures."

She gave me a sad smile. "That summer was just a flash in the pan—a stop along the way to the rest of your life."

"Some of the most important things happen when you stop along the way." I gestured with the fingers that lay across the back of my tweedy, second-hand couch. "Come sit with me, Lizzy. Let me put my arm around you."

She sauntered toward me, grinning. "Now, that's new."

"What do you mean?"

"Blunt requests. That's a new addition to your repertoire of ladies' man skills."

"I'm no ladies' man. I'm one lady's man."

She laughed. "At any rate, it's a new twist on a two-year-old game."

"It's new to me too—as in right this very minute. It's the first time I've ever said it."

"It offsets that killer smile quite nicely. Should I be worried?" She sat down next to me so our legs were touching. Although it was October, I felt my skin heat up like I'd been working in the sun.

My fingers drifted over her upper arm. "You never have to worry when you're with me, Lizzy Quinlan."

"I bet you say that to all the girls."

I slid my free hand from the side of her head around to the nape of her neck and drew her close. My lips burned to take hers, but I stopped a moment, looking at her beloved face, her eyes now closed. I kissed the closed eyelids, the cheeks, and then her lips.

"Only you," I whispered. Then I almost whimpered in dismay when she tensed and drew away.

"You don't have to do that."

"Do what?"

"Pretend like nothing's changed. Pretend like we didn't have that awful fight the last time we saw each other." Her expression hardened. "Or maybe after you read my letter, you think I'll roll over for a smile and a promise. I don't do that anymore, and you might as well know it up front."

I felt like she'd slapped me. This girl who flitted around my dreams—who I'd fantasized about since the day I set eyes on her—brought a harsh reality crashing down around us with a few ugly words. My pain must have shown on my face, because she looked away, apologizing.

"I'm sorry, Billy Ray. I know you're not like that. I don't know what's wrong with me. I guess I've forgotten what honest men are like."

"I thought you'd…well, I hoped you'd forgiven me for what I said that day."

She laid a hand against my cheek. "I have. I have forgiven you; it seems like forever ago. But seeing you again, it dredges up things from the past —things I thought I'd put away."

"So you aren't glad to see me."

"Thing is…" She knit her eyebrows in a puzzled little frown. "I *am* glad to see you. I thought I'd never want to see a familiar Orchard Hill face in this new life I made for myself, but…"

"But?" I took a finger and smoothed it over her brow, dissipating that frown.

"But seeing your face makes me smile."

"Then why can't I kiss you?"

"Well, listen to you!" she sat back and chuckled softly. "The Billy Ray who came to Orchard Hill that summer would never have asked to kiss me. You're different, that's for sure."

"Not so much."

"It's okay. I'm different too."

"You said it would be all right if I called on you. You said…"

"I know what I said!" There was exasperation in her voice. She crossed her arms protectively. "I don't know. I'm confused. I left Orchard Hill; you left Orchard Hill. What if what we had in the past should stay there?"

"Do you think it should?" My heart sank with the words.

"I don't know; I don't know. I was so glad to see you the other night, but it's been two years. Everything's different, and yet when I look at you, nothing is. You see me just the same as you always did, but I'm not that person anymore."

I turned toward her, leaning my elbow on the back of the couch and propping my head on my closed hand—studying her, as I would a problem in a book or a patient on a table. Finally, I got up and went to my sock drawer.

"Where are you going?"

"I want to show you something." I pulled out my shoebox and sat down beside her, placing the box in her lap.

"What's this?"

"Open it. There's something in there I want you to see."

She lifted the lid, setting it on the coffee table and peered inside. She took out the papers, shuffling through the half dozen or so envelopes that were there.

"Letters? To me?"

I nodded.

"I thought you said you didn't write to me."

"No, I said I didn't mail any."

"Why?"

"Why did I write them? Or why didn't I mail them?"

"Both, I guess."

"Well, I wrote them because I missed talking to you. I could scribble out those sentences and imagine what you might say. It comforted me, I suppose, to have a familiar ear listen to my stories—someone who would understand."

Her eyes were bright, and an incredulous smile burst from her. Lord, she was beautiful!

"Go on, read them." I got up, not wanting to watch her while she read. Not knowing what else to do with myself, I made a couple cups of instant coffee and brought them to the living area.

Her eyes scanned the lines of the last letter I'd written, the one right after Easter. "What on earth would induce you to sit at a bar drinking whiskey? I can hardly imagine it!"

Feeling my face flush, I told her the story about Marian Baker and the whiskey at Barney's.

"Sounds like you found an unworthy damsel in distress that night. Oh, Billy Ray, what were you thinking? Flirting with a married woman? I can only imagine how you punished yourself for that." She clucked and shook her head, just like she had in my foggy mind's eye that night, but there was no censure in her tone.

"I thought she was alone and in need of protection. I trusted what I thought I saw through whiskey goggles. And to be honest, it never occurred to me that a woman would try to make her husband jealous."

"Shame on her. She didn't deserve your pity."

"My pity? I think she did deserve that, for being so desperate to get her husband's attention. But she didn't deserve the pound of my flesh her husband was getting ready to take out of me because I was considering leaving with her."

"How did you talk your way out of that one?"

"I didn't. Donovan pulled my hindquarters out of the fire with some cockamamie story about toddies and the flu."

"Quick thinking."

"It was."

"You are too good, Billy Ray. How have you made it through the last two years?"

"I have lived in the world and learned some lessons. I'm not always so clueless. The whiskey did impair my judgment. But that night? I made it through with God's help and fate and good friends like Big Theo and Richard."

She smiled and returned to the letter. Her lips moved as she read until she murmured, "I remember this."

"What do you remember, honey?"

Her cheeks pinked at the endearment I used. That was something different, something I'd heard my friends do, calling women honey. I'd never used it on anyone though, and it felt sweet and spicy on my tongue when I said it to Lizzy.

"When I went to Orchard Hill church that Sunday and heard your father preach."

When she looked up, her eyes were shiny with tears.

"Why were you there? I've often wondered."

"I don't know. I've often wondered myself. I rarely go home now, but I made a trip that weekend for Lily's birthday because she begged me. The whole weekend in all those familiar surroundings was so odd. I walked down the street where some girls that I used to eat lunch with crossed to avoid talking to me. I used to ignore them. I strolled in front of the farm supply shop where the men used to watch me walk by with lust or condemnation in their eyes, or both. I used to stare straight at them, almost daring them to say something to me. I stood in front of the school where teachers wouldn't quite meet my eye. I remembered very well what it felt like to be dismissed or avoided.

"But you know what was so strange? By then, it was as if Orchard Hill had forgotten those days—even if I hadn't. They'd forgotten how they'd treated me. People spoke to me, greeted me, as though those other times didn't exist. Marlene Miller even asked me how I was when I went to the bank for Daddy that Saturday morning. Part of me was glad, but part of me was angry—angry that something that had shaped me so profoundly was forgotten in a year. People don't realize how the things they do and say to the young—good and bad—stay with that person for so long. How important they are.

"I went to see Mrs. G that weekend. I was so happy to see her, to thank her for what she'd done for me. The big things and the hundred little things she did by being my older and wiser friend. She made me older and wiser just by watching her. And when I realized that your dad was in the church that weekend, I wanted to hear him preach. I listened to the sound of his voice and his message. It did put me in mind of you. Your voices are so alike. I hadn't noticed that before. It soothed me."

Well, that was encouraging. "What was the message that morning?"

"Coveting—or rather, not coveting."

"Interesting."

"Yes. I don't think he saw me, and I slipped away before he made his way to the door to greet parishioners on the way out."

That explained why Dad hadn't told me he'd seen Lizzy. I wanted to think that if he had, he would have said so, but in all honesty, I wasn't sure.

"Those letters—you thought about me all those times. But not all the time—not pining away."

"No, not really. But when I had something I wanted to mull over in my head, something confusing or sad or painful, I wanted to talk to you more than anyone else." I took her hand in my two and held it. "See, it's been two years, but to me—in a way, you've been with me all along. So it seems like you saw me change. I didn't think I'd see you again, but I promised myself if I did, I'd do things right."

"Like I did at midwife school?"

"Exactly like that. And this is my chance."

"To start over?"

"If I have to, yes."

"Hello, I'm Elizabeth Quinlan." She turned my hand over and shook it with hers.

"Hello, Elizabeth. I'm Billy Ray Davenport, but most people around here call me Bill. You have the most beautiful eyes I've ever seen, and a smile that warms me from head to toe." I lifted her hand to my lips.

Heat and joy burned in those eyes when I lifted my face to hers. She brought my hand to the nape of her neck.

"You can kiss me now."

Chapter Twenty-Two

About three weeks after the night of the Community Center mixer, I found myself sitting in the hospital cafeteria, spooning sugar into my coffee, my thoughts somewhere else. Not with Lizzy, for the first time in many days, but instead, my mind drifted upstairs to the hospital room of another young woman.

Her roommate brought her in that morning with abdominal pain on the right side, nausea and cramps. It seemed like a classic case of appendicitis, but there was no fever as of yet, although she did report feeling dizzy. The staff was in the process of scheduling her for an appendectomy. Dr. Jenkins was the supervising physician, of course, and he made the call, but I had done the initial intake and examination.

Something didn't sit right though, and I had come down to get a cup of coffee and try to reason it out.

"You want some coffee with that sugar, Billy Ray? Oh, excuse me, I mean, Bill." It was Lizzy, walking toward me with a smile on her face.

I peered into my cup and laughed. "How many have I put in there, I wonder?"

"At least four that I saw." She slid into the booth across from me. "What's going on? You've got that awful scowl on your face again. You know, you never used to scowl like that when you were younger."

"There's a patient upstairs, and something's bothering me about the case."

"Tell me."

"Nah, that's okay. I'll figure it out. How are you this morning?"

She cut her Danish with a fork and took a bite, looking at me thoughtfully. "Tell me about your patient. Sometimes if I think it out loud, it helps me solve the problem."

I told her the scenario, while she nodded and sipped her coffee.

"So she was admitted this morning with symptoms that present like appendicitis," I finished off, "but no fever."

"Young woman, or older?"

"Twenty-four, I believe."

"Could she be pregnant?"

"She's not married."

Lizzy rolled her eyes at me. "That doesn't mean—"

"I know that, Lizzy," I interrupted. "I did ask her if it was possible, and she said no. Seemed really embarrassed too. And Dr. Jenkins seemed sure about the appendicitis when we discussed it."

Lizzy sat there, twirling her fork. "Hmmm…"

"What are you thinking?"

"It could be an ectopic pregnancy. Some of the symptoms are the same as appendicitis. Or it could be both, I guess." She took a sip of coffee. "I hadn't considered that."

I sat back, stunned. Ectopic pregnancy hadn't occurred to me, and it should have. I realized how biased my thinking was, given my assumptions about the patient. I had just taken the woman at her word that she couldn't be with child.

"You want me to talk to her?" Lizzy offered. "If she is hiding something, she might be more likely to tell a woman than a stern-looking, handsome guy like you."

"Maybe that would be a good idea," I mused.

A half hour later, Lizzy came to find me on the floor. She touched my elbow and drew me aside.

"You were right to ponder it some more. Your patient just told me there was a possibility, a small one, that she's pregnant. Her fiancé is in the Navy, and he was home on leave four weeks ago."

"So she lied to me?"

"I think lied is a pretty strong word, Billy Ray. She was embarrassed, and she didn't understand the seriousness of it. She'd never heard of an ectopic pregnancy before."

"How did you get her to tell you?"

She looked amused. "It helps not to go in there with a laundry list of rapid-fire questions. Sometimes you can get more out of patients if you listen for a little bit first."

"That sounds like something Mrs. G would say."

She smiled proudly. "It does, doesn't it?"

"I gotta find Dr. Jenkins."

"Find me?" The gruff voice behind me made me jump a little.

"The patient in 218, Doctor."

"The appendectomy?"

"There's a possibility she could be pregnant. We could be dealing with an ectopic pregnancy."

"What?" He walked up to the nurse's station and grabbed the patient's chart. "Why didn't you know this before?"

"I did ask, sir. She fabricated."

"Dammit," he muttered under his breath then turned around to bark an order at the nurse. "Can we get a damn x-ray here? Maybe that will tell us something."

He rounded on me. "Remember, Davenport, you can't assume anything. You should know that by now."

"Yes sir," I said, although I suspected from his expression that he had done just that very thing.

"You should consider the possibility of pregnancy every time you have a female patient of child-bearing years."

"You're right," I replied calmly.

"Good work finding out, though. I'll put a note in there for the surgeon."

"Thank you, sir, but it was Miss Quinlan's idea first." I looked over at her, but she was quietly chatting with one of the nurses and seemed not to hear us. I knew she was listening though.

Dr. Jenkins eyed her with disapproval. "Hmmph...talking about a patient with one of your girlfriends?"

"She's a good friend, yes, but she's also one of the midwife students on rotation here."

"Midwife?" he snorted.

I ignored the condescending tone. He was the attending physician after all, and I was just a lowly med student.

"That midwifery nonsense is nothing but an MRS degree in my opinion."

I clenched my jaw. "Regardless, it was her clinical skills that got the relevant information from the patient."

He shrugged and started writing orders in the chart. I glanced over at Lizzy—her lips were turned up into a smug little smile. She darted a quick, amused look my way.

Fireworks.

I saw them in her eyes and felt them in my chest. How could I have forgotten how brightly she lit up when something struck her as funny?

My fingers intertwined with Lizzy's as we walked through Glenwood City Park. She swung our hands back and forth for a minute, then held mine to her heart while she made some funny statement, then let go and tucked her hand in my elbow while she said something serious. Somehow, though, she managed to keep a constant physical link to me as we walked, which I loved. People rarely touched me, and certainly not in any affectionate way, since I'd left home. It suddenly occurred to me that my father was demonstrative like Lizzy. He was always shaking hands, patting someone on the shoulder, hugging me when we parted. I didn't see a lot of men do that, but Dad had a deep and abiding love for people and it just sort of spilled out of him. Lizzy had that love for people too, but because she was beautiful, empathy and compassion had been misinterpreted by boys and men as romantic interest. I noticed now that when she talked to men, she curtailed her earnest looks, didn't touch them, and gave men cool, refined smiles rather than warm, engaging ones. Except for me—I got all her smiles, even the steamy, come-hither ones, I thought with smug satisfaction.

"You're different than you were in Orchard Hill," I commented, extending my thoughts out into words.

"How do you mean?"

"Oh, not in a bad way. You," I shrugged, "I don't know, you've changed somehow. And people respond well to it."

She mused for a second. "I'm the same inside." She shook her head. "No, I don't think I've changed much at all really, but it's easy to look different when people treat you differently. See, in Orchard Hill, everyone had this one way of thinking about me. Lizzy Quinlan: town slut."

I tensed up in indignation.

"No," she pulled playfully on my arm, "don't get all huffy. It kind of happened before I even knew what was going on. Most of Orchard Hill thought they knew me, and they treated me according to what they'd heard. I'm just lucky I had Mrs. G to try to keep me from thinking of myself that way.

"That was one of the very best things about getting to know you, Billy Ray. For so long, I thought Mrs. Gardener was the only one who believed I could be anything but a poor, ruined girl. But you saw something more underneath all that."

"Not at first," I replied, chagrined. "I wasn't any better than the rest of them."

She leaned her head against my arm. "But pretty soon after we started talking, you were better. I remember you watching me with those big, dark eyes of yours." She led me to the bench by the big chestnut tree. Once there, she took my hand and turned toward me, her leg folded up on the bench. Her cheeks were a wind-burned pink, and the cold, crisp November air stirred her hair. She reached up and brushed it out of her face, and a brilliant smile bloomed on those rosy red lips.

"At the beginning, I thought you weren't any different than anyone else in town. Then that day after church, we talked a little—about my brothers, and your mama. We were in the graveyard out back of the church. You remember that day?"

I nodded.

"You didn't seem to disapprove of me as much, so I decided I could let myself act different toward you. And after that, you made it so easy; I just kept on acting different when we were together. You were my guinea pig; I tried out my real self on you."

I leaned in and kissed her, relishing how her eyes slid shut and her fingers inched around the back of my collar to sift through my hair. I loved her, and each day that passed strengthened the urge to put into words what I felt in my kisses and in my heart. When I thought about the rest of my life, I couldn't imagine it without her beside me—us working together, playing with our little ones, sleeping together. I wanted all that, so much so that I could taste the future on her lips and on the cold softness of her cheek.

When I pulled back, her eyes opened, and I tried to read what was in them. As the weeks went by, I knew I was beginning to see love there. Desire, I definitely saw, but it was increasingly tempered with a tender expression that made me want to melt inside. That had to be love—just had to be.

"Elizabeth," I began softly, savoring her name the way I might sample a rich, dark chocolate. I was going to tell her, make her see the obvious. She was in love with me, almost as much as I was in love with her.

She jumped up and tugged on my hand. "Come on!" she said, pulling me up off the bench.

"Where to?"

She looked across the street and back at me. "Smithy's Book Store," she answered.

I sighed and followed her, foiled in my attempt to force her hand.

We entered Smithy's, and the clerk looked up from behind the counter, straightening when he saw her. He looked like a high school kid, and like every fella between eight and eighty, he followed Lizzy with his eyes as she browsed through the bookshelves. When she approached the counter, I watched in fascination as her whole face changed; the hot, earnest looks that pulled me right out of my skin while we were sitting under the chestnut tree had cooled to a friendly smile. I put my hand to her lower back to guide her as we walked, and maybe send the guy a little message too—namely, that this woman was spoken for.

"Hello, Miss Quinlan," he said, his Adam's apple bobbing up and down.

"Hello, Boyd; how are you today?"

"I'm fine. I found that book you were looking for. It came in last week." Boyd shot me a wary look.

"You did? Thank you so much!"

"I saved a copy for you." He reached under the counter and brought out a copy of Jung's *Memories, Dreams, Reflections*. He handed it to her and cleared his throat, looking over at me one more time.

"Boyd, this is Billy Ray," she replied without looking up as she thumbed through the pages. I spoke to him, and he barely nodded a greeting.

Lizzy smiled up at the clerk as she laid the book down and pushed it back across the counter to him. "It was so nice of you to hold this for me. I wish I could buy it today, but I'm afraid I can't. If Mr. Smith wants you to put it out on the shelf, you go ahead and do that. I'll see if they have it at the library."

"It's new—they might not have it at the library yet," he replied.

"I'll just have to wait for it then. Such is the life of a student."

Boyd's features started to soften, but before he could volunteer to hold the book indefinitely or, heaven forbid, make a present of it to her, I spoke up. "I'll take it."

"Billy Ray..." she protested.

"I insist." I pulled out my wallet and handed the money to Boyd, who took it with an annoyed scowl that gave me an unholy jolt of satisfaction.

"Here you go, sir." He bagged the book and handed me my change.

"Thank you." I turned immediately and made an obvious gesture of giving it to Lizzy. "Here you go, honey." I warmed my voice to just under a steamy simmer.

"Thank you," she murmured, seeming almost embarrassed.

I had to admit, I was confused by her expression. It couldn't be the lack of funds; she'd mentioned that herself. So what was it? Had she wanted to let that pup of a clerk buy the book for her?

We walked back over to the park as gray clouds gathered in the cold afternoon. I opened the car door for her, and we drove in virtual silence over to Shanghai Shack, where I ordered take out for dinner.

She was thoughtful on the way back to my apartment and sort of quiet all during our dinner, sitting at my cozy little table for two. As she rose from her chair, washed and set her plate in the drainer, she finally spoke, trying to keep her voice light. "You didn't have to buy me the book, you know. I didn't expect it—and it made me uneasy, to tell you the truth."

"For heaven's sake, why?"

"Gifts come with expectations. I don't like being indebted to anyone."

"Lizzy," I sighed in exasperation, "it's just a book, a little thing. There are no strings attached to it. I just wanted you to have it. I wanted to see your face light up for me like it did for old Boyd when he said he saved it for you." I cringed, realizing that hadn't come out quite the way I wanted.

Eyes wide with disbelief, she stared at me. "Surely you jest, Billy Ray! There's just no way you're in the least bit jealous of Boyd the book clerk."

"Of course not."

"I mean he's Boyd. And you're—you."

"What does that mean?"

A slow, sultry smile curved her lips. "It means that you're the only man who burns my butter."

"Lizzy..." I admonished, embarrassed and amused at the same time.

"Sizzles my bacon..."

"Now you're just making fun of me." I got up and put my plate in the sink.

"Turns my crank," she went on, an undercurrent of laughter in her voice. "Wets my whistle."

I backed her up against the wall, a hand on either side. "Peace, I will stop your mouth…" I leaned against her with my body. "And that's Shakespeare, by the way." My lips descended on hers, and she made that tantalizing little whimper in the back of her throat. My whole body leapt to attention. After several seconds, I rested my forehead against hers, breathing deeply and trying to get myself under control.

"He's interested in you, you know. Boyd."

"He's just a kid." Her voice was compassionate, gentle.

"Kids have pretty serious crushes sometimes."

"I know they do. You don't think I gave him the wrong idea, do you?"

I looked into her eyes, and then I shook my head. I backed up and took her hand, leading her to the couch on the other side of the room.

"You're not 'giving' him any ideas, Lizzy. He just has them."

"Like all men do?"

"Mm-hmm."

"Except you."

I laughed softly. "Oh, I have them too."

"You do?" she asked in a breathy voice, swinging her legs over top of my lap.

"Yes, Miss Quinlan, I do." I hadn't told her about the dreams that haunted me in the night—dreams that had intensified considerably since I'd met up with her again.

My smile, the one she said melted women's hearts, was threatening to spill over. And why shouldn't I let it? This woman's heart was the only one I wanted to conquer, and I could keep control of the situation, even though we were all alone in my apartment and not a soul around to interrupt us. But I could handle this. I was a good guy: the preacher's son.

Feeling a surge of mischievous glee, I smiled lovingly at her and watched while her face flushed and her eyes darkened. I was so wickedly proud of myself when I could make her look like that.

"Now you've done it," she warned.

"Done what?" I asked, all innocence.

"You're playing with fire, Billy Ray. I'm not a scared girl anymore, and you're not a naive boy." She rubbed her foot across my thigh, and as my body responded, I suddenly began to question the wisdom of this kind of teasing.

She reached for my hand and tugged me toward her. I readjusted so I was leaning over her as she reclined on my couch. "You're a full-grown man —with a man's needs, although you'd deny it to your last breath." She ran her fingers over my lips, and I shivered almost violently. My tongue caressed her finger, and I scraped it gently with my teeth, before soothing it by drawing it into my mouth. Then I took her hand in mine and eased it down to rest over my pounding heart.

"You've waded out away from shore, and now the tide's comin' in," she whispered, right before she reached her arms around my neck and kissed me in wild, wanton waves, accompanied by sighs that were sweeter than any music I'd ever heard.

My lips curved in a smile, even as they were still merged with hers. I was remembering that day by the creek when she likened erotic love to the ocean tide.

"Dive right in," I growled. "The water's fine."

Laughter erupted from underneath me. Yes, she was lying underneath me now, our bodies fitted together.

"Oh yes, the water is *so* fine."

I slid down her body to get away from those red velvet lips that were tempting me beyond redemption, and turned my head to rest it gently on her breast. Her breath caught and I could hear the rapid patter of her heart, the erratic rise and fall of her chest. I took a deep lungful of air myself and let it out in a rapid whoosh.

A wordless cry escaped her and her hands came up to hold me where I was. I realized my open lips were sending hot air across the tops of her breasts. My hand slid up her waist and under her arm to the buttons on her blouse. Without thinking, I undid a couple and slipped my fingers in to caress the soft skin around her brassiere. Her hips jerked against my belly, and my groin throbbed in response. The most enticing scent emanated from her skin, sweet, clean, yet spicy. It made my mouth water. Her hands inched surely, confidently down my back until they almost rested on my rear. She urged me back up to kiss her, and as she pulled my groin against the soft juncture of her legs, she let out a long, low, enticing moan.

We wriggled around till we were lying on our sides, facing each other.

"How can you make me feel this way without being inside me, without even touching me?" she whispered.

I came to my senses, ever so slightly, enough to realize we were on a dangerous edge. She was lying there with her blouse open and her bra pushed to the side, revealing the pink nipple in the center of her breast. I righted her clothing, pulling the edges of her blouse together and fumbling with the buttons for a second before giving up.

"I'm sorry."

"Ooh," she crooned softly, "I'm not sorry at all."

"I didn't mean to go this far."

"But ya did, didn't ya?" Smiling a lazy, satisfied grin, she slid down my body and undid my belt. My hips moved toward her without my consent, and I was pulled under the wave of desire again, gulping air as I went. For the first time, her hand touched the bare skin under my boxers, which made me forget we weren't married. Words tumbled out my mouth without coherent thought behind them.

"Oh Lizzy, honey, I ache for you."

"I know, I know," she whispered. "But it's going to be okay now, shh…"

That's when I forgot my own name.

THE NEXT FEW DAYS WERE packed full of work for me. I barely had time to eat, or catch a nap on a hospital gurney to round out the fitful few hours of sleep I had at home. It was probably a good thing I was so busy, however, as it kept me from dwelling on my personal life.

I was, in a word, conflicted. One part of my mind was uneasy with the situation between my girl and me. Sure, we hadn't consummated our relationship that night in my apartment—not technically—but events were spiraling out of my control toward what felt like a foregone conclusion.

On the other hand, I was becoming impatient with waiting. Was I not a twenty-four-year-old man, completely grown? Some of my colleagues were married—with children born or on the way, for heaven's sake! I was the only one who hadn't had—well, it embarrassed me to even think the word. At least, I thought I was the only one who hadn't. I certainly didn't talk with the guys about it, because a gentleman wouldn't bring it up. And I knew they wouldn't broach the topic either for fear of offending me. I still carried that preacher's kid persona around like a shield. Would it always be thus? Would I ever be my own man apart from it? Should I be?

Finally, it occurred to me that part of the problem was that I was intermittently angry with Lizzy. None of this consternation would be swimming around my head if she'd just marry me like I wanted, but I was afraid to say anything to her for fear of losing her again. If I thought she'd agree to it, we'd go right across the state line to one of those wedding chapels and tie the knot. Then there would be no problem, no dilemma. We could just let things take their course—live our lives together.

I was daydreaming about that very thing when she found me in the hospital courtyard. I'd taken advantage of an unusually warm November day and sat at one of the iron-mesh picnic tables that were scattered about. While I munched my sandwich, I watched the passersby—pallid patients in wheelchairs and gowns, pushed by attentive family members, a nurse or two in starched caps and uniforms, a groundskeeper raking fresh mulch around a hedge.

Lizzy plopped down beside me with her own brown bag and a bottled soda she'd bought and opened at the vending machine outside the doctor's lounge. She offered me a swig of her drink, and I shook my head. She took a drink herself and opened her lunch bag.

"Thought I might find you out here. It's too nice a day to be cooped up inside, isn't it?" Her cheeks were glowing pink, and her eyes twinkled with affection. She had no right to be so lovely, so settled, so gosh-darn happy! Not while my own mind was so heavy and troubled.

"Yeah, it was crazy in there today. I wanted some time to myself."

She stopped in mid-bite, carefully chewed and swallowed. "I see. I didn't mean to intrude then." She wrapped up her sandwich and stuck it back in her bag, all the merriment wiped clean as her face fell, and she stood to turn away. "See ya round, Billy Ray."

As she walked off, the sunshine that had been so warm and welcoming just a minute before became thinner and cooler. I sighed, annoyed with the both of us, and went after her, touching her elbow. "Lizzy wait. I'm sorry."

She turned, but wouldn't meet my gaze. "It's fine." But her face told a different story.

It was odd. Mired in my own conflict, my first response had been to shut her out, and to my surprise, I'd hurt her. It was encouraging that I had at least enough of her heart to make her feel something. But that also meant I had a responsibility to hold her heart and protect it, even if it meant protecting it from me.

"I did come out here to be alone, but that was before you showed up. You're always welcome."

"You don't have to say that."

"Even if it's true?"

"You've been avoiding me all week."

"I have not!"

"I can only assume it's because of what happened in your apartment Saturday night."

It ticked me off that she knew me so well.

"You know, if you want to cool things off with me, all you have to do is say so."

I took it back; she knew nothing about me at all if that's what she thought was going through my head.

"You've got some weird hang-ups, Billy Ray."

"Hang-ups? What kind of new-fangled word is that?"

She pursed her lips in mild annoyance, but her expression was tinged with insecurity too. "I understand it, you know. In your mind, I can't be your steady girl *and* the town slut. Thing is—perhaps I'm both of those things, and if you try to make me just one or the other, you'll make us both miserable."

For the first time in weeks, the heat in my cheeks was the result of anger and not desire or embarrassment. "I don't think that about you, Lizzy. You're not a—loose woman, but boy-oh-boy, you aren't any sweet simple picnic either, I tell you that."

"If sweet and docile is what you want, you're barking up the wrong tree."

"It's not what I want! Don't you know that by now? I could have that a dozen times over."

"Is that so?"

"Yeah, that's so. I've turned my back on sweet and docile for two years while my dreams were full of you."

"Then I think you need to come to terms with what you want and name it out loud."

"And what do I want, exactly?"

"You've been told you should want a stale, orderly kind of life, but you don't. And you're smart enough to know it, deep down. You want to soar above the earth, yet see the underbelly of life too. You want what's exciting, what's real. I know that's what you want, or you wouldn't have decided to be a doctor. Meeting and taking care of all those different people, that's one way to see it all. It makes you experience life, puts you in the thick of humanity, with all its joy and its suffering. I know, because I want those things too. But earthly trappings make life awfully messy, don't they?"

She paused and covered my hand with hers. "Saturday night, when we were together at your apartment, you were unhappy, hurting—in your body, in your mind. I could tell, and it hurts me too. I wanted to care for you, to soothe you. It's a good thing; it's a good thing to want, and it's not dishonorable."

"You still think of me like I'm the boy you knew in Orchard Hill two years ago. You think I'm confused and ignorant about men and women and...sex."

Her eyes widened at my atypical use of the word, but she waited for me to continue.

"I'm not naive, not anymore. But no matter what you've decided about them, the rules, the guidelines I've been taught—they're ingrained in me so deep, they're part of me. If and when I decide to defy those rules, I have to be sure, and it doesn't happen without sacrificing a piece of who I am. Or who I was. If I alter the rules, I have to know I'm doing right."

"Two years ago, I said this thing between us would change you."

"You did."

"Life is change—constant adjustments, and many times, it's unsettling."

"Don't I know it," I muttered.

She smiled, just a tiny bit.

"I have changed a lot over the last couple of years, in the way I think, the way I believe. I've broadened my opinions and let go of my narrow judgments about my fellow man when I haven't walked in his footsteps. Some adjustments are easy, petty things, but there are some, that, once they're made, will alter something fundamental in me. I think sex is one of those. I wish you felt the same way about the matter, but I'm not surprised that you don't."

"'Cause I was the town slut?"

My temper snapped. "Enough! I don't want to hear you refer to yourself like that again—ever!"

She startled at the vehemence in my voice and stared at me, wide-eyed.

"I mean it, Lizzy!" My voice was vibrating with anger as I watched her, and slowly a dawning light rose from her beautiful lips to her dark eyes.

"You're right," she said. "You are absolutely right. It was a mistake—what happened with Seth—but a mistake only because of my reasons for making it, and probably the time and place as well."

Well, I thought it was a mistake regardless, but I knew she viewed it differently. Maybe she had to; I don't know.

"But I shouldn't have let it dictate who I was or how I treated people —regardless of how they treated me."

That, I definitely agreed with.

"Out of habit, I still keep the Orchard Hill gossips' view of sex—and of me." She clasped my hand and intertwined our fingers. "It's a bad habit too —one that stops now; I swear it. I'll try to see myself through your eyes, not theirs."

I didn't think it was possible to love her more, but it was. Every day, I found something more to love about her.

"You want to make love to me," she went on. "Of course you do because you're human and you're passionate, and for some reason that I can't fathom, you've chosen to be with me. But it has to be on your terms, or you risk losing a part of yourself, something that's elementally you. Do I have that right?"

"Pretty much."

"So, what are your terms? Where's the line?"

"I'm confused, Lizzy. I don't really know."

"Then how do I know if the terms have been met? Or if I've crossed a line?"

I stared at her and shrugged, helpless to answer.

She gave me a gentle, loving smile and brushed back a lock of hair that the wind had blown across my brow. "What am I gonna do with you, Billy Ray Davenport?"

I contemplated what to do, and finally spoke the only thing that made sense to me.

"Let me lead the way."

"Pardon?"

"You know everything about...physical love."

"I wouldn't go that far."

"But you've experienced it, and I haven't."

"Not sure it was really love in my case, but that's a fair statement, I suppose."

"So let me decide what steps to take and when. Let me lead us."

After a long pause, she promised in a soft voice. "All right then, I will."

I knew it would cost her to relinquish control of anything, given how hard she'd had to work to regain mastery of her life, but love shone from her eyes, and she did just that. She let go.

She did it for me.

Chapter Twenty-Three

As the days went by and Thanksgiving drew near, I began to think the time was right to broach a serious topic of discussion with Dad. Those kinds of conversations had never been easy for us, but I'd made an important decision, and I owed it to him to let him know. He was my father, and I honored him. And more than that, I loved him.

Last year, I drew short straw and had to work over Thanksgiving, but it meant that this Thanksgiving I was off for the holiday. So on Thursday morning, I climbed into the 1955 Chrysler Aunt Catherine gave me when she bought her rag top Chevy and drove the three hours to her house in the little town of Kent. Dad and I were joining her for the Thanksgiving meal, which promised to be a rigid, formal affair.

Aunt Catherine was my father's older sister, prim and proper as an old school marm. In fact, she had been an old school marm until she retired a few years back. My grandparents left quite a bit of money to them both, but while Dad kept a large part of his trust fund in the bank earning nice, safe interest to pay for his travel expenses and my education, Aunt Catherine spent her money freely: on renovating her home, or on that new rag top car of hers, for example. She liked playing the stock market too, which Dad considered little better than gambling.

But even though Dad believed a more modest lifestyle might have been more seemly, he knew he wasn't going to change Aunt Catherine's mind, and she knew she couldn't ever change his. Still, whenever my aunt mentioned that she was using her inheritance and he should as well, he would draw his lips into a thin line and quote Matthew 19:24 to her: "You know Catherine, it is easier for a camel to go through the eye of a needle, than for a rich man to enter the kingdom of God."

To which Aunt Catherine would reply, "Well, Raymond, that might be true for men, but then, I'm not a man, am I? So it doesn't apply to me."

Dad would just laugh at that, and it made me smile, too, to know that even though they disagreed so completely on this one thing, they loved and respected each other in spite of it.

I pulled up in the driveway of the old family house, built by my grandparents in the 1920s when the economy was booming, before the Great Depression. It was a burgundy brick, two stories with a wide front porch, supported by concrete columns—a symmetrical, orderly house for a symmetrical, orderly lady.

Dad came out to greet me with a warm handshake and a hug.

"Hello, son. How are you?"

"Doing very well, and you?"

"I'm well. I'm well. The Lord keeps me strong to do His work."

Dad may have been strong in his spirit, but as I looked at him, I began to realize that his body was aging. There was more gray in his hair, a few more wrinkles around his eyes and mouth, and a lack of robustness in his stride that indicated he was approaching his later years. Before, I'd always seen my father through a child's eyes, and as the years went by, I continued to see him like that—ageless and strong. On one level, I knew he was getting older, just as I was, but rarely did I let myself become aware of the fact.

As we entered the house, the smell of roast turkey and pumpkin pie baking made my mouth water. Aunt Catherine came in from the kitchen and gave me an appraising look up and down.

"You're too skinny, Billy Ray." She pursed her lips and frowned.

I leaned over to kiss her cheek. "It's good to see you too, Aunt Catherine."

She snorted. "Well, this dinner ought to fatten you up a bit. It took Zelda and me hours to fix it, and I'm sure I made way too much. You'll have to take some back with you."

"Yes, ma'am." I grinned at her, which made her face soften a bit.

"Glad you made it here safe and sound," she answered and turned to go back into the kitchen. "You two can wait in the dining room. We'll be ready to eat shortly."

We sat in the quiet elegance of my aunt's dark, somber dining room. The mahogany table and chairs, enough seats for twelve, were empty except for three settings of china and silver. A matching sideboard was filled with enough food to set those other nine places.

It was a slow-paced, silent dinner for the most part, very different from most of the meals I now took amidst the cacophony of the hospital cafeteria or in the diner. The most prominent sound was the tick, tick of the large grandfather clock in the hall—that is, until my father spoke at last.

"Are you home through Sunday, Billy Ray?"

"No, I have to work Saturday, so I thought I'd return to Glenwood tomorrow afternoon."

"Ah, I see." He picked up a dinner roll and went on. "Well, I'm scheduled to give the sermon at Corinth Hill this week. It's too bad you won't be able to attend."

"I'm sorry about that."

"You still going to church every Sunday over there in Glenwood?"

"When I'm not working, I do. Even when I do have to work, I try to slip into the hospital chapel for a bit."

"I wish you didn't have to work on the Sabbath."

"People still get sick on Sunday, unfortunately."

"That is true. Working nights and weekends is part of the doctor's mission." Dad smiled at me. "Like it's part of the minister's."

"Yessir."

"Still, if you have a chance sometime, you might want to attend a Sunday or two at Corinth Hill."

"Oh?"

"The lay minister there has a daughter about your age who sings lead soprano in the choir."

"Dad—" I began.

"Pretty as a picture, and a voice like an angel."

"Dad—"

"Just consider it, son. It's time to start thinking about those things. Medical school won't last forever."

"Sometimes it feels like it will though."

He smiled again as he cut another bite of turkey and paired it with a forkful of cornbread dressing.

I could tell from my father's expression that he noticed the way I deftly turned the topic. I had never told him any of what had happened between Lizzy and me two years ago, or why she vanished into thin air. It seemed that to tell him would betray her confidence, so I kept all that to myself. And I was sure he thought if we didn't discuss her, she wasn't real any longer —that I had relegated her to my past. To tell the truth, he was probably just relieved she was gone.

I certainly hadn't told him we were working at the same hospital, or that I spent every spare minute I could with her—or that I was getting closer and closer to a physical point of no return. Emotionally, I knew, I was already over the cliff. Knowing I was committing my heart to her was the only way I could assuage the guilt I felt when she and I pushed the intimacy a little too far.

No, I certainly didn't tell him that.

AFTER DINNER, WHILE AUNT CATHERINE went upstairs to take a nap, I found Dad in the living room, reading the newspaper.

"You want to see the funnies?" He reached into the pile to fish out the section that contained the comics. I used to always read those first when I was a boy.

"No, thank you."

I waited until he finished the article he was reading and turned the page.

"I wanted to talk to you if you have a minute."

He folded the paper and stacked it neatly on the coffee table in front of him.

"Of course, son. I always have time for you."

I took a deep breath. "Do you remember the girl I courted in Orchard Hill a couple of summers ago, Lizzy Quinlan?"

"I don't know that I'd use the word 'courting' for that situation, but yes I remember her."

"She's going to a midwife school over in Hyden, and right now she's working at the hospital in Glenwood. I ran into her at a mixer a while back."

"I see. And how is she faring?"

"She's doing very well, Dad. You'd be so proud of her. I know I am. She's one of the best students, and the patients—they love her. Her instructors do too."

"I'm glad for her, then," he said with a guarded expression, and leaned forward to pick up another section of the paper.

"I've been dating her for over a month now."

He stopped in mid-reach. "Dating her?"

"Yes sir, going to the movies and dinner and such—when we both have free time, which isn't as often as I'd like."

"Well."

"I'm going to ask her to marry me."

The tick, tick of the grandfather clock swelled and filled the room.

He sat there, elbows on his knees, fingers steepled, staring at the coffee table in front of him. He tapped his fingers against his lips, considering what to say. When he spoke, he was careful to keep his tone even. "If you're asking for my approval of your choice, I'm afraid you're going to be disappointed. I didn't think Miss Quinlan was right for you two years ago, and I don't think so now."

I was afraid that this was how it would go. He was being stubborn, not wanting to admit that he'd been swayed by gossip and innuendo, and probably aware too, as perceptive as he was about people, that Lizzy wasn't completely innocent. But if he could read people that well, surely he had to know how I felt about her—how much I loved her.

"I'm a grown man, and your approval is not required."

"So much for honoring your father, eh?"

It was an impulsive comment on his part, spoken from his hurt pride. I couldn't let it anger me, but neither could I let it pass. "I do honor you, but honor doesn't always mean obey—not for an adult."

"I don't understand, Billy Ray. You've been so levelheaded about everything in your life: school, your career, your friends, everything but this young woman. How did she get her hooks into you so tight? Or do I not want to know that?"

Lizzy's image floated past in my mind's eye—all smiles and brilliance and an electric charge all around that curvy little body that resonated with my own. It would be a lie to say what was between us wasn't physical, at least in part.

"Lizzy is beautiful, even more so than the last time you saw her. Men still look at her when she walks into a room. My friend Richard wanted to ask her out—that is, before he knew about us."

"Is that it? Does she appeal to your pride as well as your body? Because she's the woman every man wants?"

"Give me some credit, Dad; I'm not in love with just her looks. She's smart too. Like I said, she's studying to be a midwife, and—"

"I heard you, and that's a good and admirable thing for her to do. But, son, you'll have a demanding career of your own, and a doctor needs a woman who can mind the home, who can take care of his family, someone to help him, not be away helping everyone else."

I wondered if he would have said such a thing if Mama were still living and helping him care for the flock. As much as her death shaped the man I'd become, I realized it must have changed him, too, in ways I couldn't even begin to understand.

"Dad, I don't know how we'll work it all out, but I know we can. I think Lizzy is who's best for me, and I want her for my wife—if she'll have me, that is."

"What makes you think she won't?" he snorted with a humorless laugh.

"I believe she will be"—I paused, searching for the right word—"cautious about making the right decision." I left it there, still resisting any explanation, including that Lizzy turned me down two years ago.

"That's the first sensible thing I've heard since this conversation began, but it won't be an issue. She won't say no."

It was so tempting to tell him that in the past she had done just that very thing, but I hesitated to let him that close to the truth of us—not while he was still so set against her.

"At any rate," he went on, "if you're worried she won't accept you, shouldn't that tell you something? Can't she see all the advantages she would gain as your wife?"

"It's not that simple." How could I possibly explain about Lizzy without betraying her trust? "I know Lizzy's seen precious little kindness, except from a very few people, like her family and Doc Miller and Mrs. Gardener. I mean, she's made some friends at school, but that's only happened recently. Her experiences in Orchard Hill—they're why it's difficult for her to have faith in other people. I do think she loves me, but—"

"This lack of faith you speak of doesn't bode well for a lifelong commitment."

"It's hard to have faith when you've been hurt over and over again."

"No, son. The trials of a human existence aren't excuses for walking without faith—in each other, or in the Lord for that matter."

"But see, when I was child, you and Mama and everyone else in my life taught me about kindness first-hand, and I built my faith on that foundation. Someone who doesn't learn that at an early age starts the walk of faith already behind. That person has to wait until she's old enough to understand it at her Holy Father's knee, regardless of what the world shows her, and that is a rocky road to travel.

"Lizzy only got one chance from the people of Orchard Hill, and although her family wasn't cruel to her, they didn't teach her those lessons that you taught me. God's kindness—His forgiveness and mercy—seemed so far away to her. But when we started spending time together that summer, she saw compassion and acceptance from someone who wasn't her family, and I believe that was the start of a new path for her. Now, she's beginning to see kindness from other people too, and that's a few more baby steps toward a deeper faith in others, one that could last a lifetime."

"If what you're saying is true," Dad replied solemnly. "Miss Quinlan may not be able to return your love with the fervor that you bestow it, not now or maybe not ever. If she won't, or can't, she will break your heart. I don't know exactly what form the heartbreak will take—another man, a bitter heart, contempt in her words, loneliness if she leaves you—but I very much fear you will suffer because you love her." His voice diminished in strength and volume. "And I don't know if I can bear to see it."

I pondered how to explain it to him for a minute, before it occurred to me how it might make sense.

"Even if she breaks my heart—and I don't think she will—loving her will make me better than I used to be."

"How could that be?"

"When Mama passed away, you suffered, and so did I. But knowing Mama and loving her changed us for the better, didn't it? Because she was on this earth and we loved her, you and I are the men we are today. Wasn't that worth loving her in spite of the pain we suffered when she died?"

He shook his head, not willing to follow me into this painful abyss. I had never pushed him quite this hard to face his grief, but I wanted him to see that I knew the risk I was taking by allowing myself to love Elizabeth—knew it better than a lot of young men my age, and I wanted to take it anyway.

"Dad, you took the pain and grief of your loss and wrestled something good out of it. Because of Mama's love, even after she was gone, you worked your life into something worth doing—your traveling ministry. In a different way, I believe Lizzy's love will do that for me too. And I think eventually you'll see that my faith in her is not misplaced."

"It gives me no pleasure to bring this up, but I must ask you: the rumors about her past behavior—is there any truth to them? And if there is, why doesn't it bother you that other men…"

"Don't," I raised my voice and my hand, and then lowered them both slowly. "Please, sir, don't disrespect her. She entrusted me with a little of her past, her real past, not the one that Orchard Hill gossip fabricated for her. No one truly understands the road she's walked. I certainly don't, and neither do you. To say any more than that would betray her trust in me, and I won't do that."

"And let he who is without sin cast the first stone?"

I nodded.

"Well, I guess that was one lesson you learned well." His eyes held a mixture of wistfulness and pride.

"I'll admit, sometimes the ugly part of me wants to change what happened before I met her or forget it, but the only way a marriage with Lizzy will ever work is if she and I build our lives in the present and for the future and not keep looking at the past."

"Go forth and sin no more?"

A stab of guilt pierced my conscience. I needed to marry her, and soon, for a variety of reasons, but that physical point of no return was one of them. "As best we can."

"What will you do if you can't erase the past from your memory? Or if she can't?"

"I don't want to erase it, because our pasts led us to the here and now. What we have to learn is how to accept the past for what it was, and change our separate paths to one we can walk together."

"Your mother joined my path and walked it with me."

"I know."

"You should be the head of your own house, Billy Ray."

"The head and the heart have to work together, sir, or the body doesn't function at all."

"Well now, I know that." Dad sounded exasperated. "It sounds as if you're quite determined about this—path of equals."

"I am."

"I won't lie to you, Billy Ray, to make you feel better. This choice and this woman, they both worry me." He sighed. "But what you've said today has merit and it has spiritual truth. It will take a level of forgiveness beyond what many an ordinary man could muster, but you are your mother's child, and with God's help you might be capable of bestowing it. I will pray about it. I will pray for peace with your decision. And I will pray for you, and for Miss Quinlan."

"Thank you, sir." The interview was over. He had made a major concession, and it was more than I had hoped for.

Chapter Twenty-Four

The evening was going just like clockwork. I took Lizzy to Antonio's, the nicest restaurant in town. It had white tablecloths and soft music, and we talked and laughed all through dinner. Then we went to see *El Cid* at the Brandenburg theater. We strolled around town afterward, hands clasped, looking at the Christmas lights in the town square and the shop windows, simply enjoying each other's company.

And then I ruined it.

We passed Farmington Jewelers and saw a pretty display of multicolored lights and greenery in the window. A few inexpensive pieces of jewelry adorned the window too, along with those colored line-drawing pictures of women standing under sprigs of mistletoe and smiling in delighted surprise as they opened little treasure boxes. I halted, pondering the display, and covered Lizzy's hand with my gloved one. She had on thick homemade mittens so I couldn't see her fingers, but I imagined how a wedding band might look there, and a smile tumbled out of me.

"What?" she asked, smiling in response.

"Nothing."

"Tell me."

"I was just thinking; we should visit Farmington's soon."

She tilted her head to one side. "Medical students don't have money for expensive Christmas presents, Billy Ray." She started to move on. "It's a nice thought, though."

"But you'll have to have a wedding ring," I protested, knowing as soon as

217

the words were out of my mouth that I'd made a misstep. But maybe it was time for both of us to face the future, whatever it turned out to be. I hated keeping my hopes buried for fear of her discovering my innermost wishes and squashing them under her apprehension like a bug.

The smile slid off her face as she pulled her hand away, abruptly turned so I couldn't see her face, and strode down the street.

I mentally kicked myself and went after her, not fast enough to catch her—I knew it was best to give her some space when she took off like that —but fast enough to keep her in my sights.

"Gosh darn it, Lizzy!" I called. "Don't storm off!" *Again!* I thought in exasperation.

She stopped, head bowed, and turned to wait for me.

We stood there, the two of us—she with her arms folded and looking at the ground, I with my hands in my coat pocket, shifting my gaze from her dark, curly head to the few cars and people on the square.

I took off my glove and gently stroked her cheek with my fingers before I tilted her chin up to entice her to look at me.

"You must have known, surely, that I was planning to ask you about getting married."

"I suspected, knowing you. I should have set you straight right away, but—"

"What?"

"I guess I thought that when I said no, you would leave." She huffed. "It's not fair to you. I know that. I just…"

"Just…?"

"I'm selfish, I suppose."

"Oh?"

"I would miss you so much if you left." Her voice, soft and unsure, quivered like the forlorn strains of the street corner musician's violin we'd passed on Third. Then it grew stronger as she gathered her courage and spoke again. "I didn't want to let you go."

A reluctant smile spread across my face, because in spite of my frustration, I considered this a step forward. "I don't care if you're selfish about keeping me close. In fact, I welcome it." I kissed her cheek, pushed her hair behind her ear, and on impulse, kissed right below her ear, feeling my blood simmer up and boil over as I tasted her skin, soft as flower petals. My lips found her mouth and my arms found their way around her, holding her close. Every part of her seemed to soften and melt into me, and my pulse kicked up another notch.

I put my hands under the soft curtain of her hair and held her forehead against mine. Then I let the inner corner of my heart out into the evening air, my words a blazing torch slicing through an uncertain darkness. "I love you, Elizabeth."

Her body stilled. "I'm not ready for this," she whispered.

I wondered if that was meant for me or only for herself. Darn it, it hurt that she didn't say the words back, although somewhere in the depths of my soul, I believed she did love me. Still, her lack of reciprocation provoked my temper.

"What part of 'calling on you' did you not understand? Where did you think this was going?"

"I don't know," she fretted. "Not to this, not this soon. So many things can go wrong. What happens when I graduate this year? You still have another year of medical school. And then you have residency. Am I supposed to put a halt to my work, pick up and go wherever you go, just because you're there?"

"We'll cross that bridge when we come to it. We'll work something out that's best for both of us." She'd led me by example to that idea; it was the main thing I learned when she turned down my first proposal.

"Easy for you to say now, but when it actually happens, you'll conveniently forget all about this conversation."

"I won't forget."

"You will forget. Every man—"

Exasperation finally won out. "I know, I know. Every man forgets. Every man wants to pigeonhole you into being something you're not. Every man, every man, every man. I'm not every man, Lizzy. I know what I'm signing up for with you."

She looked at me and raised one eyebrow.

"Okay, I don't know *exactly* what I'm signing up for. But I know enough to know it's worth it."

She folded her arms across her chest and stared at me, trying to frighten me off, but it wasn't going to work this time. I gently took her elbow and we strolled the three or four blocks to her boarding house. When we got to the front porch, I led her to the glider and we sat, facing each other, a tense silence between us.

But saying those three little words out loud to her had given me strength, and now I knew what I had to do. "I know what the problem is, honey." I gave her my best smile and watched with smug satisfaction as her face softened and her eyes got all dark and dewy.

"You do, do ya?"

I nodded, caressing her bottom lip with my thumb, lulling her into that warm, languid place where we'd been just a few minutes before. And then I let her have it. "You're afraid."

The effect was instantaneous. She bulled up, anger bursting from her eyes. I half expected bolts of lightning to shoot out her fingertips and the ends of her hair. But she had to face the truth if there was any chance for us at all.

"I'm not afraid! I just know I'm not cut out to be anyone's wife."

"I agree."

She stopped, staring at me.

"You're not cut out to be anyone's wife. You're cut out to be mine."

"You'll believe that while you're all worked up, but words are cheap, Billy Ray."

"Okay, I'll concede that much, Miss Know-It-All, but you answer this —how can I ever show you I mean those words if you don't let me stick around long enough to back them up with actions?"

She didn't have a ready answer. Encouraged by the silence, I went on.

"You think because someone hurt you in the past that you can't trust kindness, that a man's love isn't real. But I'm telling you, Lizzy Quinlan, my love is real—so real, it hurts." Unconsciously, I brought my fist to my heart. "And a love like mine is forever if you'll let it be."

Hope ignited in her expression for a fraction of a second, and then I watched in frustration as she extinguished that hope in the blink of an eye.

"It's wrong to punish me for what some other man did to you. All that does is make us both miserable. I deserve to be happy—and so do you."

"No—"

"No? You don't deserve happiness? Lizzy, we've all made mistakes."

"I know."

"Or do you not deserve to be happy because, when you were young and foolish, you trusted the wrong person and put yourself on a destructive path for a time?"

"Not exactly, but—"

"You've taken yourself off that path now, right?"

"Yes, but that's not what I—"

"We all deserve forgiveness for our mistakes. You, me, our parents, the Orchard Hill gossips, the Neanderthals who used to ogle you from their pick-up trucks, even that low-life who hurt you in the first place." I hesitated, but I had come too far to turn back now. "Let me ask you, do you forgive" —my mouth twisted with the effort of saying his name—"Seth Corbett for what he did to you?"

"It doesn't matter. He doesn't matter. I've moved on. I made a new life for myself in spite of him."

I wanted to draw her into my arms and hold her like I'd hold and comfort a little child. "But see, it *does* matter. 'Cause until you forgive him, you can't move on to the life you're supposed to have—with me by your side."

I stood up then, and paced back and forth in front of the glider. "I've spent two years thinking about this—about how I felt two years ago when I wanted to marry you and how I've changed. I know I wasn't ready to be a husband that summer. I asked you to marry me for the wrong reasons. I had to become a man who could love a woman worth pleasing. I had to forgive Corbett and accept what happened to you. I can let go of my jealousy and anger now—and forgiveness wrenched from malevolence has power. Do you want to hear me say it?" I felt bile rise up in my throat. "I forgive him. I forgive him for seducing you, for leaving you, for hurting you. I forgive him for stealing a part of you that should have been given to me. I forgive him because what he did, in part, made you who you are, and I love who you are." And as if I'd thrown water on a flame, my anger sputtered and went out. All that was left was a peaceful quiet as the bitterness of my rage dissipated like campfire smoke into a cool, spring morning.

"You know, Corbett was a lucky man who didn't know what he had. For a little while, he was blessed with your divine spark, and then the fool trampled on it. I'm grieved that he hurt you, but in the end—well, it was his loss, not yours. He might have been the first man to see the light you carry in your heart, but he didn't own it. It belongs to you, given to you by God, and you can bestow it on whomever you wish. And if you honor me with that light, I won't be foolish enough to waste it, you can be sure of that. I'll use it to fill up my heart and my life, and bask in its warmth for the rest of my days. You make my heart feel warm again. Did you know that, Lizzy?

And you seem to be the only one who can.

"You're right that I don't know what will happen to us in the future. I can't promise everything will be easy, but I can tell you that no matter what comes our way, I'll love you through it all."

I sat back down next to her and drew her into my arms, very gently. The words I'd just spoken were hard, so my touch had to be soft. She grasped my shoulders and held on tight, her head on my shoulder, her voice choked.

"I know I should jump at the chance. I'm an idiot, a stupid little fool, Billy Ray. But what if I can't be what you want, what you deserve? And I'm afr —I worry I won't get to be who I am either."

"From the time I was a little boy, I was taught to take steps in faith; you weren't. You are afraid we'll make each other sad and miserable in the long run, and I'm here to tell you, with every ounce of conviction I have, that you're wrong."

"This"—she pointed between us—"it overwhelms me."

"You could try just diving through the wave—or letting go and floating to the ends of the earth with me. The ocean isn't always punishing and harsh, you know. Sometimes, it's peaceful."

She looked shocked that I'd turned her own analogy back on her.

I held her face in my hands and kissed her slowly and sweetly, pouring everything I felt into that kiss, and wondering if it would be the last time I kissed her like that or the first time of many.

I drew back and looked deep into her eyes. "I want you to be my wife. I can wait for you, maybe for a long time; I don't know. I'll hold my heart open as long as I can, but time passes, and whether we like it or not, time changes us. Neither one of us will be able to wait for the other one indefinitely. At some point, you'll have to decide."

"And if you want something I can't give you?" The vulnerability in her face broke my heart, but she was the one who had to take that final step. I couldn't drag it out of her. All I could do was hold out my hand and wait as long as I found waiting tolerable.

"I know you're worried, honey, but don't be." I stroked her hair and held her close, and then I turned her loose, which was most likely the hardest thing I'd ever done. "You'll figure it out. Come find me when you know." I leaned down and kissed her cheek, and then I left her on her porch, arms around herself as if to block the icy December wind from freezing her heart.

THREE DAYS AFTER CHRISTMAS, I was trudging home through the snow after a long night at the hospital. It was a bright, sunlit morning. Crisp and cold, the world was covered in a blinding white blanket that had arrived sometime after I'd buried myself in the hospital but before I'd emerged this morning.

I had taken extra shifts, trying to keep Lizzy off my mind. This waiting for her to decide on our future was agony, and staying busy was the best way to make it through the days—and nights. I couldn't keep up this frenetic pace forever though. I prayed that she would accept her love for me soon, so we could move forward with our lives.

On the way home, I stopped at the diner for a bagel and cream cheese, and a coffee to go. My plans included a solitary breakfast in the quiet of my apartment and maybe catching some shut-eye before I started my reading for the afternoon.

About ten yards from my door, hot coffee sloshed through the lid and onto my bare hand, scalding me. I nearly dropped the cup, but somehow managed to transfer it to my other hand. I did, however, end up dropping the bagel bag in the snow at my feet.

"F-f-f-f-...fiddlesticks!" I murmured, looking around to make sure no one heard me. I'd been around Donovan too long and was beginning to pick up his bad habits. I wasn't sure what embarrassed me more, the impulse to use the word he would have used or the fact that it dissolved into a silly, feminine sounding by-word like 'fiddlesticks.' A giggle emanated from up ahead, and I squinted in the sunlight to see who witnessed my foolish moment for the day.

A pair of worn out boots and the hem of a long, olive green, wool coat stuck out from the behind the holly bush beside my apartment building's steps. The person wasn't actually hiding, but whoever it was had made an effort not to be observed by any passers-by. The boots took a couple steps and pushed the coat and the rest of the person forward enough to peer around the big holly.

"Dare I face your wrath, son of a preacher man? Those were some mighty fearsome words comin' out your mouth just now."

I stood there in total shock. It hadn't been that long since I'd last seen her, maybe a week, but that week felt like years and years. She approached me and picked my bag out of the snow. Opening it, she peered in, taking in a deep whiff of the contents.

"Mmm," she said as she closed her eyes. "Bagel." Her eyes popped open. "I love bagels. Care to share it?" She grinned and turned on her heel, walking toward my stoop. I followed her without a word.

She held the storm door for me while I pulled out my key, and then I grasped the handle and motioned her inside. "Hurry on in, Lizzy. It's cold."

She walked up the stairs that led to my second floor studio and sat down on the couch, putting the wet paper bag on the coffee table in front of her. Turning to me and giving me that come-hither smile, she patted the couch beside her, and like a dutiful pup, I walked right over. Setting my coffee next to my bagel, I unbuttoned my coat and unwound the scarf from my neck, laying them both on the chair that sat catty-corner to the couch. I looked up to find her eyes roving up and down my frame, carefully detailing every move I made.

"Can I take your coat?" I held my hand out to her.

"What?" she murmured a little dreamily. "Oh, yes, of course." She removed her own coat with my help, and I laid it on top of mine. That faraway look on her face confused me. I was absolutely sure I hadn't thrown my best smile at her. I didn't feel like smiling. I was too afraid of what she was about to say.

"Did you have a good Christmas?" I sat down on the edge of the couch, creating a buffer of space between us.

"Yes, I did. How about you?"

"It was quiet but good."

She chuckled. "My holidays are never quiet with Susie and Lily around."

I was impatient with all this politeness. "So, what brings you to my door, Ee-lizabeth?"

"I've come to find you, 'cause I know."

"What?"

"I know. You told me to come find you when I know."

"About getting married?" I asked, disbelieving.

She nodded.

"I don't understand. It's only been a week. How much can possibly change in a week?"

"Quite a lot, actually." She folded her hands primly in her lap. "Especially when events conspire to make you think about something really hard."

"What events?"

"Mostly just me having time to think. And I prayed some. I even read

224

the Bible a little too. And being home with my family, considering how different your Christmas with the Reverend and Aunt Catherine must have been from my noisy holiday. Walking around our old haunts in Orchard Hill, remembering the good and bad things that happened there. That was all part of it."

"I see."

She reached over and took my hand, and for once, I felt her shiver at the contact instead of me.

"The day after Christmas, I went up to the post office to get the mail for Mama and Daddy, and guess who I saw?"

I shrugged and looked down at our hands, clasped fast.

"Doctor Miller."

"Oh? And how is he?"

"He's fine, just fine."

"That's good."

"Yes. So we were walking along together and chatting, he and I—up to where his path went off to Cavanaugh Street and mine went the other way to Linden Road."

She stopped, remembering in her mind's eye, and I waited patiently for her to continue.

"After we finished the small talk, I had this burst of curiosity to know what he really thought about being a doctor—now that he was on the other side of all the schooling you're taking now."

"What do you mean?"

"Did he think it was worth the hard work, the pressure? Did he enjoy the life he'd made? Would he do it again, if he knew then what he knew now? So I just asked him outright, 'Doc, have you been happy—being a doctor in a small town like this?'"

"And what did he say?"

"He looked off in the distance for a long minute and then he turned to me with a sad smile. 'Yes, Lizzy,' he said, 'for the most part, I have been happy being a doctor in this little town. I get to really know my patients. I care for them from the cradle to the grave, some of them. My life has been good here. The people in town have respect for my work, and I have my family, but...'

"'But?' I asked him.

"'But at times, being the only doctor around, it can be lonely too, especially in a small town like this. It's a demanding life, being a physician, a life people outside of medicine don't always comprehend. I know Martha—well, sometimes it's hard for her to understand when I have to miss supper, or go out in the middle of the night. Sometimes, I wish there was someone to work with, someone to share that…that burden. It was a godsend when I was finally able to talk with Mary Gardener a little about the patients we share…'

"And then he just kind of trailed off, looking wistful." Lizzy stopped for a minute, lost in her thoughts. Sadness crossed her expression as well, but then her face brightened, and her gaze snapped back to focus on me. "And after he said that, all of a sudden, everything made sense to me."

She sought to read my expression, and her eyes burned with a fierce intensity.

"See that's when I realized something that totally changed how I thought about us, Billy Ray. You and me, we understand something important about each other. We know what it means to carry that burden Doc was talking about, because both of us carry it too. So as the years go by, we'll be able to help each other." Joy suffused through her face, so bright and hot, I almost had to look away. It stole my breath.

"Don't you see? *That's* what I can bring to you. I can give you something all those other perfect girls can't. I can't give you a virgin for your wedding present. I can't be what I'm not, but I can be what I am, which is something that will outlast a wedding night or medical school or even raising children. I can give you myself, and in the long run, when you're as old as Doc, you won't feel the least bit lonely. We can still share our lives and talk about our work and go through it together—and that will make you happy, yes?"

"Yes, Lizzy," I said, grinning because I could see the reasoning behind her words. I couldn't believe I hadn't thought of it myself. "That will make me happy. As long as I know you're with me, we can work the rest out. We'll learn to be husband and wife our own way. Maybe our marriage will be different from everyone else's, but that will make it even more precious, something worth keeping."

"I do love you more than anything, Billy Ray." She laughed. "And it feels good to finally tell you so."

My heart swelled to bursting. "I love you, too."

"Will you marry me?"

I choked on a surprised laugh. Lizzy Quinlan made the most topsy-turvy ideas—like a woman proposing to a man, for example—seem perfectly logical.

"I believe I will—if you'll have me."

"Oh, I'll have you all right," she teased.

My heart burned in my chest, and I felt my blood pumping through my veins, but my mind reached back to a long, hot summer two and a half years before, and I remembered the thrill of teasing back.

"Miss Quinlan—I'm shocked. Is that a double entendre?"

"I'm not sure what a double entendre is exactly, but if you're talking about all the ways I can have you, then, yes, Mr. Davenport, it is."

We just sat there, looking at each other, her expression alight with challenge, and me grinning from ear to ear.

After a minute or so, I opened my arms, and she rushed into them. I pulled her into my lap, holding her tight and thanking God that she was who she was, and that she was mine to love.

"You were right, Lizzy, that morning I first asked you to marry me way back in Orchard Hill. It took me a while to see what you meant—because I was angry and hurt and embarrassed. Back then, I thought loving you weakened me, but that was wrong. Because now, I believe I could topple the walls of Jericho."

Chapter Twenty-Five

Although I accepted Elizabeth Quinlan's marriage proposal in early January, it was way up in the spring before I told Dad that I was going to marry her for sure. I wanted to tell him in person, not in a letter, and he and I were both busier than ever. After Christmas we didn't see each other for about twelve weeks until one Sunday when I did finally make it to Corinth Hill for his sermon.

He packed the church that day, and the music was spectacular. Dad was right about the lay minister's daughter—she was a pretty girl with an angelic voice. But I also saw the looks she exchanged with a young man who'd just moved in to manage the glass factory, and she wasn't going to be available for too much longer if they were any indication.

Dad was joking about it as we took a walk around the park after church that day.

"You missed your chance there, son. That young fella blew into town and swept Cheryl Ann right off her feet."

"I guess there's no fighting true love," I replied, grinning.

"S'pose not."

An awkward silence opened like a chasm between us. I stuck my hands in the pockets of my jacket and slowed my pace. Dad stopped when he realized I'd fallen back and turned to face me, his eyes asking the question he dreaded asking aloud.

"Dad," I began in a gentle voice, "I asked Elizabeth Quinlan to marry me, and I'm happy to say she said yes." That wasn't exactly the way it happened, but it was the gist of it—and would make more sense to him that way.

He stared at me a long minute, his face unreadable. "I see." He turned and continued a couple steps down the path. "Well, then…I guess congratulations are in order." His voice was flat, so unlike the rich, warm tones that typically carried his words. It broke my heart that I was breaking his.

"I don't need your approval," I began.

"Yes, you've made that very clear."

"But," I interrupted, "I'd like to have it anyway."

He sighed and walked over to the corner of the churchyard and sat heavily on the cold wrought-iron bench, looking out over the headstones in Corinth Hill cemetery.

"And I'd like to give my approval. It's just…"

I sat beside him, running my thumb over the intricate curves of the metal, and waited for him to ponder his next words.

"Sometimes," he began, his voice sounding weary, "sometimes, I think I've just seen too much—too much evil, too much heartache, too much betrayal, too much sin. I look into your future with Miss Quinlan as your wife and see so many ways it could go wrong."

How ironic that Lizzy had used those very words once upon a time.

When I didn't respond, he went on. "You know, you could have almost any woman you wanted. You're what all the church committee mamas call a 'catch.' I've overheard them say it."

I chuckled. "They do, huh?"

"Yes, they do," he said, smiling in spite of the seriousness of the conversation.

"But Dad, they're just looking at the outside of me—what the world sees. Lizzy sees my heart."

"Like the Lord saw David's in First Samuel?"

"Yes, very much like that. She loves me, she wants me to be happy, and I believe she may be the only woman who could make me so. She sees the world in a different light than…well, than anyone I've ever met. To her, it's a bright and colorful, and interesting and scary place. Getting a glimpse of that through her eyes makes me feel alive in a way I've never felt before or since I met her."

"And is that enough to base a marriage on?"

"Perhaps not on its own, but like me, she has this calling to take care of people. We're going to answer that calling—together."

"That career of hers also concerns me. I don't understand how she can be a so-called modern working woman and be married at the same time. What kind of mother will she be if she's not in the home? Who will take care of you, of my grandchildren?"

"Without her work, she wouldn't be the woman I love. Surely, you understand this, given the way you've chosen to spend your life. I would lose her if I separated her from her gift to the world. It wouldn't be right—not for her and not for the world either."

"But I'm worried about what's right for *you*—and for your unborn children."

"If the children come, we will love and care for them, but we will have to figure out the day-to-day particulars together."

"Try as I might, I can't see how that's going to work."

"I don't think it can be seen right now. You need something more to believe in it."

"Something more?"

"You need faith."

He stopped short.

"Trust us to do what is right. Take that leap of faith with us, Dad. She's worth it—you'll see."

His voice sounded agitated, frustrated and impatient. "I can't see my way clear to take that step. All I can see is how many ways I could lose my son."

"The only way you will lose me is if you force me to choose."

I realized then that sometimes even a preacher man is just a man, and he has to actually see the next step with his own eyes and hear it with his own ears. He has to be shown the walk of faith, at least as it regards the people on earth he loves. How could I illuminate that step for him though? How could I show him that Lizzy was a woman of integrity whose actions supported her beliefs?

"I never told you this, but I asked Elizabeth to marry me two summers ago."

He looked at me in shock. "You did?"

"I did. And I did it badly and for all the wrong reasons. She turned me down."

"Because she had plans for this big career of hers?"

"No, Dad. She turned me down before she even knew she was going away to school. She turned me down, knowing that I was her easiest and fastest way out of Orchard Hill. She took a chance on being trapped there forever, in a place where people disdained her and wouldn't forgive her or let her be anything but a ruined girl. She said no to me because she wanted what was best for both of us in the long run."

"Well…" he mused. "Well…"

I let him turn that over in his mind a minute, watching his face as he went deep in thought, the way he did when he was trying to reason out a particularly thorny problem. A robin landed on the path in front of us, tilting its head this way and that before it picked up a stick and flew off into a nearby tree.

"I had no idea," he murmured.

"Please don't make me choose between my only parent and my only soul mate."

He sat there, looking out over the chilly spring day. The redbuds and forsythia were just beginning to bud under the warmth of new sunshine. Finally, he spoke.

"If you and Miss Quinlan will allow me, I would be honored to conduct the marriage service."

My throat closed up so tight it hurt to swallow. This was his leap of faith —in me, in Lizzy, in God's plan for me, whatever it might be.

"Thank you, sir."

"Yes." He put his hands on his knees and leaned forward, as if to stand up.

"Dad?"

"Yes, son?"

"You should start calling her by her first name."

"Lizzy?"

"She has a beautiful given name, a Biblical name—Elizabeth." It rolled off my tongue in a spellbinding cadence, like a prayer.

Dad nodded. "From the Hebrew. It means 'God's promise.'"

"It does, at that," I answered, smiling.

We each sat there a while longer, letting the sun warm our bones and listening to the bird song.

"I'll let you in on a secret, Dad."

"What's that?"

Leaning toward him, I whispered, "The church committee ladies say you're a catch too."

"They do not!" he protested.

"Yessir, they do—I've overheard them."

Dad grinned and pushed at my shoulder. "You shouldn't kid an old man like that, young whippersnapper!" He stood, shaking his head while he indulged in a soft chuckle, and started walking back toward the church.

I laughed out loud and followed along behind him.

Chapter Twenty-Six

I ambled up the beach, water splashing around my ankles as I watched the sand swirl, a kaleidoscope of patterns wherever I stepped. The late afternoon sun blazed across the water, but it was not nearly as blinding as the sight of Lizzy, sunbathing in a very appealing two-piece bathing suit, bright red with white polka dots.

It was the last day of our honeymoon. My father had given us a long weekend on the Carolina coast as a wedding present. It would have been nice to take a little longer trip, but a weekend was all the time we could spare. Lizzy would start her new job as a nurse midwife at the Tri-County Health Department in two weeks, and soon after that I'd start my last year of medical school.

After much prayer and thought, Dad had suggested that we marry in the little church in Orchard Hill, which I thought was a grand idea. Lizzy wasn't sure about it, but I wanted to prove to her, and to everyone else there, that she had risen from the ashes of their toxic rumormongering. I wanted them all to know that forgiveness and joy lay on the other side of transgression—at least for people who strove to overcome it—and Lizzy Quinlan Davenport was the shining example. She had rebuilt her life, she was strong and she was loved. Oh yes, almost beyond the limits of the human heart, she was loved.

In the end, the pull of having her family and Mrs. Gardener in attendance was enough to convince her. I'll never forget how lovely she looked as I stood beside my father and Richard at the front of Orchard Hill's rustic sanctuary. She glided toward me in that candlelight satin dress, her pretty calves peeping out from beneath the hem, a shoulder-length veil covering her dark curls, and joy radiating from her face like rays from the sun. Mrs. G had told Lizzy she should wear a white dress if she wanted, no matter what anyone might say, but my precious wife-to-be looked at me with a shy smile and said, "No, white is a cold color. I want to wear candlelight, because Billy Ray says there's a light inside me that's mine to share with whoever I wish. And I want to show everyone that I choose to share it with him."

So here we were, on the last day of our wedding trip, lounging on the beach. My wife (how I loved calling her that!) eased back, tilting her face to the sky and trailing her fingers in the sand. I settled beside her, soaking her in: the satisfied hint of a smile, the windblown curls, soft, creamy skin along the hourglass curve of her waist, the well-formed muscles of her legs. Powerful little things, those legs, I'd discovered in the past couple of days. Strong, when they wrapped around my hips as I made love to her. Soft, as they smoothed down the back of my calves, while I held her against me and lost my soul in 'the little death' of sexual completion.

I had read about the act, of course, but the experience itself was life altering, like the earth turned upside down. I now lived in a world very different from the one I'd inhabited during my bachelor days. I was going to greatly enjoy being a married man. And it seemed I had a talent for it too. At least Lizzy said I did.

Somehow, some way, we had managed to wait until the marriage vows to consummate our union. It hadn't been easy, but the agreement we had made after that night in my apartment actually brought us much closer. Even though Lizzy assured me that she was only trying to care for and comfort me, I could hardly reconcile my behavior that night with what I'd been taught. But she accepted my convictions and what they meant to me, and as she promised, she let me call the shots about our intimacies from then on. All the way through the rest of our courtship and engagement, even on our wedding night, I led the way or stopped the train. Although now that we were married in truth, I didn't feel that need to rein us in anymore.

In fact, I had to admit it was exhilarating to let the horse have his head, so to speak. The first time was a blur of clothes and breath and heat—and over in a matter of minutes, I remembered with a laugh. But it didn't take me long to get the knack of slowing things down and prolonging the agonizing joy of lovemaking. If I thought the soft, dark looks she gave me when I smiled at her were ego boosting—well, that was nothing compared to the conceited pleasure I felt when some subtle change in the stroke of my fingers made her cry out to her Maker and beg me not to stop. It aroused me just to imagine her in my mind's eye and hear the faded echo of her voice inside my head.

So much so that when we headed back to our everyday lives, as we were planning to do Monday morning, I wasn't quite sure how I was supposed to concentrate on working all those long hours. Now that I was married, all I could think about was the next time I might have her soft and warm and writhing underneath me, or on top of me, for that matter.

I couldn't believe my good fortune; Elizabeth Quinlan was mine and I was hers. So many things could have derailed our love along the way: If I hadn't talked to her that morning so long ago in the graveyard, if she hadn't agreed to let me befriend her after the laundromat night, if we had let bitterness and sorrow win out over the joy of seeing each other again at the Glenwood Community Center. And Marlene's nasty little trick of taking Lizzy's address out of my book when I moved from Orchard Hill? Well, even that had served a purpose in that it gave us time—to miss each other, to learn our trades, to become ourselves, selves worth giving to the other person.

"Lizzy," I continued my train of thought out loud, "when did you first begin to love me?"

"Hmm?" she murmured.

"I know now that you love me, and have for some time, but how did you ever start to see me, not as the preacher's son, but as a man," my voice roughened with suggestive overtones, "As a lover."

She smiled a secret smile, one I thought I saw only when she looked at me. "I'm not sure I can say. It was more like I discovered a feeling that was already there."

"You fought my feelings for you for a long time, but I just kept after you anyway. Now, be honest—did you love me for pursuing you so ardently?"

"For your bravery in the face of everyone's disapproval, I did. And for your loyalty to a friend."

"You may as well say I was stubborn, for that was part of it."

She laughed. "You always were a soft touch for lost causes."

"What do you mean?"

"A lost cause—I could have been one before you came along."

"You were never lost, Elizabeth."

"Maybe, maybe not." She shrugged, digging her toes into the sand. "You know the lyrics to the old hymn as well as you know your own name. 'I once was lost, but now am found.'"

"I didn't save you…" I started to reply, but she interrupted me, a thoughtful look on her face. I'd learned quickly to just hush and listen when she had that look, because it usually signaled some unique idea was about to come out of her mouth. Something I'd probably get a kick out of.

"You know, I prefer to think of myself as 'found,' rather than 'saved'—as the Reverend might call it."

"And why is that?"

"Because 'saved' implies that all the hard work and the challenges are over. Being 'found' means that the journey has just begun, and the joys and hard knocks are all unseen, hidden around bends in the road. That seems more like real life, don't you think?"

We were quiet for a minute, but then it was my turn to be thoughtful.

"The fact is you were remarkably courageous. You didn't know that much good of me. I could have been just another Neanderthal in gentleman's clothing. You took a chance on me."

"You? Not good? There's so much good in you; it's overwhelming at times!" Her eyes were shiny, although I wasn't sure if it was from tears or from the brightness of the sun. "You're the best person I've ever known, Billy Ray." Her voice caught a little, just at the end.

"Thank you, my love. I feel the same about you."

"And there are a million little reasons I love you now: you're good, and you're smart, and you care about people—really care about them—and you're handsome, and you have that killer smile. But mostly, Billy Ray, I want to be with you because something inside you made me light up here." She touched her heart. "And here"—she touched her temple with one finger and her tone turned mischievous—"and other places too."

"Lizzy," I admonished, embarrassed, but amused at the same time.

She leaned forward and put her arms around my neck. "I adore you. And now, I'll have to spend the rest of my life showing you just how much."

She looked at me for half a minute, and then, as if I had just asked, she answered my original question.

"So, when did I begin to love you?"

I smiled and leaned over to place a kiss on her mouth.

"It must have been that day you and the Reverend came out to help my daddy fix our barn. You hit your thumb with the hammer and had the tip of it in your mouth to soothe it."

"I remember."

"I wondered if I would be able to lead you around on a string like I did all the Orchard Hill boys. I hardly knew you, and you being from out of town made you even more of a challenge. I sauntered over and gave you my most provocative smile, rubbing your thumb to try and stir you up. But something happened when I looked up into your eyes."

"What was it?"

"I saw my future. It just took me a long time to have enough faith to believe it could come true."

I stared at her, captivated and speechless by the light and beauty that was my beloved wife.

"I love you, Billy Ray Davenport."

"And I love you, Elizabeth Quinlan Davenport."

She took my face in her hands and kissed me, as if to promise me a lifetime of that love. Then she drew back and got to her feet, tugging me by the hand. "Come on."

"Where to?"

"For a swim."

I followed her into the water, until we were in about waist deep, playing and splashing in the waves.

"Here comes a big one!" I shouted over the sound of the surf.

"Don't let it knock you down!" she called. "Dive right through." She looked over her shoulder with a come-hither smile, and through the wave she went.

I was right behind her.

The Bookend on the Right

AN EPILOGUE

October, 2012

From time to time, the young people comment on how admirable we are, a couple who weathered the twentieth century's major cultural upheaval with our marriage still intact. We've been married now for over fifty years, clinging to each other during the days of ever-climbing divorce rates. When asked, I say that I don't have any secret to a successful marriage, at least not one that played well with the seventies' Me Generation, the eighties' Yuppie Crowd, or today's disillusioned youth that Occupy Wall Street. At any rate, people are more inclined to listen when Lizzy tells the story. They call her life a treatise on women's changing roles in the workplace and in the home—but my views always come off as old-fashioned. I'm an outdated relic from the 1950s.

In my opinion, Elizabeth is no modern women's crusader—she's too busy living out her dreams, even to this day. Our life together has been a thousand little journeys, just as Mrs. Gardener predicted—medical residency, and babies, starting the family health center when we relocated to the Carolina coast—and by the time our fourth and last son came along, we were well settled into what my father called our 'Bohemian lifestyle.'

It wasn't the life Dad envisioned for his only son, but my Aunt Catherine reminded him that Davenport men were always set on choosing their own paths, and I was only the latest example of that. She told Lizzy and me how

238

my grandfather, a shrewd businessman, hadn't been too happy with Dad's decision to be a minister. My father forged his own road, however, and in the end, he realized he had to let me do the same.

They made a peace of sorts, my father and my wife. He never did understand how our marriage could possibly work, but when we descended on Aunt Catherine's house with his grandsons, he would comment that it must be working at least on the 'be fruitful and multiply' front! The boys adored him and he them, and that went a long way with Lizzy. Over time, my only surviving parent and my only soul mate found a measure of faith in each other.

From the outside, I'm sure it looks like Dr. Elizabeth Davenport is a pioneer among modern women, leading by her carefree example. In some ways, I suppose that's true. Lizzy always embraced change, and our lives have never been dull or ordinary. But believing our path was all brilliance and easy adventure discounts the tough choices we had to make along the way. After I finished my medical training, I was offered a prestigious position in Philadelphia: big hospital, a thriving practice, a house in the suburbs. Then we got the call that changed our lives forever: Lizzy received an offer to serve a working class and indigent population as a nurse midwife on the Southern coast. We could have lived a more traditional life up North, but there just weren't the same opportunities for my wife there, and we had both fallen in love with the Carolinas on our honeymoon.

We gave up financial advantages to stay in the Southeast, but the advantages we gained were priceless to us: warm climate, relaxed living, family close by, and the knowledge that our work really mattered.

People insist I believe in women's rights because I contributed to—even encouraged—my wife's achievements. In the next breath, they tease me about tossing besotted looks her way and turning the tale of a momentous cultural shift into just another sappy love story.

There is nothing sappy about it, however. I'm a simple man who loves his wife. Sure, we relocated to the Carolina coast because of that job offer, and there were all sorts of adjustments to make when she decided she needed to get her medical degree to grow our family practice. But Lizzy made countless concessions, too, every day of our married life.

I may not know much about the Sexual Revolution or Women's Lib, as they called it, but I *do* know my wife like the back of my own hand. She always marched to the beat of her own drum—and it was an exotic, intoxicating rhythm of life that enticed me to stay in step beside her through every song and cadence, every silence and storm. Our thousand journeys intertwined into something strong, something worthy—something that was made beautiful in His time.

I wish the same for you.

CPSIA information can be obtained at www.ICGtesting.com
Printed in the USA
LVOW07s1950121115

462271LV00003B/396/P